The Blue Look of Fear

The Blue Look of Fear

By

Dewitt L. Edenfield, Jr.

ISBN # 1-58721-100-9

1stBooks – Rev. 3/8/00

About the Book

Captain Benjamin Guron is pushed from a rock out-cropping and falls to his death in Georgia's Tallulah Gorge, and David MacGruder must find his killer.

Private Investigator David Michael MacGruder — ex-SEAL and ex-cop — is faced with the baffling murder of a long-time acquaintance. Fearful of what might happen to critical but fragile evidence at the scene, MacGruder calls on the Georgia Bureau of Investigation and finds himself engaged to investigate the murder. His immediate superior, GBI Agent Brenda Carlisle, is a brilliant professional. She is also tall and lithe and beautiful, and MacGruder suddenly finds himself entangled in the case, and enthralled by Agent Carlisle.

This case takes MacGruder from Fort Lauderdale, Florida, to Georgia's Smokey Mountain's where he matches wits with a dangerously cunning and cold-blooded killer.

Dedication

To my daughters, Deanna and Suzanna, for putting up with their father's moods and moments.

Chapter One

I parked Tucker Markum's four-wheel drive truck in the pull-off at the top of Tallulah Gorge just behind a red Chevrolet four-wheel drive pickup truck. I looked at the tags; it had Habersham County plates. Then I looked around for Ben. There was no one in sight, but there was a blue Mercedes-Benz parked up the road. I didn't take time to read the license plate — there was no reason — but I knew it was a Georgia plate. I suppose, in the mist of the morning and the expectation of meeting a prospective client at that particular spot, it didn't seem important to check either the cars or the license plates.

Funny place to have a meeting, I thought to myself. Not the weirdest place I've ever met someone, not by far, but funny nonetheless.

I had flown up from Miami, leaving just one hour after I got the call. Wiley Frazier met me at Hartsfield, the international airport in Atlanta, and drove me to his new home. It had been almost a year since I had seen him and his wife, Virginia, the doctor. Wiley and I had been friends for almost thirty years; twenty-plus years as sailors wearing the navy blue of our country, and nine as civilians; cops and private investigators. We had this business; now a corporation; MacGruder-Frazier Investigations. Wiley was good at it, while I merely plugged along. He had a way of making businesses believe he could cure their ills, and he could. We had struggled in the first few years after our early departures from law enforcement; Wiley from the Dade County Sheriff's Department and I from the Broward

County S.D. I had left the B.C.S.D because of an automobile accident that left me impaired, or so the department doctors said. Wiley had left Dade County because of a disagreement he had with one of the senior administrative officers.

Our struggles had paid off and Wiley had departed south Florida for the antebellum hospitality of Atlanta, Georgia. It had not taken him long to land several lucrative corporate accounts. From that point, the bud blossomed. MacGruder-Frazier, once counting the pennies between cases, was now a seven-figure enterprise, although you couldn't tell it from the way either of us lived.

I live aboard a boat that I acquired years ago as a second home, when I was still married. Since that time my forty-one-foot Mainship has been my girl when there were no others. I call her *The Other Woman*, a moniker my ex-wife assigned because she said the boat was my mistress, and I guess she was — and is.

She was one hundred forty-seven thousand dollars when anything over fifty grand was a lot of money to pay for a boat. Now it isn't. If you bought her new, she would cost twice that much. Used, she'll still bring one-twenty or so, maybe more if the buyer knows what he's getting.

So I had her when I was a cop and my yearly earnings qualified me for food stamps in most states. I had her when MacGruder-Frazier Investigations didn't bring in enough to pay the slip fees. I still have her even though the Frazier half of the corporation has boosted our yearly revenues past the one million mark. Virginia had set us up with a very good accounting firm, and they, in turn, had steered us toward an investment brokerage firm, and they, again in their turn, had invested the money in very secure and lucrative stocks and bonds and money market accounts and ... it all bored me to tears. The bottom line is even without the few bucks I managed to dump into the accounts,

MacGruder-Frazier Investigations was rock solid and profitable, and both Wiley and I could retire and enjoy the fruits of our labors, if we so elected.

The doc, better known as Virginia, or Doctor Virginia, or Mrs. Wiley Frazier, was a practicing psychiatrist, and damn good at it. She had moved her practice from Miami to Atlanta, yet she retained quite a few of her south Florida patients. So good was she at unraveling their problems and putting them on the road to mental recovery they boarded flights from Miami to Atlanta just to continue their medical relationship with the doc.

The doc and Wiley lived in Powder Springs, one of Atlanta's many suburbs. Their house was a rolling, rambling mastery of brick masonry and hooded archways. When I stepped to the door, it sprang open and the doc came bursting out and into my arms. Her lips tasted of cinnamon and licorice candy.

It was the kiss of close friends, comrades, and a sweet reunion. When it had lingered longer than the three seconds big, burly Wiley allowed, he cleared his throat. "You two want me to go away and let you have some time alone?" There was no malice in his voice.

I pushed Virginia out to arm's length. "You haven't changed at all. You're still the same beautiful lady I remember."

Her ebony face glowed and her smile was infectious. "David, you clod, it's been a year! Don't you ever visit your friends?" she asked.

I grinned around at Wiley. "Not when she has a two hundred and fifty pound bodyguard."

"Two forty-seven," Wiley stated. "I've been on a diet."

I turned to my friend and hugged him, too, only there wasn't a kiss. "You old sea dog, I've missed you, too."

I felt a soft, warm hand on my shoulder. "So why didn't you visit?" Virginia asked.

I turned to her. "The airplanes fly both ways, Doc, or had you forgotten?"

"It's easier to drag an elephant into the desert than to get Wiley into an airplane." Virginia laughed, "Or has it been so long that you've forgotten?" Then she turned and opened the door. "All right you two, let's go inside. I've got bottles chilling and glasses ready." Wiley and I followed Virginia into the house.

It was almost midnight. Wiley had gone plodding off to bed after promising he would see to my transportation needs in the morning. I felt pleasantly relaxed. Virginia had fed me a large steak and lots of lettuce and tomatoes and sweet Vidalia onions. While we ate, Wiley had talked business, and I had been curiously inert, aware of the impact of the multiple six-figure accounts he talked of, but the gravity of the newfound bonanza didn't really strike home until Virginia and I sat in comfortable padded chairs out in their glassed-in family room.

I took a small sip of the brandy I was holding. "Guess all this makes it easier on you and Wiley."

She turned her dark brown eyes on me and I thought I saw a glint of sadness in them. "It certainly makes it easier to keep Cherrise up at Boston University, and Thomas over at the University of Georgia, but it's not so easy to keep Wiley contented — not like when he was working what he calls 'real cases.' He misses the intrigue, David. This corporate security isn't Wiley. He misses getting out on the streets, but more than that, he misses you. We're making all this money, living the American dream, and my husband hates every minute of it. I think he'd trade all this for five minutes of danger, if he could." She paused for a brief moment. Then, "And, David, you aren't helping matters any."

"So what are you saying?"

"I'm saying that Wiley moved us up here because he thought it would make things better for us — Cherrise and Thomas and me — and for you. That's what he thought, but you don't even take your share of the profit he shows."

I shook my head. "That isn't entirely true. I do get a salary, Virginia. To me, that's more than fair."

"David, you dummy, your corporate salary is over a hundred thousand dollars a year, and you take only thirty thousand dollars. Whether you know it or not, your pride — if that's what it is — is making Wiley feel guilty."

"What do I need with a hundred grand a year? I live cheap, Virginia. You know that. And anyway, how many times has Wiley told me to keep the case fees I get?"

"Don't you know why he does that, David?" She watched me through brown eyes that had started to turn to cold black. "I suggest you think about it."

I sipped the brandy again, and gave her an embarrassed smile. "Okay, so he thinks he's living in all this splendor and I'm living like a bum, but we both know that isn't the way it is, Doc. Hell, you're still driving that old Mercury and he's still driving that old, beatup Datsun 510. So maybe Wiley's having some problems adjusting to his newfound wealth."

She gave me a slow, sad smile. "That's part of it. He still sees himself as a poor black kid from North Carolina. He forgets that he's worked like hell his whole life. So now, all of a sudden he's rich, and he has no idea what it means." She paused for a moment, her eyes clouding. "But there's something else, too. He doesn't feel good about himself anymore, not the way he used to feel."

I shook my head at her, trying desperately to erase her words. Then, after a few moments, knowing she knew better than I, I asked. "All right, so what do I do to help?

She exhaled softly. "I don't like saying this. I love that man and I hated it when he did all those dangerous things.

5

I want him around a long time, but the way he is, he won't be. He'll fret himself into a stroke or a heart attack ... or worse. I want you to get him involved again. I want you to make him a part of MacGruder-Frazier Investigations one more time."

I sat forward, my elbows on my knees. "That's a dangerous place out there and people get hurt. Are you really sure about this?"

"Damn it, David, no, I'm not sure about it, but that's where Wiley was happiest, out there, out in that danger, and if that's what it takes to make him happy again, then I'll live with the fear."

I finished the brandy and set the glass on the table. "All right, Virginia." I stood, looking down at her. "It's late and I'm tired, and confused, but maybe you're right. I'll give it some thought, and if I can, I'll bring Wiley in. Right now though, I'm tired. I have to meet someone tomorrow over at Tallulah Falls and it's a long drive." I left her sitting there, her eyes full of dread.

I stepped down from the truck and walked to the guardrail. It was dented as though some crazy driver had tried to take a quick trip down into the gorge. I leaned out and over the steel rail and looked down. A thick, gray fog filled the gorge so that I couldn't see more than fifty feet down. I checked my watch. It was nine-fifty-eight. Ben had told me on the telephone to meet him here — down on an outcropping about a hundred feet below the roadway — at ten.

He had also told me I would find a path leading down the face of the gorge at the west end of the guardrail. I found the path and started down the embankment. It was easy going for about ten steps — then it turned not-so-easy. I inwardly thanked God I had elected to wear the cleat-soled hiking boots.

6

I turned a corner, holding a pine sapling, stepped across to a granite boulder that sat precariously out over the drop, and felt the cold chill in the middle of my back. I dropped to a hunch and slithered back against the rock face, snaked my head around, but saw nothing. For some reason I found I had retrieved the Colt Ace from my belt. Subconscious reactions are funny things. I have learned to trust my instincts. They had served me well through the years. On more than one occasion, the inward voices that tell us to take care had warned me just in time to prevent my certain demise.

It was the same this time, so when I heard the voice, I tried to inch my way into a one-inch crack in the granite. I didn't manage it. What I did manage was to remain still for what seemed to be an eternity. When I checked my watch, it had only been a few seconds. When I finally moved farther down the slope, I did so very slowly, very carefully and very, very quietly.

The path was made up of boulders, tightly fitted to the edge of the mountain. To move downward, I had to step-leap from one boulder to another so it was a precariously slow, step-by-dangerous-step process.

I was inching my way around a large rock when I sensed more than heard what sounded like a frightened "Oh." It was exclaimed softly and was followed by the sounds of pebbles falling down the face of the rocks. A few moments afterward, there was an audible *thunk*. It sounded like something heavy and soft-solid had struck a hard surface. I remember thinking at the time I heard the muted outcry it was almost as though the speaker was caught unawares and had whispered the sound silently so as not to frighten anything, like a hunter who stumbles and crunches a shin tracking the wily beast, but forces himself to hold the cry of pain-fear inside.

I thought instantly of Ben Guron, but shook the thought from my head. I knew something was very wrong as the same cold chill I had felt earlier returned, centering itself in the middle of my back. I remained still for a few more seconds, listening for sounds. There were none. I eased myself upright and moved around the rock and down the face of the cliff until I reached a place where sand had collected on the granite outcropping. I felt the hairs on the back of my neck standing, but I shook myself. I could see no one around, and the morning was still as quiet as a tomb.

Something told me to stop. I looked down. There were foot prints in the sand; two very distinctly different prints impressions; one set of prints were of the type hiking boots make, like the ones I was wearing except these had vee-grooves in the soles; the other prints were common sneaker soles, almost like boat shoes. Some of the prints were facing each other, as if the two people had been talking. Then the vee-grooves stepped aside and to the rear of the sneakers, and there was a foot-long scuff that led to the edge of the rock.

I forced myself to step to the edge, careful not to disturb the prints. When I peered down into the mist, a light wind swirled the fog and touched my cheeks. As I looked down into the gloom, the haze began to clear, and something began to materialize below me on another rock outcropping.

At first it was merely an outline, a vague resemblance of something I could not at first identify. Then I could see what appeared to be darker appendages that sprang from the center; two at the bottom and two from what seemed to be a little distance from the top. When another puff of wind blew up from the canyon floor, I saw the vague image was a body.

It was lying on the rock twenty-five feet below where I leaned out. The arms were out-stretched and raised in a gesture of surrender. One leg was bent at a precarious angle out to the side of the body, as though the person was in the midst of a ballerina's pirouette, the other bent and crooked obliquely beneath the first, the foot hanging out over the edge of the boulder, the canvas sneaker of which was dangling delicately from the toes.

I stared at the mass of torn and bloody tissue below me. The head rested crushed and flat against the rock, mashed until the shattered cartilage and bone no longer resembled what had once been a handsome, almost alluring face. The blood soaked gray-black hair fanned outward as though it was some terribly humorless death-mask halo. The blue eyes I had known so well stared up at me vacantly and without any sign of life.

I inched my way down the face until I stepped onto the precipice. Even before I reached the ledge, I could smell the foul odors of violent and sudden death. My hand was shaking as I touched the neck just below the ear where the carotid artery is closest to the surface. There was nothing, not a pulse or a throb, or even a quiver; but I had known that before I touched him.

The body had not been dead for long, no more than five minutes. My mind replayed the sounds I had heard. The "Oh" had been the death cry of this person.

There was no face, just a flat, lifeless mask that had once been full of life, of laughter, of that special mischievous grin that only Ben Guron could have flashed. I peered down into those now-dead blues eyes, and I felt a sudden shiver ripple through me. The eyes, now lifeless, stared up at me through that endless distance, and in them I saw the blue look of fear, that immediate knowledge that death was certain, and there was no escape.

I sat beside him. I felt the hot tears filling my eyes. I whispered to him, "I'm here, Ben, I'm here. You called to me and I came, only I was too late to save you."

I felt as though the lifeless form that had once been my friend was trying to speak to me, so I asked, "Who did this to you, Captain Ben? Who pushed you over the edge? Was it the same person you said was after you? When you called, you used the word *they*; who are *they*, old friend? And why were they after you? What is it you knew but would not tell? And now you can't tell."

I removed my jacket and placed it over him. I climbed the twenty-five feet back up to the ledge. When I got there, I sat. It wasn't cold, but I felt myself shivering.

When I felt the sadness turn to anger, I looked at the prints again. The vee-grooves were about nine inches from toe-to-heel, as though the boot was small. I looked around. There were cigarette butts — four in all. I lightly touched each of them. The last was still warm. And there was something else; a paper stick, like one of those that holds a candy sucker. I touched the end. The tip was wet while the rest of the stick was dry. In this fog, the moisture would have drenched the paper in an hour or so. Whoever had eaten the candy had done so not long before I had arrived.

I made my way back up to the guardrail and east to the gift shop. Absentmindedly, I noted the Mercedes was gone. There was a telephone on the wall just outside the door. I made three calls. The first was to Wiley. I used his private number. His secretary answered and put me through to him when she heard my name.

"Dave?"

"Wiley, listen. I have to make this quick. I'm over at Tallulah Gorge. I came over here to meet Ben Guron ... "

"Captain Guron?" he asked.

"The same," I said, hurrying on. "He's dead. Someone pushed him off a ledge." I paused, then went on. "I need you to check some things out. He lives ... " I corrected myself. "Make that lived in a town about eight miles south of here called Harlanwood. I need your help on this one,

Wiley. I need to know what he's been doing since he retired. You'll have to dig deep. I have to know if anyone was after him, if there is anyone who might want him dead, and if so, why. Can you get someone on it?"

Without hesitation, he said, "I'll do it." Then, after a brief pause, he asked, "Are you okay, Dave?"

"Yeah, I'm okay. I'll get back to you." I hit the bar and heard the line go dead. When I released the bar and heard the dial tone, I dialed 911. A female voice answered after the second ring. "Habersham County Sheriff. This is an emergency line."

"My name is MacGruder — spelled M-A-C-G-R-U-D-E-R, first name David. I'm at the overlook at the top of Tallulah Gorge, off old 441. Someone has fallen over the cliff. I went down as close as I could get — I didn't get to the body," I lied, "but it's apparent I was too late. My guess is the person was killed in a fall. I'll wait here until your deputies arrive."

The female voice said, "Yes, sir. They'll be there in ten minutes."

I tapped the bar again. I dialed the number of Boone Swabble. A curt, business-like voice answered, "Georgia Bureau of Investigation."

"This is Dave MacGruder. I need to talk to Agent Swabble."

"I'm sorry, Mr. ... "

"MacGruder," I informed the voice.

"Mr. MacGruder, Agent Swabble is out of town. Is there someone else who could help you?"

I thought quickly. "When do you expect him back?"

"Could you hold please?" He didn't give me time to respond. I was about to hang up when a female voice came on the line. "This is Agent Carlisle. You were asking about Agent Swabble?"

"Listen, I don't want to waste a lot of your time. My name's MacGruder. Boone and I spent time in Vietnam together, and I need to talk to him."

"I'm sorry, Mr. MacGruder. Agent Swabble is in Washington. He won't be back for several months. Was there some reason ... "

I cut her off. "Agent Carlisle, this is going to sound crazy to you, but I may need Boone's help on something that's completely out of your jurisdiction. I want you to get word to him that Captain Benjamin Guron has been killed. It happened over in Habersham County, or at least I think it happened there. Maybe it was Rabun. I don't know. I called the Habersham County Sheriff, and they're responding, though none of that matters. What matters is that you get in touch with Boone and tell him Captain Ben is dead. Can you do that?"

There were a few seconds of silence. Then, "Mr. MacGruder, Agent Swabble is ... out of service for a while. I can't go into it, but you'll have to understand I can't reach him. I'm sorry. Perhaps I can help?"

I could hear sirens off in the distance. I breathed loudly into the phone. "Agent Carlisle, I'm a private detective; the Florida half of MacGruder-Frazier Investigations. Ben Guron was an old friend. I came up here to meet him, only I didn't get here soon enough. I have a suspicion by the time the rescue boys and the deputies get finished, all signs of the murder will be gone. Ben called me because he thought he was in danger, and I don't want this to go down as an accident. Do you understand?"

"Are you certain it was murder?" she asked.

"That's what the signs say. Two sets of prints, then one set moves and the other drags a foot to the edge, and that's enough for me, Agent Carlisle."

There was no delay as she said, "Did you call the state patrol?"

12

"No, I haven't had time."

"When the deputies get there, you tell them you are acting on behalf of the GBI, tell them you are a special agent on detached duty. If they want ID, you have them call me. You tell them you are taking control of the scene until the state patrol arrives." A short pause, then, "You are certain this man — this Ben Guron is dead?"

"As sure as I'm talking to you."

"We have a resident agent up in Clayton, but it'll take him a while to get there. The state patrol officer who responds will know what to do. You stay there until he arrives, then you show him the crime scene. He'll do the rest. And Mr. MacGruder?"

"Yes?"

"I'll want a written statement from you."

"Yes, of course you will." Then the line went dead.

Chapter Two

The two deputies who arrived in the four-wheel drive vehicle were understandably and it appeared morbidly eager to get down to the body, but when I told them I was a GBI special agent on detached duty, they nervously went back to their truck.

The blue-and-gray Ford with the Georgia State Patrol emblem on the driver's door arrived about five minutes later. The officer was in his mid-forties, with a stocky build and gray short-cropped hair. He got out of his car and came over to me. "I'm Burns. You MacGruder?" When I nodded, he said, "They said something about you being GBI. Got some ID?"

When I gave him Agent Carlisle's number, he looked at me for a moment, then went to his car. I saw him pick up the cellular phone and make a call. He spoke into the phone and then he listened for a full minute, after which he hung up. When he came back to me, he said, "All right. Let's you and me go down and take a look." To the deputies, he said, "Looks like we might have a murder, so you boys get on your radio and call for the crime scene truck. Me and ... Agent MacGruder here are going down to take a look." Then he turned to me. "Let's go."

When we had reached the outcropping where I had crouched and heard the cry, we were out of ear shot of the sheriff's deputies. "So let's have it," he said to me.

I gave it to him, including the bit about the Mercedes. He took it all in, jotting a few notes in his notebook. When

I was finished, he said, "You stay here. I'm going down to take a look." I watched as he disappeared over the edge.

He was gone a full thirty minutes. When he came back up, his color was bad. "Not a pretty sight." He took out a cigarette and after lighting it, he asked, "You knew him?"

I nodded. "We were stationed together in Vietnam. That was a long time ago, but we've remained friends since then."

"And he called you and asked you to meet him here?"

"Like I said, he told me he thought someone was after him."

"But he didn't tell you who it was?"

"No, and he didn't tell me why he thought someone was after him." Then, "You saw the second set of footprints?"

He nodded. Then, "Just for the record, MacGruder, what size shoes do you wear?"

I smiled ruefully at him. "Size eleven."

"Do you smoke?"

I smiled again, and produced the rumpled pack of Camels from my pocket.

He nodded. "Just for the record, you understand. So what do you make of the second set of footprints?"

I shrugged. "A small man, maybe."

"Why do you say maybe?" He asked, his eyes on mine.

"I estimate the size at six and a half, or seven, and from the indentations, I'd say the person weighs only one-ten to one-fifteen pounds. I knew Ben Guron and if it had been a man, he would have been careful, especially out on that rock. A woman? Maybe he would have been a little less careful. Anyway, whoever it was, that person caught him with his guard down. There was no struggle, just a quick push, and Ben was over the edge."

"All right, MacGruder, I'll buy that."

I shuffled my feet. "Something I don't understand."

"Yeah?" His eyes suddenly became alert.

16

"Where did she — or he — go?"

It was Officer Burns' turn to shrug. "There's a path leading up the face from where you found the prints. You have to jump about four feet to another rock, but if you make it, the path is easy up the face and back to the pull off. It would have been simple for someone who knew what they were doing."

I looked at him. "So it could have been anyone? Is that what you're saying?"

"I'm saying it could have been anyone who was in reasonably good shape and wasn't afraid to take a leap across to that rock. I wasn't, and I'm not a rock climber, so, yeah, I guess you could say it could have been anyone."

"Great," I grunted.

He looked at me, his eyes watching me intently. "So you kept in touch with the deceased after Nam?"

I nodded slowly. "Yes I did. We were both in the Navy. He was my boss back in the early seventies. I liked him and he liked me, so we stayed close."

"Friends?"

I shook my head. "Acquaintances," I lied again. "When we were in the Navy, we traveled in different crowds. I liked him. I admired his leadership principles, but no, we weren't exactly friends."

"So you can't tell me anything about him? His life, that sort of thing?"

"No, not really."

His eyes narrowed. "Then why are you here?"

"I'm here because he asked me to be here." When Burns looked skeptical at my response, I added, "Agent Carlisle may have been a little quick to make me a special agent. I'm a private detective, Trooper Burns, and Captain Guron wanted to talk about a problem he'd been having. I'm here because he selected this as the place to meet."

He paused for a few seconds, and then asked, "What sort of problem?"

"I don't know. He didn't have a chance to tell me. But I think it had something to do with someone being after him."

Burns watched me for a few seconds. When he spoke, his eyes were wary. "You wouldn't be keeping anything from me, would you, Mr. MacGruder?"

"Two things I've learned, Trooper Burns. The first is to be honest whenever possible. The second is there is no client confidentiality when the client is dead."

He smiled ruefully. "I don't know this Agent Carlisle, but I guess she's a pretty good judge of character, MacGruder. So you and me, we've got this murder on our hands, and we are going to make damn sure that it goes down as a murder. The Habersham County Sheriff — his name is Hawthorne — he's good, and he might not need us, but we are going to be available if he does, if you get my meaning."

I returned his rueful smile. "I read you loud and clear, Trooper Burns. If Sheriff Hawthorne needs me, I'll be there."

He nodded slowly. "Make sure you are." He retrieved his notepad from his rear pocket and wrote a few words, then he asked, "Your local address?"

"You can reach me through MacGruder-Frazier Investigations, 117 Commercial Park Place, Atlanta."

He wrote, then smiled and winked at me. "Or through that Ms. Carlisle?"

I returned his wink and said, "Yet to be seen, Burns. Try the Commercial Park address first."

He smiled and nodded, then turned and walked off.

I drove back to Atlanta, my mind only occasionally on the traffic that zoomed past me on the divided highway.

Murder is a definite act, an act sometimes committed as a result of some indefinite emotion. I have heard all the arguments as to why this one takes the life of that one, and how it should be excused because of these or those mitigating circumstances. But when all the noise of argument and complaint dies away, the fact still remains a living, breathing, caring human being lost all the opportunities of life because another felt that he — or she — should live no longer.

I have killed, both as an lethal human-instrument of my country and as a result of my civilian labors. I have never enjoyed causing the death of another, even at those times when the death was to prevent my own or someone else's death. And I have taken it upon myself to administer the ultimate punishment without giving the courts of our land the opportunity to fairly judge and sentence as the jury and the judge deem fit. I do not try to justify my actions to anyone, for I have been and will be judged ultimately by my Creator, in His court of total venue.

I thought about Ben Guron and contemplated the painful reality that he had been killed. Then I thought about the red pickup truck and the blue Mercedes — both with Georgia plates, and recorded a slightly blurred vision of the truck and the automobile in my brain. Next came the hiking boots with the vee-grooves in the soles, and the images of prints in the sand and the foot-long scuff leading to the edge of the rock.

All that and driving through the hubbub of Atlanta traffic.

117 Commercial Park Place is an impressive, steel, cement, marble-facade and glass building that soars twenty-six stories skyward. I found a parking space a block down the street and walked up to the front door. When it opened automatically, I stepped into the dry coolness of the foyer.

A clean-cut middle-aged man in an official looking blue uniform stepped from behind a desk and smiled at me. "May I help you, sir?" I noticed the gold badge. It read *MacGruder-Frazier Investigations, Inc.* Hard to accept I was a part of an established corporation. There was also a nametag. It read *B.G. Maldin.*

"David MacGruder, Mr. Maldin. I'm here to see Mr. Frazier."

Maldin eyed me for a few seconds, faint glints of recognition in his eyes. Then he walked back around to the rear of his desk and pick up a metal clipboard. His eyes looked down at the paper and then back up at me, and there was a slight reddening on his cheeks. "Oh, Mr. MacGruder, sir. I'm sorry I didn't recognize you."

I shook my head at him. "No reason why you should have, Maldin. We've never met, at least I don't think we have."

His hand fumbled across the top of his desk and he came up with a glossy plastic badge which had a clip on one end. He handed me the badge and said "No, sir, we've never met, but I see your picture every time I inventory the security badges, so it's like I know you already."

I looked at him questioningly, then I looked down at the tag. Sure enough, laminated between two sheets of plastic was a one-inch square picture of me. "Is this really necessary?"

His eyes were unwavering as he responded, "It's our building security clearance. The government requires us to check everyone who enters, and we have identification tags for everyone who works here."

I watched him for a quick second, then smiled. "Of course, Maldin."

He looked relieved. "Mr. Frazier's office is on the top floor, Room 2610. I'll let Ms. Norton know you're on your way up." He pointed at a bank of elevators at the rear of the foyer. "Use number four. It's a private lift and it's an express."

I nodded, clipped the identification tag to my shirt pocket and walked to the elevator.

When the elevator door slipped open, she looked up and smiled broadly at me. "So, you've finally come crawling back to me."

"Am I crawling? I didn't notice."

She gave me a crooked smile. "No, but you should be."

I moved across the room and stopped beside her. Mickie Norton was still a big, beautiful, red-haired, green-eyed woman. She stands almost six feet tall, without shoes, and, as I have so often said, she's more woman than most men see in a lifetime. Mickie has always been one of those big, brawny, buxom Irish females who will stand toe-to-toe with most men and win every time.

Wiley and I hired her down in Ft. Lauderdale because Virginia thought we needed a trustworthy secretary, and because Mickie needed a job. There was one other reason, too. Virginia thought Mickie would make a nice permanent addition to *The Other Woman*, my boat and my home. I gave it some thought and Mickie gave it some thought, and we gave it some thought together, but it always added up to the same thing; there just wasn't enough emotion to supplement the lust. There was an awful lot of that, and it was good, very good, but it wasn't great. Even so, Mickie and I shared an emotional tie that was still very alive, and we both knew it.

"Do I get a hug?"

She slipped her chair back and stood, moved the few inches that separated us and threw her arms around my neck. "You big, ugly old bastard." And then she was pressing her lips against mine and molding her muscular female frame against me.

There were gentle pressures and obscure perfumes and the taste of lipstick, and when she stepped away from me, her eyes were slightly out of focus. "Whew," she exclaimed. "You do such naughty things to me, David MacGruder."

"And you do the same to me, girl."

"Yes, I guess I do at that." Her eyes cleared and she sat back in her chair. "Do me a big favor, MacGruder?"

I gave her a gallant bow. "Anything you want, sweet lady, just ask."

"Get away from me before I lose control."

I dutifully went around to the front of her desk. "This better?"

Her smile was rueful and wicked. "Barely. I can still smell your aftershave."

I sat on the edge of her desk and placed my hand atop hers. "You okay up here?"

"Umm," she said. "I'm getting used to it. It isn't Lauderdale, but that isn't so bad. And you and Wiley are very generous, so I live a lot better up here. Still . . ." She let her words trail off.

"Still what?" I asked.

She gave me a searching look. "Don't you know?"

"Know what?" Then I saw it in her eyes. "Oh. Well, maybe you aren't missing much."

"The kiss said that isn't true."

I smiled down at her. "All that kiss said, Mickie, was we are both very much aware of who — and what the other person is."

She looked down at her desk for a few seconds, then back up at me, her eyes bright. "Okay, so I miss being hugged, and being hugged by an old friend is better than nothing."

"Sometimes it's better than anything."

She nodded slowly. "Can I see you?"

"I can think of nothing I'd rather do. Dinner tonight?"

She smiled up at me and nodded. Then her face changed and she gave me a very professional glance. "Mr. Frazier is waiting."

I nodded toward a highly varnished oak door. "That the master's office?"

"It is." Then, "Dave, can you please get him involved in something ... "

I cut her off. "You and Virginia been talking?" Before she could answer, I went on. "I promised the doc I'd get him out in the field, and I'm telling you the same thing. Damn! Why isn't there someone who worries about me like you and the doc worry about Wiley?"

She rolled her hand over beneath mine and her fingers curled around my hand. "There are, David, and you damn well know it."

I smiled, lifted her hand to my lips and kissed the back of it. Then I slipped from the desk and strode across the room to the oak door, gave two quick knocks, and opened the door.

Wiley Frazier was seated behind the largest mahogany desk I had ever seen. His eyes smiled up at me as I entered, while the rest of his face reflected no emotion at all. "Well, will you look here. The MacGruder half of MacGruder-Frazier Investigations has finally decided to show his face."

"You forgot to add in the word *Corporation*." He muttered a four letter word, but I let it pass. "You never were very good at acting, and you don't do well with hostility, old chum."

"You know, Dave, half the folks that work for us think David MacGruder is just some white bread I dreamed up so the rednecks would take MacGruder-Frazier seriously?"

I gave him a conciliatory smile. "Wiley, in case you haven't heard, this is the age of equality and racial opportunity. Most folks realize that black is a skin tone and not a disease. And a few of us rednecks have even learned that brain power and intelligence are not affected by skin tone."

His ebony face contorted and he burst into laughter. "Damn it, MacGruder, you could have called me before you came."

"For what?"

"So I could show you off."

I shook my head. "Wiley, just how the hell do you think I would feel being escorted through this fancy building being introduced as the M part of the M-F?"

"Damn it, Dave, this is our comp ... corporation. Ours. In case that honky brain of yours doesn't recognize the word, it's spelled O-U-R-S. It was money we both made that financed the move up here."

I held up my hands. "Okay, so I surrender." Then after a moment, I asked, "So why don't you tell me what this is all about?"

The broad shoulders slumped and the handsome black face drooped. "Hell, I wish I knew."

I took a seat across from him. The burgundy leather was soft. "Okay, so partner, you and me, we go back a long way. We've been through some rough times together, but we always managed to come through it all right. We did it by talking it out. So talk to me."

His eyes appeared sad. "I shouldn't be here, Dave. I should be back down in Lauderdale with you. This isn't me. I'm a black man. Black men don't make it in this country. Pop was a share-cropper all his life. He never made more than a hundred dollars a week, and he could never afford any of the things he really wanted. He died a pauper and we all had to scrape enough money together to bury him in something besides a cardboard coffin." He paused and shook his head. "I've got more money right now than ninety percent of the black people in this country.

24

Hell, I'm married to a doctor. For most of our marriage, she held back her career so I wouldn't feel like she was better than I was." He paused for a moment. "Guess that's something we black men share with you redneck bastards, Dave. Ain't no woman ever going to be the bread-winner in our homes. We got to be *the man*, or we ain't going to be nothing." I knew he was serious, but he had spoken the words with a smile.

"It's a new age, Wiley, and it's okay if the wife makes more than the husband."

He grinned at me. "I know that. Virginia has been giving me that lecture for years, and if I live to be ninety, I might just believe it." Wiley paused again, then turned his eyes toward me. "You know we banked two-and-a-half-million last year? We, Dave, you and me. I took one-hundred-and-fifteen-thousand for salary, and you took thirty and we have almost doubled our bank account in the last five months."

"Okay, so we're making a lot of money and we both live like human beings. So?"

When I looked at him, his eyes were tearing. "So, I hate this and I hate this office and I hate trying to act like I'm some kind of corporate tycoon."

I watched him for a few seconds, then said, "No. That isn't it."

His eyes flashed anger. "What the hell do you know about it? You and your white upbringing. You have no idea what it's like."

I shrugged. "No I don't know what it's like, but that doesn't mean I'm blind. Virginia sees it, Mickie sees it, and I see it. You're a very talented man who is stuck behind a desk and who wants to be back out where the action is." Then, "And maybe you feel a little guilty about being successful."

His eyes had the sudden appearance of defiance, but then they softened. "Yeah, I guess you would be the one who figured it out. I do feel guilty, like I'm letting my people down. I'm black and I'm making it, and they aren't."

"So take all that money we have in the bank and donate it to some worthwhile charity. Send a few kids to college. Pay a few medical bills. Help Habitat for Humanity build some houses. Find some homeless people and put a roof over their heads. Find some church that does something worthwhile, and give them a huge check. Find some old people who are trying to get by on what little our social security system pays them. Find some people who are really trying to get out of the welfare trap and help them crawl out of that rut. Wiley, what in the hell do you need to hear this from me for? My ex-wife is married to a guy who keeps her in diamonds and silk. My kids are all out of college and have careers and families of their own. I'm a happy-go-lucky beach bum who doesn't need a whole lot to live on. So give the damn money away, and I don't care who gets it: black, brown, red, yellow, or white. If you have the urge to show some good old human kindness, then do it, for God's sake!"

Wiley leaned back in his chair, clasped his hands across his stomach and looked at me. "You really feel that way?" When I nodded, he said, "And you don't care how I handle it?"

I shook my head. "Not as long as it goes to someone who really needs it."

After a few moments, he said, "All right then, that's what we'll do."

I shook my head. "You do this in your name, or in Virginia's name, or anonymously. Leave me out of it."

"You afraid someone will see through that crust and recognize MacGruder isn't the tough guy he wants everyone to think he is?"

I gave him a small, crooked smile. "Something like that."

"Okay, if that's the way you want it."

"It is."

He nodded, sat up and looked over at me. "I'll have the accountants set it up, but it will have to go in as MacGruder-Frazier, Incorporated. We need the tax dodge."

I looked at him and he looked at me, and then we both laughed. What a way to put one over on Uncle Sam and his "infernal" Revenue Service.

When the laughter had faded away, I said, "Were you able to dig up anything on what Ben Guron has been doing since he retired?"

The old Wiley was back. "Georgia's growing. Some people think it's growing a little too fast. Others think becoming the new retirement capital wouldn't be so bad. The lottery helps. Hope Grants, and all that. And the Olympics didn't hurt, either, and it's funny how greed can make some folks blind. Land speculators took advantage of the greed and used the games as a way of enticing some unsuspecting investors into land deals they wouldn't normally get involved in."

"So what's it got to do with Ben?" I asked.

He shrugged and said, "Nothing directly, but everything indirectly." Then his eyes narrowed. "You know anything about his wife?" When I shook my head, he went on. "I guess you already know her name, but just in case you don't, it's Gloria. She's a little thing, but only from her toes to her head. Every place else — every place that matters, anyway - she's a big girl. And pretty. Very pretty. My operative tells me she's an eleven on a ten scale, and coming from him, that means a lot. Her maiden name was Spence. She's from a little town south of Tallulah Gorge: Harlanwood. She came from a questionable background — mother and father not necessarily married when she was born — and the books make her as being wild as a teenager. Had a sister named Mary Jane. She was a big name in porno for a few years before AIDS caught up with her. Died a few years ago. From what I've been able to learn Gloria was into porno too, but she got out before it was too late. After that, she got herself set up well in Washington. She was somebody's mistress, and it was a *somebody* high up. Anyway, Ben met her at a party in Washington, and they hit it off. Word has it they were seen around quite a bit for five or six months, and then they got married. When Ben retired, he invested some money in a development company and came down here as overseer. From that point on, the trail gets a little too tangled to follow."

"That it?" When he nodded, I said, "Think maybe you could fly up to Washington and check Gloria out?"

"I can leave tomorrow."

"Good. First thing in the morning, I've got to make a statement for the GBI. After that, I plan to go back over to Habersham County and do some checking."

"You'll keep Mickie informed?" When I nodded, he asked, "We going to see you tonight?"

"Can we play it by ear?"

Wiley smiled. "Got something lined up?"

"Thought I'd take your secretary out to dinner."

His brows raised and his mouth formed an 'O'. "Mickie?"

"You got another secretary hiding behind your desk?" Before he could respond, I went on. "Do me a favor and don't tell the doc. You know how she feels about me and Mickie. I wouldn't want her to get her hopes up for nothing."

There was a vulgar glint in Wiley's eyes as he said, "MacGruder, we do have a rule about office relationships."

"I'll keep that in mind."

I stood and walked to the door. Then, just as I was opening the door to leave, Wiley called after me, "Thanks, Dave."

I turned to him and said, "You and me, we've been near death together. You've saved me and I've saved you. Guess that makes us brothers, of a kind. And Brother Wiley, just in case you never knew it, I love you, my brother." I opened the door and stepped out of the office, pulling the door shut behind me before he could respond.

When I walked out of Wiley's office, Mickie handed me a slip of paper. "My address and phone number. Seven o'clock?"

I read the paper. *10441 Peach Tree Lane, 777-4000.* I folded the paper and put it in my shirt pocket. I leaned over and touched my lips to hers. "Seven it is, love." Then, my face close to hers, I said, "Just for the record, what you said earlier, about the hug?"

"Yes?"

"You made reference to it being nice to be hugged."

"Yes, I did."

"What we did when I came into this office, that wasn't a hug."

Her brows went up. "No? Are you sure?"

I nodded. "I'm sure."

Her brows came back down and she smiled sweetly. "Well, it's been so long. A lady forgets those things."

I stood. "In that case, it might be the gentlemanly thing for me to warn you that if you forget again, I won't be held responsible for the consequences."

Her eyes widened. "Promise?" she asked.

I smiled at her, my fingers touching the smooth skin of her cheek. "Promise."

Chapter Three

Tucker Markum and my father were friends. They were in World War II together and served in the Army Air Corps. They, along with many thousands of other American youth, were in the India-Burma-China campaign. All those millions of tons of cargo that were airlifted across "The Hump" were loaded by soldiers, of which they were but two. The way they tell it, they played very insignificant roles, but all veterans tell it about the same way. If I ever get the opportunity, I'll ask them what would have happened to the Allies if the two of them, and every other soldier, sailor and marine just like them had decided not to go. What would have happened to the world?

Tucker owns one of the best supplied gun shops I've ever seen. What he doesn't have on display, you don't need. But if you happen to need it, he probably has it locked away in a one-hundred-square-foot steel vault in his storage building. I have used his services before, when I needed something a little more powerful, and a little more high powered than my usual S&W or Colt Ace.

Old Tucker Markum is one of those youthful types who has never found it necessary to grow up. He was married for the seventh time — this one a young redhead with enormous breasts and the longest legs I've ever seen. Nothing at all odd about that except that Tucker has spent more than seventy years on this earth, and the redhead — her name is Carlie — has only spent eighteen. When I picked up the truck, Carlie was in her eighth month with their first child, and I wondered if she could manage more than a few more hours, much less another month carrying a baby that would weigh in at ten or so pounds. She smilingly told me in a thick southern drawl that it was a boy and she and Tucker were going to name him Carl Tucker. Appropriate enough.

Old Tucker does one thing that gets to me; he tells anyone who will listen he's known me since before I could tell the difference between a fake and the real thing. When asked exactly what that means, Tucker takes great delight in telling how the story originated. He says when I was still in diapers and my mother was trying to switch me from breast milk to the bottle, she would wrap the warm bottle in a soft feather pillow, and I would go right on suckling, my small fingers gripping the pillow as if it was my mother's skin, just as nothing had changed. I don't mind the story, even if it isn't true, and even if he does wait to tell it until I am escorting a pretty lady around. They seem to enjoy hearing it, anyway. Trouble is, none of them has ever defended me. Sometimes I wonder if I do have a problem with telling the real from the false.

When I returned Tucker's four-wheel drive truck, he met me at the garage. "You see your friend, Dave?"

I handed him the keys and said, "Yes, I saw him."

There must have been a painful grimace plastered on my face because he quickly asked, "Something wrong?"

I gave it a moment before I replied. "Tuck, the man I went to see was killed."

He placed his hand on my arm. "Sorry to hear that, son. Anything I can do?"

I shook my head. "You into bringing people back from the dead now?" I put a little too much sarcasm in the words.

He looked hurt. "Didn't mean to pry, son, but I was thinking you might need someone to hear you out."

I mentally castigated myself for the harsh words. I laid my right hand on his shoulder. "Sorry, Tuck. It came as a shock and I guess the reality of his death is just setting in."

"You want to talk about it?"

I started to say no, but then stopped myself. "Yes, I guess I do."

"Then come on in and sit. Carlie is back in the bed resting, so we'll have the den to ourselves."

I followed Tucker into the house and through the living room to the back where he had built a room that looked more like an English pub than a den. There was a pool table, a dart board, and in the front corner a dark oak bar complete with sink, tap and refrigerator.

"What can I fix you, son?" He asked as we entered the room.

"Rum — black if you have it — over ice." While Tucker was making the drinks I wandered over to the back corner of the room where one of those monster projection TVs was set up. There was a video cabinet sitting beside the large screen which held an impressive array of titles. I looked at the end-flaps of the covers expecting to see what most people would display. Tucker was not most people. The titles ran the gambit; *Jill and Jack Fall From the Sack, Blow Like the Wind, The Parting of Dolly's Thighs,* and so on.

A man and woman in the throws of passion is a magnificent thing, but only for the two of them, and only when viewed in reality as a participant in the act. Voyeurism is not my cup-of-tea. Like most men, I have seen the gritty, slightly out-of-focus celluloid reels of man or men doing woman or women, and several variations on that basic story line. And I will admit to a certain vile-beast reaction to the squirming, thrashing, sweat-soaked bodies in their few minutes of stardom. However, as I got older, I began to view such flicks with a too-critical eye, catching the mistakes, the miscues and the painful grimaces when the orifice was not quite ready to accept the probe. And then I came to the place where I felt embarrassed at the antics, as though I was peeking through a keyhole at some unsuspecting couple, contorting themselves in their private moments, unaware anyone, especially one David Michael MacGruder, was viewing their ministrations.

After that, it was a small step to feeling soiled by watching, and I simply said "No more." I did not suddenly become a puritan. No one suddenly awakens to find themselves aghast at what he — or she — considers to be immoral. It is a slow process, much akin to aging.

I did not condemn Tucker. I simply hold some things sacred, and one of them is those moments of physical love between male and female.

Tucker brought the drinks. "Some collection," I said.

"They ain't mine, son. Belong to Carlie's brother. Me and her, we bought this here television from him, and they just sort of came with it. Carlie hates 'em, and she's been after me to get them out of the house. Says she won't bring our son back here until they're all gone. You want 'em?"

I took a sip of the dark liquid, then shook my head. "Not my style, Tuck."

He sipped his drink and sat back in a tall, pool-room chair. "Mine neither, but I have watched one of them. Made me damned tired watching that little girl on the screen doing what she was doing. Dave, I got me the prettiest wife in this world, and I like seeing her ... naked. But watching them folks on that screen, it makes me too aware of just how ugly men and women can be. So, I ain't watched no more of them, and I don't plan to, neither." He paused for a moment, took another sip of his drink, and then patted the chair next to his. "You sit on up here, son, and let's talk. What did you say your friend's name was?"

"Guron. Ben Guron," I said as I took the seat.

Tuck watched me for a second, then his eyes opened a little wider. "Guron, you say?" He paused and his eyes narrowed. "That name sounds familiar to me. Let's see now ... " He let his words trail off. "Well, it'll come to me in a while. What did you say happened to him?"

"I didn't say. Someone tried to push him off into the gorge, but they didn't push hard enough. He only fell twenty feet, but it had the same effect."

His gray eyes watched me. Then, "He — this Guron fellow — he lived up there?"

I shrugged. "I don't know where he lived, but it stands to reason it was somewhere close to where he was killed."

"Why'd you go up there to see him?"

Again I shrugged. "Sounds a little crazy, Tuck, but I went there because he asked me to go. I have no idea what it was all about. If I did, maybe it might help me to find out who killed him."

Tuck averted his eyes, sipping at his drink. "Ain't that a job for the police, son?"

"It is, but he was a friend, so it's my job to make sure they do theirs."

"Yes, I guess it is, him being a friend and all. How long you know him — this Guron fellow?"

"I met him while I was in the Navy. He was my skipper. Captain Guron ... "

Tucker interrupted me, snapped his fingers and jumped down from the chair. He disappeared into the dark of the house, returning a few seconds later, an envelope in his right hand. "Damn it all, son, I knew I'd heard that name before." He handed me the envelope. "Read that."

I pulled the folded paper from the envelope, unfolded it and began to read. Embossed across the top in heavy gold leaf was *Gorge Investment and Development Corporation, 115 Highway 441, Harlanwood, Georgia*. In smaller print, two spaces below was imprinted *Marvin Dubois, President and CEO*, then beneath that was *Benjamin Guron, Captain, United States Navy (Retired), Vice President.*

The letter was an advertisement, espousing the Tuck's good fortune at being allowed to invest in a growing corporation and at being given the opportunity to become one of the growing number of Georgia residents who had ventured their capital in this once-in-a-lifetime, never-to-be-repeated offer. For the meager sum of five thousand dollars, Tucker Markum would become a voting member of the board of trustees, and would hold one thousand shares of corporate stock, and a one-half-acre parcel of beautiful property overlooking Georgia's breathtaking Tallulah Gorge.

It was all very neat and tidy, and very persuasive, but it had the same smell as ten thousand identical schemes that touted the water-front properties that could be purchased in various parts of Florida, or the *ranch-acreage* that could be procured in Arizona. The problem with them all was the same; buy the land, and if it could be accessed, and if it fell above the Florida flood plane, or if the arid Arizona desert could be forced to yield enough potable water to sustain life, and if the purchaser could afford the cost of getting the electricity to the homesite, and if there were suitable roadways to support the builder's vehicles, then possibly a habitable home could be constructed. The bottom line was that pre-building costs could be ten-to-twenty times the cost of the property, which was always above the current market value.

"Tuck, when did you get this?"

He scratched his head. "Oh, I guess maybe two-three weeks ago. Man my age, being retired and all, and with enough money in the bank so that my credit report shows everything paid in-full — or at least paid up to date — gets lots of this sort of thing."

"You keep everyone you get?"

He laughed. "No. Don't keep hardly any of them. Funny thing about this one. When I saw Guron — I guess it was your friend — was a retired navy captain, I just thought this one might be up-and-up. With the baby coming and all, and me not getting any younger, I got to thinking about leaving Carlie and the baby something besides this old house. Oh, I got me some money saved — a good bit, too — and there's the farm down in Ware County, but a man can't do enough for his family when he goes. He's got to make sure they're taken care of. Guess maybe I thought that one might be the right thing to do. Anyway, I just hung on to it."

I read the letter again, and then a third time, trying to convince myself the name *Benjamin Guron* was not the same Ben Guron I had known. It couldn't be. The Ben Guron I had known was honest and brave and reliable. Whoever this Benjamin Guron was, he was anything but honest.

But there was a voice in my brain telling me there could only be one Benjamin Guron, Captain, United States Navy (Retired). Why? I asked myself. Simple. Tucker had said it. You stick a title behind the name and suddenly it all becomes very plausible and very palatable. Would a retired military officer allow his name to be used if it wasn't all legal and ethical? No way.

So why would Ben be involved in it if it wasn't legal and ethical? Maybe it was. Maybe he wanted to invite me into the flock, give me the opportunity to invest some of my hard-earned cash in something that would make me rich. Maybe he had waited for me out there on the pull-off, and he got bored, walked down the sloop onto the outcropping and slipped. Maybe the second set of prints had been there for a long time, and I was just seeing things. It wasn't murder at all. It was an accident. Ben Guron had slipped and fallen to his death, and I couldn't accept it, so I invented the rest.

Come out of it, MacGruder. It was no accident. He was murdered. And just as that is true, it is also true he was involved in a land development scheme that was perhaps designed to bilk the unsuspecting investors out of their money.

I didn't hear him at first, so he repeated his words. "Dave, are you all right?"

I shook myself. "Yeah, I'm okay." Then, "Tuck, you said you thought about investing in this ... " I opened the letter again and read the words from the top. "Gorge Investment and Development Corporation. Did you invest?"

He gave me an embarrassed smile. "No."

"Why not?"

His eyes never wavered from mine as he said, "Like I told you, a man wants to leave his family in good shape when he goes. I generally have these things checked out before I go putting money in them."

"Why, Tuck?"

"Well, because there are a lot of unscrupulous bastards out there, ready to take all they can get without any regard to who they get it from, or what hardships it causes by them taking it."

"And did you have this checked out?"

His eyes narrowed. "Why you asking me that, son?"

I shook my head. "I don't know. Maybe I'm looking for something."

His eyes narrowed even more. "You thinking maybe this Gorge Investment and Development Corporation ain't exactly legal?" His eyes softened. "Son, your friend is dead, and it ain't right to think harsh about the dead. Anyway, if you can call him a friend, then he was okay and maybe you just should put that out of your mind."

I shook my head. "Tuck, just answer me; did you have it checked out?"

He slowly nodded his head. "I did, son."

"And?"

"And my lawyer-son tells me the whole bunch of them officers in that corporation are as slick as eels, and I shouldn't be wasting my time or my money on them."

"And Ben? Did he ... did your son mention Ben?"

His eyes saddened. "He didn't exclude any of them."

I smacked my fist into my palm. "Damn it!"

"Now Dave, just 'cause my boy didn't tell me your friend was all right, it don't necessarily mean he was dirty."

I leaned back and closed my eyes. When I spoke, my voice was almost a whisper. "He wasn't dirty, Tuck, but he was involved, and that's almost as bad."

I felt a warm, rough hand on my arm. "Ain't necessarily so, Dave." I opened my eyes and looked at him. "People can be like sheep. They can be led to the slaughter without ever uttering a word, or even a sound. Happens all the time." He paused, seemingly weighing his next words carefully. "Your friend, was he married?"

I nodded. "To a very luscious piece, or so I've been told."

The old man chuckled. "Long time since I heard a female referred to as a *piece*. When I was a kid, you call a girl that, it meant only one thing; that she was available to anyone who wanted her. Those were the kinds of girls we snuck around and saw, and then only for one reason. A good boy would never take one of those home to meet his mother. Most of them ended up marrying some poor unsuspecting lad they managed to convince had fathered their unborn child. Sometimes that was true enough, but most of the time not. The ones who didn't get married ended up working down in Jacksonville, and the work they did was all done in a bed with soiled linen." He paused and sipped the last drops from his glass. He arose from his chair, eyed my glass, and when I shook my head, went over and fixed himself another drink. When he came back to the chair, and had settled himself in, he asked, "Reckon you might have something there? Calling her a *piece*, I mean? What you know about her?"

"Her name's Gloria. She was a Spence. May have done some time on the streets. Ended up in someone's bed — may have been a politician — but without any legal bonds. My guess is she saw Ben Guron and figured he would be a good one to latch onto. Ben had never been married. He was older and she was pretty. They courted — in Washington society — the right parties, the select social events — and then married. Ben retired and they moved back here. Somewhere along the line, he got involved with the Gorge Investment and Development Corporation. The rest you know."

Tucker Markum thought about that for a good two minutes before he spoke. "So maybe she opened more than her heart to him. Young pretty woman takes a liking to an older man, it does something to his ego. Maybe she opened her arms — and her legs — and offered him something he needed. She's all warm and ready and willing, and he goes a little crazy. He's thinking he's old and worn out and she just shows him a little thigh, or some silk panty filled with soft woman-flesh, and he goes all dumb and stupid inside. Then maybe she does a few things that make him feel young and renewed, and then when he thinks he can't react again, she shows him something else that awakens him. He ends up feeling like he was a young buck. He begins to feel almost the same as he did when he was a teen, and before he knows it, she's sort of roped him in. Maybe he was too blind in love to see her for what she really was. When he finally did open his eyes, maybe he called you. Maybe he was going to ask you to help him get out."

I had always liked Tucker Markum, even when I was a kid, but suddenly I saw in him what my father surely must have seen. Tucker possessed an innate goodness that made him search for reasons that would logically explain why a man might make a mistake.

I was about to reply when a sleepy voice called from the doorway, "Tuck, sweetie, why didn't you tell me David was here? You should have come in and got me up. I could have fixed you something to eat."

Carlie stood framed in the doorway, her eyes red from sleep, the unborn child seemingly about to burst from her womb. When she glanced at her husband, I saw a deep affection and a need that I had never known, and I knew that whatever Carlie was, she was not a Gloria Spence. In this home, age was not defined in years. It was a state of mind and of being, and for Tuck the years had rolled back, while for Carlie they had rolled forward, until the two of them met in that age which can only be described as mutual devotion.

I arose from the chair, setting the half-empty glass on the table. "Kids, I have a date tonight with a very lovely lady, and I don't want to be late." I turned to Tuck. "Thanks, old friend. I listened and I heard." I moved to where Carlie was standing in the doorway, put my arms around her and hugged her close. "You take care of Tucker, your baby, and yourself, and if you are looking for a godfather, keep me in mind."

I walked from their house leaving them both staring wide-eyed after me.

Chapter Four

I made my way down the lane to the highway. I had visions of hitch-hiking back into Atlanta, but as luck would have it, a cab just happened along at the right time. I hailed it and had the driver take me to the airport. He dropped me off at one of the large green signs directing pickup and discharge of passengers, and went on to tell the drivers that violators would be prosecuted. Something about southern hospitality that warms my heart.

I walked through the door and up to the counter. I rented a compact Chrysler convertible from a pretty young woman with bright green eyes who smiled up at me, took down all the information and passed the keys across the counter to me. When I walked out into the parking area, the blast of heat stunned me. I could feel sharp trickles of perspiration beginning to run down my back.

I had no trouble finding the convertible. It was exactly where the girl said it would be. When I started it up and turned the air conditioner to full cold, I felt the chilling breeze coming from the vents within a few seconds. By the time I had the seat adjusted properly to allow my long legs some stretching room, the interior of the car was approaching the freezing point. I adjusted the temperature, pulled the gearshift down into reverse and backed out.

I had to stop only once to ask directions. I had expected an apartment, or at the most, one of those small townhouses that seem to attract the youthful set. 10441 Peach Tree Lane was neither of those. It was one of those zero lot limit, patio homes which seem to be springing up all over the countryside today.

The driveway led to a two-car garage, so I parked on the cement about ten feet from the garage door, leaving enough room for Mickie to get her car out if she was the designated-driver for the evening. I checked my watch. It was five-forty-five. Damn, I thought. Early. I was about to put the car in reverse and back out, when the garage door started to rise. I turned in the seat to see a smiling Mickie behind the wheel of an impressive Detroit roadster. It was a red Mustang GT convertible, and I had the sudden inspiration to applaud Mickie on her choice.

I got out of the car and walked into the garage as she was pulling in. When she got out of the car, I was going to tell her I could go away and come back, but the door came down as soon as she stopped. She came out of the car all warm arms and soft lips and hot body pressed against mine, and I felt my head starting to spin. Her lips tasted of sweet rouge and her arms held me tightly. There was an urgency about the kiss that signalled trouble, but I was too dizzy to care. And then there was just a little too much female body molding itself to me to give the signal any more thought.

When the embrace ended, I stepped back unsteadily and looked at her. "You always greet your dates that way?"

She gave me an impish smile. "Only the ones who are going to stay the night."

The surprise was not feigned. "Oh. Am I staying the night?"

She leaned back and nodded slowly, her arms around my neck. "You are if I have anything to say about it." Then she kissed me again and I felt the dizziness coming back.

This time when the kiss ended, I could see its effects in her eyes, too. She leaned her face against my chest and

44

spoke in a soft, willowy voice.   "David, can we do something we've never really done before?"

I stroked her hair. "Depends on just what it is," I said.

I felt her chuckle against me. "Oh, don't we have a dirty mind."

"Excitable, yes, but not dirty," I said. "What is it you wanted to do?"

I felt her tense slightly, then she moved away from me, her eyes searching mine. "Talk."

"Talk? Mickie, we've talked a million times before."

Her eyes glazed. "Yes, but never about us."

I stepped away from her, my hands holding her arms. "Lady, as I recall, we've had the *Where-are-we-going-with-this-relationship* conversation before, so if that's the *us* you want to discuss, we've run the subject up the flag pole before, and there was no wind. I think we've run out of words on that particular subject."

Mickie looked as though she wanted to protest, but instead she smiled. "You're early."

I nodded. "I know I am. Want me to go away and come back when the lady is properly dressed for an evening on the town?"

"No," she responded. "I've changed my mind. I don't want to go out with you."

"Oh?"

She smiled. "No. I want us to stay right here tonight and see if we can solve a problem I've had for a long time."

"And just what might that problem be?"

Her soft, pliant, desirably warm female body pressed against me. There was a slight, lewd-sexy grinding of hips against mine. Then her face was only two inches from mine when she whispered, "I remember a delectable naughtiness about you and me and us, and I want to know if it was real, or if it was just some silly trick my mind was playing on me."

I opened my eyes widely in a mock pained expression. "Do you mean you asked me here so you could take advantage of me?"

She giggled softly. "Something like that." I felt the pressure of her loins against me. Her eyes glittered and her voice dropped half an octave. "And something tells me that you have almost the same thing in mind."

I stepped back a few inches and took her hand. "I don't know the layout, or I would lead the way."

She smiled and pulled me into the house, through a maze of neatness, feminine adornments and faintly soft female scents, up a flight of stairs and into a loft bedroom overlooking the living room. The drapes were pulled, but the room was lit by the evening sun. She gave me an excitedly-embarrassed smile and began unbuttoning her blouse. It dropped to the floor, and was closely followed by her skirt. She stood, a look of defiance on her face, the black slip shrouding her while conforming to her every curve. It was a tantalizing sight. I felt my head spinning as I looked at her. There was a lot of tanned female skin showing under, around, and below the satin slip, and I gazed at it all.

In a deft motion, she raised the slip and removed it, standing before me in black lace bra and panties. Then the bra dropped and the panties slipped down, and she stood before me naked. Her lips parted and her tongue licked out seductively, but the smile was questioning.

I slipped into the bed beside her and she came into my arms, our mutual excitement evident and urging. I kissed her and she rolled over, pulling me atop her. I felt the sting of moist heat and the pliant resilience of her against me. Then, suddenly, almost imperceptively, I knew something was wrong. She was willing, even eager, her lips against mine, open, sweet, pleading, but there was a slight reluctance to culminate, a downward movement of hips as I pressed against her.

I propped myself up on arms shaky from desire, looked down into her face, my body poised against her, ready to make the onslaught. "Want to tell me?"

Her eyes opened wide. "What?" she murmured in a whisper.

I rolled from her, pulling her with me. When we were on our sides facing each other, I asked, "Why you resisted?"

Her eyes narrowed. "I ... I didn't."

I smiled. "Yes, Mickie, you did, and it was as obvious as something like that could be." I reached out and touched her cheek. "It's okay, though. I mean, you and I, we have this thing. We've talked and we've loved — in our own way. A while ago, there was something inside you that said it just wouldn't be right. I felt it. Now, you want to tell me why?"

She tried to look incredulous, but the tears filling her eyes betrayed her. Then she was nestled against me, her body quivering, but not from desire. She was crying softly, her face buried in the crook of my neck.

I stroked her hair and kissed her cheek, tasting the salty moisture that ran from her eyes. It all came out in a rush. There was a guy, a nice guy. He said he loved her. He wanted to marry her. She thought she loved him but she was unsure, and every time he held her, her mind would play those silly tricks on her. She wondered about me, about her, about us and the way she remembered thinking it could be, and she didn't know about him.

She had never slept with him. "He's a nice guy, David, and he makes me feel wanted, but somehow I can never bring myself to sleep with him ... to make love to him. At first I thought it was just me, just some old reluctance coming back to the surface. But then, when I couldn't do it,

I began to think maybe there was something wrong with me, something that kept me from responding. That's when I remembered the way you made me feel, and I ..."

I cut her off. "You thought maybe you'd see if it was different with me."

I felt her head nod against my neck. "But I couldn't do it with you, either." I felt her tremble. "There must be something wrong with me. Every time he wanted it to happen, so did I, but when it came time, I stopped it. I would make excuses and he always accepted them. Then he would go away smiling back at me. I keep thinking he'll stay away, but he always returns. Always."

"So why me, Doll?" Dumb question, but it slipped out before I could stop the words.

And then the tears came back and she told me she had to know. She had to know if there was something wrong with her, and if not, whether she and I could be a couple. So she had made up her mind to have me, just to see if it was real or if it was only her imagination that made it so good.

"But Dave, when I felt you almost in me, I knew I couldn't do it. I felt cold and dirty and cheap."

"And maybe you finally found out you love this guy."

"I do love Tom and I want to marry him." She snuffled. "And I just can't do this to him. I could never face him again, and I could never forgive myself."

"Shhh. I know. I understand."

After a few seconds of silence, she said, "Now I'll never know ... about me."

I brought my hand down and touched her breast. She shuddered and caught her breath. I let my hand slip lower. When I touched her, she shuddered again and sighed, her hips arching toward me. I kissed her quickly on the tip of the nose and said, "Nothing wrong with you, lady, except conscience, and that's the best quality to have."

I left her on the bed, slipped into my jeans and went downstairs and out onto the rear deck. I had finished my third cigarette when she came out into the moonlight. I could see the flimsy hue of white silk covering her.

"David?" she called to me from the other side of the deck.

"I'm here, Mickie."

She came over to me, and leaned against the rail. "I'm sorry, David."

"About what?" I asked.

"About ... about what I did."

"Hey lady, we're friends. We've been friends for a long time. You don't owe me anything except honesty. That's all. I figure we're even, Mickie."

"Even? How?"

"Well, let's just say if we had gone through with it, you wouldn't have been able to marry this guy you're in love with. And sooner or later you would tell me, and I would feel guilty so I'd have to marry you. You would hate it and then, after a while, I would hate it. We'd get a divorce and I'd feel compelled to pay you lots of alimony. The way I see it, you saved us both a lot of grief and me a lot of money."

She wasn't touching me but I could feel her stiffen, and I had the sudden urge to run. I had witnessed her Irish temper before. But I stayed put, bracing myself in the dark for the blow I was certain would come. Then I felt the rail begin to shake. I thought she was cold, but then I heard her teeter in the dark. And I started to laugh, too.

After a while, she said, "David, you are a bastard. What the hell do you mean saying I saved you money, damn you? Couldn't you have said your heart was broken, or you would never let me go?"

"Doll, if I thought that it would have made any difference, that's exactly what I would have said." I paused for a moment. Then, "But we both know it wouldn't have made a difference."

She moved the few inches separating us, her face an inch from mine. I could feel her hot breath on my cheek. "No, I don't suppose it would have," she whispered.

I felt the pain of loss and I wondered why. I had never had her, so how could I lose her? Then, as suddenly as the pain came, it left, and as it went, I knew it wasn't the pain of losing her, it was the pain of the failed conquest, and that was a pain I could certainly live with.

I held her for a few moments, then I asked, "Got any coffee in there?"

"Got some of the best instant coffee on the market, provided you like the cheapest thing they put on the shelf."

"I do." I patted her warm rump as she walked away.

We were seated at her table. Somewhere during the minutes that had passed, I managed to get dressed. I sipped at the steaming mug, choking the bitter brew down.

Mickie's mood had changed. She was the professional again, and I suddenly knew this was the Mickie that I was attracted to. She placed her elbows on the table, stifled a yawn and said, "David, Wiley asked me to pass something along to you."

"Yes?" I asked.

"He said he thinks he knows how your friend got involved in that Gorge Investment and Development Corporation. It's headed by a man named Marvin Dubois. This Dubois is Gloria Guron's cousin. He also said to tell you there's another Dubois involved — Marvin's brother, Cleet Dubois, and Wiley said word on the street is this Cleet Dubois is a real bad character."

"He tell you anything else?"

She shook her head. "That's it, except he was taking the early morning flight to Washington. He also said he would try to get back as soon as he can."

I finished the coffee and stood. "Well, it's been a long day and I'm tired. Guess I'd better be running."

She looked up at me, her eyes veiled. "You can sleep on the couch if you'd like."

"Aren't you afraid I'll start thinking about how close it was?"

She smiled. "I'm more afraid I will." Mickie stood. "I'll get some sheets and a pillow."

"You sure?" I asked as she was walking to the door.

She stopped, her back to me. "Yes, David, I'm sure."

We went through the motions and when the couch was readied, Mickie gave me a quick kiss on the cheek, then headed off up the stairs. In the time between crawling beneath the sheets and awaiting the arrival of sleep, I thought about Mickie, and her warm female flesh just up the stairs. In my mind, I saw her beckoning me toward her, but every time I took a step, she would disappear, only to reappear behind me. I gritted my teeth and cursed, and found it difficult to keep myself from climbing the stairs. It promised to be a long, fretful night.

I had just slipped off into semiconsciousness when I felt a warm body nestle close to me on the couch, warm hands touch me, then a tentative testing followed by a nervous shifting of weight. I felt warm lips touch mine and I had the urge to take her in my arms and take her up on the offer. I fought the urge back and feigned sleep even though I was ready. Then I felt her move and felt her weight on me, then a moment of uncertainty, then warmth engulfing me. Then, after another moment, I gave in to the closeness of the moment.

I held her gently, tasting the sweetness of her tears, then the eagerness of her need. When I kissed her, I felt the knowing awareness this moment was special, for her and for me.

It was a slow, even, testing time, and neither of us spoke. It was almost as though we were in some kind of trance, each aware of all that was happening, yet somehow disembodied, viewing it from some high place. There was no thrashing, no screaming, no hurried, uncontrolled movements when it came, merely a quickening of pulse, a tensing of muscle, a strain and a sigh, and still no words.

When it was over, there was no awkwardness, no tears, just a soft, warm kiss and an embrace. And then after a while, I felt the warmth leave me and I heard her pad up the stairs.

Chapter Five

I was up and dressed before Mickie awoke. I didn't feel like facing her. I didn't want the apologies that might come, or the embarrassed smiles that would surely come. I guess I'm just a coward at heart.

When I walked from her house, I felt as though I had stolen some obscure prize from her. I could have stopped it. I should have, but I didn't. I wondered why I had let it happen, why I had been so docile. It had started being that way for me lately. Something within me was gnawing at my inner self, screaming for more and more. The years had slipped by, and as I looked back on them, I didn't like what I saw: one ruined marriage which had given me four daughters I didn't even know; another child — a son — born out of what should have become a marriage but didn't; too many pretty ladies in and out of my life as though through some dilapidated saloon, its swinging doors swaying loosely from ripped hinges. I was no adolescent male-child any longer, able to excuse my liaisons as forays into masculinity. I wasn't even young any longer. I was approaching fifty years, and middle age was looming ever closer.

Perhaps I could excuse my reluctance at saying no to Mickie as a moment of questioning where the answer could only be given in tenderness. Even as I said it to myself, I knew that was not so. Oh MacGruder, you fearless bastard. You strove directly into the lion's den and devoured the lioness. Only the lioness was not wild. She had been tame and docile and had needed warmth and friendship. And what had you given her, MacGruder? Sex. You had set the trap and she had wandered into it, her eyes clouded with fear of what might lay somewhere out in her dim future. You had rumpled her mane and scratched her head, and she had licked your hand, and once you had her there, you took her rather than relate to her. Afterward, you didn't even have the nerve to stay and comfort her in the light of the new morning. You really are a snake, MacGruder.

I drove out to Powder Springs, the mental abrasive scarring my ego. But I deserved it. The doc had given me a key just in case I needed to get in. As I unlocked the door, I blessed her thoughtfulness. I needed a hot shower, a close shave and some clean clothes. Then I needed a cup of coffee.

The phone rang as I was about to leave. I got to it and picked it up. "Frazier residence," I said into the mouthpiece.

"David?"

I knew the voice. "Hello Mickie."

There was a brief silence at the other end. "About last night ... "

I cut her off. "Listen, I'm sorry. I shouldn't have let it happen."

There was another silence. Then, "You shouldn't have let it happen? As I recall, it was all my doing."

"Yes, but I could have stopped it," I said, my voice full of self-loathing.

"Why you egotistical ..." The anger was evident. Then I heard her laugh. "I called you to apologize for using you. After the first failed try and our talk, I got the notion to finish what I had started." She paused for a moment. "David, when are you going to realize it doesn't have to always be the man who controls the act. Once in a while, the woman can take the initiative. I used you because I needed you. I think it's the first time in months I've slept really well. If you hadn't slipped out this morning like some silly school boy, I would have told you that to your face."

"Mickie, you don't have to ..."

It was her turn to cut me off. "David MacGruder, why is it all men think when it happens, it's all their doing? Most women have the same drives as men. We have the same needs, so why can't it be up to us once in a while?"

"I ... guess ... I guess it can be."

She laughed again. "It can and it was, lover. And at least I found out that I can still respond."

I smiled into the phone. "Yes, you can certainly do that." Then, "So now you can marry Tom and live happily ever after."

"No, I can't."

"You can't? Why not?" I asked.

"Because of last night."

I tried to make my voice light. "Wait a minute, doll. We went through all that. Remember?"

She gave a knowing laugh. "Oh, now don't expect me to become some godawful red-headed Irish albatross hanging around your neck. We frolicked and I enjoyed it totally and without regret, but that does not mean this lady wants MacGruder as a husband."

"And Tom?"

A brief pause punctuated her next words. "Maybe it's Tom that's the problem, David. Maybe the reason I couldn't ... sleep with him is he's just too nice. See, every time I considered ending it, his manner made me feel guilty about it, like I should have done it even though I didn't want to do it with him. Last night, when I stopped it, you accepted it and you said words, but none of them made me feel guilty about saying no."

"I told you we are friends, and I meant it. Friends don't have to give reasons for saying no."

"And that's it. Tom loves me, and I ... well, I suppose I love him, too, but not in the same way. I love him like a child would love a wet puppy. I want to hold him and dry him and pet him, but that's all. See, MacGruder, Tom and I aren't friends. And because of that, he could never really understand why I might say no to him. But, damn him, he would smile and say it's all right, then I would feel guilty, and if I gave in because of the guilt, sooner or later I would begin to detest him because of it. And if I didn't give in, I would begin to detest myself."

"So that's what it was all about?"

"Last night?" she asked. Then before I could respond, "I suppose last night was a closing of one door and an opening of another. You made me a little too aware there is a very human side of me, and I had to find out if it was a good thing."

And is it?" I asked softly.

She laughed gently. "It is, and I just wanted to say thank you for teaching me I am human enough to be tender." Then, "I wanted to say something else, too."

"What is it?"

"David, you are my friend, and my door is always open to you."

Somehow I knew she had more to say so I kept silent. "But only as a friend."

I felt my heart grow heavy, as though I had lost another good one. But I kept my voice light as I said, "Mickie, last night was a beautiful moment which I will never forget."

There was a moment of silence on the other end of the phone. "David, I just wanted you to know I'm always here for you if you need a friend."

"I'll keep it in mind, doll." I heard the phone go dead.

Atlanta is an easy enough city to motor through, but only as long as you know exactly where you are going, how to get there, how to avoid the usual traffic snarls, and so on. Even so, I had no trouble finding the GBI building, and even less finding the person I hoped would be my contact.

When I asked directions, I was told where I could find Agent Carlisle. The door of the office was open. I stopped just outside, a throwback to my courteous military days. She was standing beside an orderly desk, digging through a file cabinet which had been placed a foot or so from the corner.

Georgia Bureau of Investigation Agent Carlisle looked to be in her mid-thirties. She was a brunette with sparkling brown eyes and good, strong features. She was also pretty, but not in the Barbie Doll sort of way. There was absolutely nothing fragile about this woman. She was large boned and stood almost six feet tall. Her features were not soft or subtle, yet they were feminine and pleasant. Hers was a beauty that was innate, apparent only at a second or maybe third or fourth glance. At the first look, you would see her nose was crooked and one of her eyelids drooped slightly, and there was a small scar at the right corner of her mouth. If you took a second glance, you would see her mouth was full, her smile could be generous and her teeth were straight. If you took any follow-on looks, you would see she had a body complete with all the curves, valleys and rises so attractive in the female gender. If you took one last look, you would see the hint of physical power and inner strength.

"Agent Carlisle?" I called from the open doorway.

She turned. "Yes?"

I took the few steps separating us, extended my hand, and said, "David MacGruder."

Her handshake was firm and the intensity of her stare forced a smile from me, which she returned without hesitation. "I didn't expect you so early." The light blue blouse and dark blue skirt she was wearing showed full breasts, narrow waist and nicely rounded hips. The calves, encased in dark hose, were muscular and firm, the ankles smooth. The navy blue pumps had three-inch heels, but there was no hint of awkwardness as she stood in them.

She motioned me toward a chair and I sat. "Actually, I'm not here to give my statement, at least not until after we've talked."

There was a brief moment of raised eyebrows. "Is there a problem?"

I shook my head. "No, not really, except I have a few questions that need to be answered."

She watched me for a few seconds, then smiled. "All right. There's plenty of time." Her brown eyes darkened. "I get the feeling I'm about to be interrogated. Maybe you should tell me why I should answer your questions."

"Because I have a stake in this investigation, and because you made me more than just a witness."

Her dark brows raised. "I did?"

I nodded slowly. "You did."

"How?" she asked.

"Let me quote you: *When the deputies get there, you tell them you are acting on behalf of the GBI. Tell them you are a special agent on detached duty.* Those were your words?" I asked her.

She nodded. "Sounds pretty much like what I said. So?"

"So, in effect you deputized me."

She shrugged. "Maybe I was just trying to make it easier on you, in case the questions got a little too heavy."

"Or maybe you know more about this than you are letting on."

Again the shrug. "I've known Boone Swabble long enough to know when he says a person is all right, he's all right."

"And he said I'm okay?"

She nodded. "He told me a story about something that went on over in Milledgeville, and how you handled it so all the loose ends were tied up. He said you could be trusted. He has your name in his special file, and when he took the assignment with the ..." She let her words trail off. "When he went on detached duty, he gave me his special file. I have an excellent memory, so when you called, I knew who you were. I acted accordingly."

"Where is Boone?"

She shook her head. "I can't tell you."

"I could find out."

Her eyes watched me. Then she took a deep breath and let it out slowly. "I guess you could at that." Her eyes watched me for a few moments, then she got up, went around the desk and to the door, closing it. When she was seated again, she put her arms on her desk and said, "That action you set off down in Milledgeville cut into the Drug Enforcement Agency's resources pretty badly. That agent who got killed ... ?"

"Fimms," I cut in.

She nodded. "Yes, Fimms. He's the one who caused the investigation. Seems he was one of many. Those DEA boys are pretty proud of their record. They don't like it when one of their own turns bad. Anyway, you got one of the bad ones, and they got the rest, so they had a few holes in their organization. Boone Swabble is one of the best investigators I've ever known, and apparently the DEA felt the same way because they borrowed him from the GBI. Satisfied?"

I nodded at her. "So now I know what happened to Swabble. So now why don't you tell me why you suddenly decided to make me an unofficial Georgia Bureau of Investigation agent."

Those big, brown eyes watched me for a few seconds before she sat back, pulled the top drawer of her desk open and handed me a neatly typed, official State of Georgia form. "Read that and sign it." She slid an ink pen across to me. "We'll wave the oath because it's the same one you took when you got your private license, except for a few words, so you are already sworn to abide by the laws of the state."

I read the form. It stated in so many words David Michael MacGruder was being duly sworn as a special agent of the GBI, and by signing the form, he swore to uphold and defend the constitution of the State of Georgia, and to obey all legally issued orders from his superiors; all nice and legal and binding. I tossed the form back on the desk. "What in hell are you doing?"

Her brown eyes softened. "I'm ... we're making it easier for you to find the killer."

I surveyed her from across the desk. "And you're putting me in a position where anything I find out will be the property of the state."

Her eyes hardened. "Need I remind you that you have a legal responsibility to hand over anything you find out about this murder?"

I returned her hard glance. "Ever hear of client confidentiality?"

Her eyes softened and the corners of her mouth turned up a millimeter. "Your client is dead, Mr. MacGruder. His confidentiality doesn't matter any longer." Then she leaned forward. "Is there some reason why you won't help us in this matter?"

There was an edge on my voice that surprised me when I said, "Agent Carlisle, Ben Guron — the man who was killed — was an old friend. I went up there to see him, at his request, and finding him ... dead was quite a shock."

"Of course. I understand." After a moment, she added, "You went there on a business matter." She had said it as though she assumed that's what it was, but there was an

60

underlying question, and she waited for me to confirm or deny her assumption.

"I went there because an old friend I hadn't seen in a long time wanted to talk to me. Whether it was a personal or business matter, I don't know."

The right corner of her mouth lifted slightly. "Oh, I see. He called you and you came up from Ft. Lauderdale, Florida — at no small expense — and you have no idea what is was all about."

It was my turn to raise my brows. "You sound as though you find that hard to believe."

She leaned back in her chair, curled the fingers of her right hand and touched her lower lip. Then she brought her hand out a little and raised her index finger. "Can we say that I find it unusual?"

"Unusual? How?" I asked.

"Mr. MacGruder, you're in business. Airline tickets and rental cars cost money. A friend you hadn't seen in a long time calls and you come. You didn't even bother to ask what it was all about. I find that an unusual thing for a business person to do, especially when that particular business person is a private investigator of your caliber." She must have seen my eyes widen because she added, "I've already told you about Boone Swabble's file, and it was easy enough to check out MacGruder-Frazier Investigations. Just to make sure, I made a few more calls. You seem to be quite a celebrity with the county and city agencies in south Florida."

"Okay, so I have this thing for friends. They call and need me, I come without asking questions. It's a flaw in my personality, but it isn't illegal, immoral or unethical."

She did the thing with her fingers again. I found it very disconcerting, a little too attractive and a bit too distracting. "Maybe that's why I think your time will be better served as an agent than on a private basis."

"Agent Carlisle, why is it so important to you?"

She sat forward in her chair. "Because, Mr. MacGruder, a man was killed, and I want to know why so I can find out who did it."

"A little out of your jurisdiction, isn't it?"

She shook her head adamantly. "No, not really. The GBI is chartered to assist in these matters when the local authorities don't have the manpower or the expertise."

I watched her from across the room. "So the locals have asked for your assistance?"

She smiled. "Let's put it this way; we have reason to be interested in the deceased. His death may be tied to some other illegal activities which fall within our purview."

My mind weighed her words for a few seconds. Sometimes it's better to lay your cards face up on the table at the end of a hand, just so everyone will know you didn't bluff your way through. Something told me this was one of those times. "I want to know who killed Ben as much as you do."

She eyed me for a few seconds. "You may have more reason to find the killer than we do, and that's what this is all about." She pushed the paper across to me. "Maybe, together, we can find out who did this and why. Maybe I can help you."

I watched her for a few seconds. I had no doubt that I could find out who had killed Ben, and why, but once I found out, what could I do? With the backlog in the courts, and the justice system the way it is, even if I found out who killed Ben, there was no guarantee it would ever go any further than that. As a private citizen, I might get away with administering punishment on the guilty party — or parties, but it would certainly bring a certain amount of negative notoriety to MacGruder-Frazier Investigations, or maybe worse. If it brought discredit, Wiley and Virginia would suffer. They would be innocent bystanders who are punished because the law fails to adequately punish the guilty.

I glanced down at the form. Maybe this would allow me to get to the killer and ensure justice was served without endangering the lives or livelihoods of people I love.

I picked up the pen and signed my name on the line at the bottom of the page. I slid the paper across to her, and asked, "What next?"

She opened the drawer again and took out a leather badge holder and tossed it across to me. "Your badge, Special Agent MacGruder."

I picked up the holder and opened it. Inside was a gold shield with the words *Special Agent, Georgia Bureau of Investigations.* The number *1192* was engraved in the center of the badge. I closed the folder and slipped it into my shirt pocket. "Okay, so I'm on the payroll."

Agent Carlisle laughed. "As a special agent, you'll make exactly one-half of what I make, which means that you are entitled to $67.31 a day, plus reasonable expenses, and welfare if you're so inclined."

"I'll get rich." The sarcasm in my voice was evident.

Her eyes darkened again. "No you won't, no more than any of the rest of us do. If you are injured, the state will cover the expenses. If you are killed, we'll all turn out in our Sunday best to say good-bye to a fellow officer."

"Sounds better and better all the time," I said. "I can't think of anything more to wish for."

"MacGruder, the most you can hope for is you'll find out who killed your friend. If we are lucky enough to find that person ... or persons, it may make the streets a little safer for the people of this state."

I watched her for a few moments. "And is that why you do this?"

Her eyes grew suddenly sad. "My dad was a deputy sheriff down in Ware County. He was strictly by the book.

If it was illegal, he wouldn't bend. He ruffled a lot of feathers down there. He took my mother out on a picnic one Sunday afternoon. The next day they found them. Someone had tied them to a tree and killed them. The good old boys who killed my father are still out there somewhere." Tears had filled her eyes. "That's why I do it."

I tilted my head. "I'm sorry."

When I looked up, she was staring at me defiantly. "Sorry? Why?"

"Because I tend to forget I was once a cop. Sometimes I have to remind myself there is a reason to serve and protect."

She had regained her control, and her smile was warm. "We all do that at times." She reached across the desk, her hand outstretched. "Agent MacGruder, let me be the first to welcome you to the Georgia Bureau of Investigation." Her hand was warm and her grip was firm.

I held her hand longer than I should have. "You and I, are we partners?"

She did not try to pull her hand away, and her eyes smiled into mine. She nodded. "Yes, I guess we are."

"Then I'm David," I said, releasing her hand.

"And I'm Brenda."

Chapter Six

Brenda Carlisle had gone through all the motions of introducing me to my newly acquired compadres, but through all the introductions, she made certain that I was infinitely aware my services to the State of Georgia and the GBI would be through her and her alone. She would be my contact and my superior, but that was okay with me.

Somewhere along the line, I had my picture and my prints taken. I was presented with an official GBI identification card, which I put it in the holder along with the badge. Suddenly I was beginning to feel like the people's servant.

When the introductions had been completely, Brenda suggested we adjourn to a more secluded spot. I told her that was fine by me. She found us adequate seclusion in a restaurant called *The Farm House*.

When we were all settled in, and the waitress had taken our order, I informed her, "I think it's time you told me something about what's going on."

She smiled. "Aside from the murder, you mean." When I nodded, she shrugged and said, "It's a long story."

"You seem to have arranged it so I have got all the time in the world."

"You could have declined my offer."

It was my turn to shrug. "Turn down all that money? Not on your life." After a moment, I went on. "It has something to do with the Gorge Investment and Development Corporation, doesn't it?"

Her eyes narrowed and she placed her elbows on the table. "How much do you know about them?" she asked.

"I know they are a land development syndicate, and I know Marvin Dubois is president and CEO, and Ben Guron was the VP, at least on paper. I'm smart enough to know that although most land development syndicates are above board, some aren't. My instincts tell me that Gorge Development isn't."

Brenda studied me for a few moments from across the table. "No," she said. "Gorge Development isn't."

"How dirty are they?"

She smiled ruefully. "Oh they've made it all appear clean and legal. Lots of good family names on the board of directors, and lots of good old Georgia money backing them. But it stinks like a truck load of dead fish."

"So why not just go in and arrest them?"

She shook her head. "It isn't that easy, and you know it. It's all quite legal and effective at separating the small time investor from his — or her — money, most of whom can't afford to lose the money in the first place."

I nodded at her. "I've seen it before. Let me give it a stab." I paused and took a sip of water. "They do it this way," I started. "A couple of big-dollar types — or big banking types — buy options on properties that look as though they'll appreciate in value, or will become prime for development. They set it up so it will be attractive to the small investor; someone who has a few thousand to put in the right place. They do it right. They set up corporations and investment syndicates. They buy all the right licenses and they pay the taxes on time and up front. They get fancy offices and give each other titles such as vice president for field operations and secretary for internal audits, and so on. Once they have everything in place, the sharks go hunting. They target people who don't have a lot to invest, so they have to get out quickly. And the sharks find the people who are ready for the easy buck, the quick turnaround, the large profit on the small investment. There are lots of them everywhere, and Georgia is no exception. Take out a few adds in the right papers, and mail out a few flyers, and the get-rich-quick types will flock to the door, only most of them can't afford the loss."

Brenda nodded her head. "And this thing is set up so there won't be any profits, except for the ones who get in up front."

"The obvious question is if the backers invest like the others, don't they stand to lose?"

Brenda shook her head, her brown hair swaying with her movement. "You know how it goes; promissory notes and no cash, not ever, not from the corporate people." She raised her eyebrows in a forlorn question. "And that's the part I don't understand."

"It's simple. A scout finds a piece of property. Then some sleazy lawyer writes a contract that goes something like the parties of the first part promise to pay the parties of the second part X dollars on a certain date as an option to purchase the property described below. Et cetera. You dig deep enough through the maze of corporations and pseudo corporations, and at the bottom you'll most likely find the parties of the first part already own the land."

The waitress brought our lunch. After it was set out before us and she had gone, Brenda watched me. "So how do they bilk the investors?" she asked.

I dug at my food with my fork. After a few seconds, when I was certain I was in no mood to eat, I let it drop to the plate. "You have to understand the contracts are written so that if one of the investors fails to come up with his or her portion of the cash-call, their interest in the corporation is reduced by that amount. The corporate heads are allowed to write a promissory note for the amount due, so they still haven't invested any money. If they do come up with the amount required, so much the better. The bank account has just increased. Put the buy-in at five-to-ten thousand, find a hundred people who want in, and you have five hundred thousand to one million dollars in the bank. The first sting — cash call — comes when it's time to buy the option. If the property already belongs to one or more of the corporate heads, that's all the better. Let's say this is only a three thousand dollar call. Put another three hundred grand in the bank and it's all profit. The next cash call comes when it's time to buy the property — at a higher value than it's worth. Let's put this one at five thousand. That's another five hundred grand, but some of the investors won't be able to come up with the cash, so their interest in the corporations is reduced. Someone who invested five thousand up front has now lost sixty per cent of his or her investment, while the corporation has a bankroll of at least one point three million. If the cost of the land was, oh let's say, one point three million but true market value is only five hundred thousand, the corporation is technically eight hundred grand in the hole, and that makes them insolvent. They can't borrow against the property because its paper value is more than its actual value. So what do they do? Another cash-call. Maybe this one is for improvements to the property, such as roads or sewers or utilities, or maybe all, and all going to one — or all — of the corporate officers under a subsidiary company and charged at two or three times the going rate. If the sharks did their job correctly, this will finish the remaining investors. They don't pay, they lose their interest in the corporation, and they say good-bye to their investments. Maybe some do pay. If so, there will be other cash-calls, and they'll keep right on until they fail to meet the deadline, and they're out, too. The only ones who have made any money are the officers in the corporation through loopholes in the laws. And in the end, the corporation is bankrupt.

Oh, maybe there's enough to pay a few cents on the dollar to those who stuck it out, but not usually."

She thought about that for a few minutes, then her eyes clouded with something I took as disbelief, but she said, "That's the way I have it figured."

I looked up at her, my eyes impressed. "So this was all a test?"

She gave me a wan smile. "Call it an evaluation. I had to know just how astute you are."

"And did I pass?"

She smiled. "Yes. As always, Boone Swabble was correct."

It was my turn to question her. "So what's your theory on what this all has to do with Ben Guron's death?"

She shrugged. "I think he had enough money to stay in until the last. And when things turned sour, Ben started asking questions. Keep in mind that Gorge Investment and Development Corporation was headed by Marvin Dubois, Cleet Dubois' brother. And Gloria Guron is their cousin."

I shook my head. "That doesn't fit. I have it that Ben was married to her for five years before Gorge Investment and Development Corporation was formed. If you're saying that she married Guron just to get his money, it's bad timing."

"I don't know why she married Ben, but I do know she's involved in some way. Maybe she believes blood is thicker than water. Or maybe she got bored with her marriage. I don't know, but I do know I'm going to find out what happened."

"Brenda, suppose she was involved; we've already decided the corporation was all legal. So maybe Ben was killed because he found out too much about Gorge Investment and Development Corporation." I gave her time to respond. When she didn't, I said, "I know it's a big *if.* Sometimes that's all we have to go on. We have to assume something, don't we?"

She nodded. "Okay, so we assume Guron wasn't directly involved."

"Knowledgeably," I added.

"All right. He had no knowledge that something illegal was going on. That makes him a dope."

I winced at her word. "Ben was a lot of things, but he wasn't a dope."

Her eyes tilted down. "So maybe he was in love with his wife and he let her talk him into doing something illegal."

I shook my head. "I don't buy that, either."

Her brows raised and I thought I saw something about her that reminded me of my mother's eyes when she was about to lecture me on the difference between right and wrong. "David, I know he was your friend, but you have to admit he was involved in this thing up to his ears. You've already said he wasn't stupid, and I'll accept that. So he must have known what was going on."

I felt the sting of hot tears in my eyes. I shook my head. "That's something I can't believe, Brenda."

She reached across and covered my hand with hers. "It happens sometimes. Good people get involved in bad things."

"Not Ben Guron," I said adamantly.

"Why not Guron?"

"Why not your old man? Why not explain his death as a payback because he balked at the bad guys? Maybe he wanted more money and it got him killed."

She drew her hand back so fast that it took me a full second to realize it wasn't still on mine. As soon as I understood, I wanted to retract the words. "Hey, I'm sorry. I shouldn't have said that."

Her eyes were hot coals burning their way into my soul. "You made your point."

Real great, MacGruder, so you made your point. Why is it knowing you did what you set out to do didn't make you feel any better about it?

I reached across and took her hand, fully expecting her to pull away from me again. I was surprised when she didn't. "Brenda, Ben Guron was one of those rare human beings who was just plain good. He had more integrity than a hundred other people just like him. When he said something, you could count on it. That's how I know he wasn't involved in any of the dirty stuff." I paused for a second, took a deep breath, then went on. "Sometimes I say things I don't mean. That was one of them, and I'm sorry for saying it."

Her eyes cooled. "Like I said; you made your point. I'll accept that Ben Guron wasn't involved."

I took my hand away from hers. "So can we agree we think Ben was killed because he found out what was going on?" When she nodded, I said, "Now all we have to do is find out who killed him."

Her eyes had a strangely sad look in them. "What do you plan to do?"

"Maybe I can infiltrate their ranks." At the question in her eyes, I explained. "I'll go undercover. I'll become one of their dupes, only I'll do it with enough money where they'll have to let me in at the top. Maybe I can become a vice president of the corporation. Once I'm inside, it won't be hard to find out what's going on and who's involved."

She shook her head slowly. "And it might be just as easy to get yourself killed just as your friend did."

"Maybe you weren't listening, Brenda. Ben was one of the good ones. I'm not. I can't be fooled as easily, and I don't see everyone as being good. I'm cynical, Brenda, which makes me wary, and that, in turn, makes me careful. And I've managed to stay alive this long by being careful."

Her eyes signaled acceptance. "And once you're inside?"

"I guess I plan to smoke out whoever killed Ben. While I'm at it, maybe I can get some money back for some people who couldn't afford to lose it in the first place."

She watched me for a few moments, then she nodded. "All right," she said. "How can I help."

"I need to know who invested in that corporation. I need to know where they live and how much they lost. I'll talk to them, each one. The official power you presented me with will help. I may have to put a little pressure on some of them."

Her eyebrows came together above her eyes, while deep furrows creased her brows. "You aren't planning to do anything stupid, are you?"

"This special agent stuff, what authority does it give me?"

"It gives you the same authority I have, and the authority any other agent has."

"I can ask questions and demand answers?"

She watched me as she nodded. "Within the confines of the law, yes. You can't beat any heads, legally. And you aren't a vigilante. You have to operate within the laws of the State of Georgia." She gave me a very official stare. "You do understand that, don't you?"

I nodded slowly. "I understand that as an underpaid consultant ... make that as a special agent ... I can get into doors that I couldn't otherwise. The losers in this scheme will be more likely to talk if they think I've got a state agency behind me."

She turned her hand over and clasped mine. "David, promise me you won't do anything ... rash."

I raised my eyebrows at her. "Me do something rash? Why, Agent Carlisle, you know I wouldn't do that."

After a moment, she smiled. "I think I'm going to be very sorry I convinced my boss you would be right for this job. And he wasn't easy to convince. He has this thing about amateurs. To him, anyone who isn't a GBI agent is an amateur, so don't take that personally."

"But I am a GBI agent," I said.

She smiled again. "You are now. Let's just hope I'm still a GBI agent when this is all done." The last was added as an afterthought.

When we got back to her office, Brenda motioned me into a chair. When we were both seated, she asked, "You do have a gun, don't you?"

"I can get one."

She opened one of the drawers of her desk and took out a nasty looking Remington 9MM auto and handed it across to me. "It's already registered in your name, David." She tossed hand-cuffs and keys across the desk. "And so are these. I'll expect a daily report from you until this thing is closed."

"And if I need backup?" I asked.

"Just call."

There was a lot more in her answer so I decided to play it out. "And if I need cover?"

Her brows raised. "What kind of cover?"

"Well, maybe I might get a lot further if I went in as John Doe who had a wife and wanted to invest some money for the family's future."

She watched me, her eyes curiously smiling at me. "If that comes up, I'm sure we can find an agent who can act as your wife."

"Might be better if it was an agent I knew and I trusted," I responded.

The smiling eyes began to laugh. "Then we'll see if we can find an agent you know and trust."

I shrugged. "Only one agent can fit that bill."

The laughing eyes mocked me. "And just who might that be?"

I smiled at her lewdly. "Why, it's you, Agent Carlisle."

Her eyes continued to laugh even though a soft, red hue crept up her face. "We don't really know each other well enough to play house, even during an investigation."

"We might after we have dinner tonight."

The red hue faded, but the eyes didn't stop laughing. "There's a rule against fraternization, Special Agent MacGruder."

I tried to look incredulous. "It wouldn't be fraternization, Agent Carlisle. You are my contact, and I'm new at this, so it would be a training session. I still have a lot of questions that need answers."

Her eyes stopped laughing. "Oh," she muttered. It was a simple enough response, but it held a startled realization I just might be on the up-and-up. "Well, certainly, yes, I suppose ... that would be all right."

I smiled triumphantly across the desk at her. "Good. You'll need to give me your address and phone number." When I saw her brows raise, I quickly added, "Only in case I need to get in touch with you in an emergency, of course."

"Of course," she responded, and handed me one of her cards.

I placed it in my shirt pocket and arose from the table. "Seven o'clock?"

She smiled at me and nodded. Then she added, "But you'd better call before you come. My home number is on the card. I get stuck here a little too often to make promises about ... dates." She had spoken the word awkwardly, as though she didn't use it too often. Then she added, "You owe me a report." When I looked at her questioningly, she answered, "About yesterday." She opened her drawer and handed me another official GBI form. "You can give it to me tonight."

I took the form. "Of course," I said and left her office.

Chapter Seven

I found the parking garage and checked out a late-model, plain blue Ford sedan from the pool. It was complete with radio, telephone, computer keyboard and screen, shotgun rack — without the shotgun — siren, and blue lights, which were hidden behind the grill. Decked out across the top and trunk was an impressive array of long, thin metal antennae.

There is something about an unmarked police car which screams UNMARKED POLICE CAR! I had no doubt anyone who saw that particular car would be very much aware I was an official law-enforcement type. I made a mental note to turn it in before I infiltrated Gorge Investment and Development Corporation, which was presumably still located at 115 Highway 441, over in Harlanwood, Georgia. They might not be so willing and ready to accept a partner who drove an unmarked police car.

Before I left the GBI building, I called the rental agency and told them where they could pick up their car. I left the keys with the attendant.

My first stop was MacGruder-Frazier Investigations. The same security guard, B.G. Maldin, was on duty when I came in. "Morning Mr. MacGruder." He gave me a warm smile.

I leaned my elbows on the top of his desk. "Can we make a slight alteration in protocol?"

His eye went blank. "Sir?"

"It's the Mr. MacGruder thing. My first name is Dave." I held my hand out to him. "And yours is?"

He stared at my hand as though I had offered him a fish that had been out of the water long enough to begin to smell. After what seemed an eternity, he took my proffered hand. "Beaufort. It's Beaufort, Mr. MacGruder."

"Make it Dave."

He looked around. When he was certain there was no one close enough to hear him call me by my first name, he relaxed. "Okay, Dave."

"Now that we have that all taken care of, let's try this. What do you say to Mr. Frazier when he arrives in the morning?"

His eyes darted around. "I ... I don't understand."

"Beaufort, I'm asking what you say to him."

His eyes held that dull look of incomprehension. "Well, I say *Good morning, Mr. Frazier.*"

I smiled. "Beaufort, this isn't a test of security. I know you do your job well. If you didn't, Mr. Frazier wouldn't keep you. So relax." He gave me a tentative smile. "See, Mr. Frazier and I have worked together since the mid-sixties. You might say we grew up together, literally. And I know him very well. I think it might be nice if instead of saying Mr. Frazier, you said Chief Frazier, or just chief. See, Wiley is one of those rare persons who is real. Did you know he's a retired Navy Chief Petty Officer?" When he shook his head, I went on. "And did you know he was a cop?" Again he shook his head. "He was both. So he knows what the hell you are going through sitting behind that desk. He understands security and he knows sometimes it's a real pain in the ass. So what I want you to do is give him a quick pass down on what's been going on. Doesn't have to be more than a few words, just let him know he's the boss and he deserves to be involved in what's going on around here." I paused for emphasis. "Can you do that?"

The dull light behind his eyes slowly faded, and a large smile spread across his face. "I'm retired Atlanta PD, Dave, so I get the picture. The boss has been kicked out of the field and behind a desk, and he hates it."

I nodded. "You got it, buddy."

"Get him involved without bogging him down with the BS." He nodded. "I can do that, and I'll makes sure the word gets around."

I shook his hand again. "Thanks." He handed me my identification and I clipped it to my lapel. "Could you call up and tell the boss's secretary that I'm on my way?" I turned and walked toward the bank of elevators before he could respond.

Mickie glanced up when the doors opened and gave me a smile. There was no hint of embarrassment or uneasiness. She was the cool, calm and collected Mickie that I had always known once again. "Wiley called. He told me to have you call him as soon as you got in."

I walked to her desk. "Get him on the phone for me, will you?" Then as she picked up her phone and started to dial, "Can I use his office?"

Mickie's smile broadened. She hung up her phone and stood. "Why, Mr. MacGruder, did you really think that MacGruder-Frazier Investigations would not have an office for one of the partners?" She showed me into an office across from Wiley's. It was just as luxurious as Wiley's, and had a better view. Mickie told me it was because Wiley felt guilty about working out of such a nice office while I was stuck aboard my boat.

I had an impish desire to see her squirm. I waited until she was about to leave and asked, "Does the company have rules against fraternization?"

I saw a faint red hue creep into her cheeks, but her eyes remained steadily on mine, and she didn't squirm, not even a little. "As far as I know, none of that is going on."

I gave her a hardy laugh. "Good girl," I said. She stood at the door as I sat in the leather chair behind the desk. I looked up at her. "Was there something you wanted to say?"

She shook her head. "No. I was just wondering if you needed anything."

I leaned back in the chair and closed my eyes, clasping my hands behind my neck. "What I need, sweet lady, is three inches of rum over five cubes of ice."

When I heard ice cubes crash into the bottom of a glass, I opened my eyes. Mickie had opened two doors in one of the walls exposing a very impressive and well-stocked bar. When she had filled the glass, she brought it over to my desk and placed it in front of me. When I sipped the amber liquid, she asked, "That okay?"

"Fine," I said.

"You want anything else, pick up the phone and press the first button."

I sat the glass on my desk. "Efficient."

"Yes, it is," she responded.

"I meant you."

She smiled. "I know you do, but I don't take compliments too well." She took a step toward the door. "Will there be anything else?"

I nodded. "Who makes the assignments? For the field operatives, I mean."

"I do. Why?"

"Because I want you to pass some of them to Wiley."

Her eyes opened wide. "David, this isn't the old MacGruder-Frazier agency. We do business in the millions now. Wiley is the boss. It wouldn't be right to have him do field work."

I sat up in my chair. "Mickie, let's get this straight. Wiley and I are equal partners in this corporation, or am I wrong?"

"No, you aren't wrong."

I gave her a cheerful smile. "Good," I said, quickly followed by, "So if I can do field work, so can he. Right?"

A knowing glint flared in the backs of her eyes. "Certainly."

"So what I want is for you to find some way to convince Wiley that you have more work than the operatives can get done. I want him out of this office every day. Understand?"

A smile turned the corners of her mouth up. "I understand completely, and I'll make sure he gets out of here. Now, if you'll excuse me, Mr. MacGruder, I'll go get Mr. Frazier on the phone for you."

When Mickie left the office, I sat back in the chair, sipped the drink and waited for the phone to buzz. I was swallowing the second sip when it did, and it startled me a little. I picked it up and heard Wiley's booming voice on the other end. "Dave, our girl tells me that you've made yourself right at home. Better be careful or the easy life of the corporate executive will get to you."

"I doubt it. I'm not as good at this as you are, Wiley, but then I haven't had the practice you have." I let him hurl a few choice four-letter words through the lines and then asked, "Find anything out about Gloria Guron?"

"Yeah, but you aren't going to like it."

"Try me, Wiley."

"Some of this you already have." The phone was silent for a few seconds. I could hear papers being shuffled as Wiley sorted his notes. "Gloria Guron, born Gloria Louann Spence. Age 34. Date of birth, April 12, 1961. Born in Emmanuel County, Statesboro, Georgia, to Harkness and Beverly Spence." He paused for a moment. "My contact tells me she's a little spit of a thing, says she doesn't stand five feet tall, but built like she was a whole lot taller. And he says she's very, very pretty. Says she's more than most men ever get the opportunity at — his words, not mine."

He paused again and I said, "Keep going."

"Her father, Harkness Spence, came from a well to do family up in Harlanwood. Mother was a Dubois. Family not so well to do. Street rumor up here — and you can take this for what it's worth — has it that Beverly Dubois was five or six months along with child when Harkness married her. I called a friend over in Statesboro, and he told me that Gloria's father was killed in '62 in a farming accident. Told me that Beverly slipped back into the alleys of Statesboro and Vidalia, and that she had a good clientele. Anyway, she died in '75. Killed by a drunk driver in Vidalia. One sister: Mary Jane. Died in '88 from a strain of viral pneumonia; AIDS related. She was a porn queen, and made a fortune at it. My IRS contact told me that her last return listed pre-tax income at over five hundred grand."

I whistled into the phone. "Wiley, sounds like we may be in the wrong line of work."

"No way, pal. Ain't no amount of money worth dying for, and that's what's out there. Anyway, Mary Jane left everything to her sister, which made Gloria even richer, which was only fair because Gloria got into the sex scene with her sister, and probably at her insistence. Gloria was at it up until late '82 or early '83. She started young, maybe at age sixteen. Got into the films and then moved on into prostitution. She was one of the high-priced callgirls in D.C., and when I say high-priced, I mean big-dollar. She didn't work 14th Street. Gloria worked out of Arlington, Virginia, out of one of those high-rise apartment houses in Crystal City. You remember Billy Jenkins?"

"Billy Jay of SpecWars fame?" I asked.

"Yeah. The same. He tells me he spent a month's pay on Gloria in just one night." He paused, then added, "And he told me it was worth every penny. Says she had a specialty."

I cut him off. "That information I don't need. So how did she come to know Ben?"

"She was twenty-one when she quit and best I can find out, she had a sizable bank account. Her trail turns cold for a few years, but the word on the street is she was a live-in for one of the power brokers on Capitol Hill."

"Any guesses as to who it was?"

He chuckled into the phone. "Our very own Senator Bumgardner."

"Barry Bumgardner?"

"You sound surprised." He chuckled.

"Shouldn't I be? Wiley, Bumgardner must be in his seventies."

"Actually he's eighty-three, but that hasn't seemed to curb his appetite any. Word up here is Senator Bumgardner has round heels and he'll roll for anything in skirts, as long as they're young, beautiful and available. Everyone seemed surprised when he took up with Gloria. His usual female companions are still in their teens."

"Any word on the rift?"

"Only that they parted friendly. Rumor has it that old Barry saw a wrinkle at the corner of Gloria's eyes and decided she was getting a little long in the tooth for him. What makes it interesting is that he stayed with her for almost eight years. Maybe there's something to what they say about her specialty." He let out with a particularly dirty laugh.

"Okay, so you tracked her into the nineties. What next?"

He said simply, "Ben Guron."

"From a senator's bed into a navy captain's bunk? That sound plausible to you?"

"It wouldn't if I didn't know the story. Ben was working as an advisor to the Senate Armed Services Committee, and old Barry is right there, and has been for years. Word has it the transition was set up by Barry, with Gloria's consent. Ben just got taken in by her charm, or so I'm told."

"Wait a minute," I interjected. "Ben was married, wasn't he?"

Wiley said, "Yeah, but Martha died in '86, and they tell me he was all broke up about it. Said he didn't start coming out of it until he met Gloria. They tell me after the two of them got together, he started acting like his old self, only better." Wiley paused for a few seconds, then said, "Maybe she was good for him, Dave."

"Maybe, but something tells me if he had never met her, he would still be alive."

"Yeah, maybe, but Billy Jay tells me a night with her was like ten years with any other woman. So maybe Captain Ben died a happy man."

His laugh stabbed at my sensibilities and I couldn't keep the irritability out of my voice when I said, "This is Benjamin Guron we're talking about, Wiley, not some gutter-bum sailor. He was family first and navy second, and he never chased the skirts. He's dead. Someone pushed him off a cliff and it wasn't a nice way to go. My gut tells me his new wife had something to do with it, so don't give me any of the dying-a-happy-man crap!"

He was quiet for too long. "Dave, you sound as though you're a little too close to this one. Maybe you should let me handle it."

I shook my head, knowing that I had been too rough on him. "Yeah, well, maybe I am a little close, but he was a friend, and I don't like it when my friends go out the way he did." I waited a moment before asking, "You have anything else?"

"Only that Ben and Gloria Guron moved into the Spence family residence in Harlanwood, Georgia."

"Inheritance?" I asked.

"Nope. Seems the Spences wouldn't have anything to do with Beverly and her daughters after Harkness was killed. If the record is true, I can understand their reluctance. Anyway, guess maybe little Gloria had it in for them. Seems the good family ran into some financial problems a few years ago and Gloria bought their home and all their properties right out from under them, and at about forty cents on the dollar. She did it through a dummy corporation, just in case there was any problem. After the sale was final, she tossed the old couple — her grandparents — out into the street. Caused quite an uproar in that little town, or so I'm told. I made a call to the police department in Harlanwood and spoke with a ... " I heard more papers being shuffled. " ... an Officer Ryan. He told me the good people of Harlanwood would have nothing to do with Gloria, said her husband was an all right sort of guy, but his wife was trash. He mentioned Cleetice Dubois, said he had taken up residence with the newlyweds just after they had moved back into town. He also said local gossip had it Gloria and Cleet Dubois were carrying on ... before Ben's death, but they had kept it all very discreet. Since his death, they haven't been discreet at all. Officer Ryan had more to say on the subject, but I'm sure you'd rather get the gossip for yourself."

"Wiley, sounds as though we might have ourselves a couple of suspects."

"Maybe we do at that," he responded.

"You got a lot accomplished over the telephone."

This time his laugh was happy. "You should know I do my best work over the phone lines, partner."   After a moment, he said, "I've been doing all the talking. Anything new on your end?"

"Nothing except that I've been drafted into the GBI."

"What?"

I laughed. "It'll wait. When you coming home?"

"I'm booked on a Delta flight out of National at four-thirty. You'll be at the house when I get there?"

I laughed. "That might spoil Virginia's homecoming plans for you."

"Brother, what Virginia has planned for me is a nice hot meal, a warm bath, a back rub, and sleep, and I promise you won't spoil any of that."

"Even so, I think I'll find someplace else to be. Might be in later, though, if that's all right."

"It is and you know it."

We said our good-byes and hung up. I checked my watch and found it was a little after one. I had almost six hours to kill before I was to pick up Brenda. I remembered the report, took the folded form from my pocket and set about putting in all the details about what had happened the day before. I had forgotten just how perfunctory and succinct a law officer's reports had to be. A private investigator's clients expected long, detailed explanations. The prosecutors did not. All they wanted were the facts. I chuckled to myself remembering those old lines from a television program ("Just the facts, ma'am") and wondered if that pseudo Los Angeles police department sergeant knew that he was telling it like it is for a thousand cities across the country. Funny how art or popular culture could imitate and even echo the real world.

I shook myself back into the reality of writing the report, and kept my statements factual.

When I walked out of the office, Mickie gave me a funny smile. "Leaving so early?" she asked.

I gave her a blank stare. "The hired help isn't supposed to ask the corporate staff questions like that."

Her smile vanished, but her eyes still held the mirth. "Oh? I didn't know. If I offended you, I deeply apologize."

"You didn't, but I just thought I'd remind you."

"Putting me in my place, are you?"

I shook my head. "No way, lady. I'd be afraid that you'd get up on your haunches and put me in my place first."

Her eyes grew solemn. "You were on the phone with Wiley a long time."

I shrugged. "He had a lot to tell me." I gave her a quick rundown on what Wiley had said and what I surmised.

Her eyes searched mine. "This thing you are working on, it sounds, well ... dangerous."

I gave her my best nonchalant look. "No more than any other case we take on."

She didn't buy it. "You're too reckless for your own good, you know that?"

I nodded. "It's my nature, doll. You worried about me?"

Her face grew tense. "Should I be?"

I smiled. "No, not really. I'm a big boy and I can take care of myself."

Her eyes didn't change, but she forced a smile. "All right. Just promise you'll be careful."

I leaned across her desk and kissed her softly on the cheek. "You think I want you to lose a friend?"

A tear came to her eyes. "Sometimes I wonder."

I stood and walked to the elevator doors. When they opened, I stepped in. As the doors were closing, I turned back to her and said, "I'm the last person you have to worry about, Mickie." I could see in her eyes she didn't believe me as the doors closed shut.

Chapter Eight

I drove through the early afternoon traffic, wedging my way out onto the freeway, and north to Powder Springs. I rang the bell, thinking Virginia wouldn't be home, but not wishing to walk in uninvited in case she was. To my surprise, she opened the door and smiled up at me. "Hello stranger," she said.

"You always get home in the middle of the afternoon?" I asked as I followed her into the house.

"I'm a doctor. Male doctors play golf on Wednesday afternoon. Female doctors come home and play housewife and mother."

She led the way back through the house and into the den. "Drink?"

I nodded. "Beer?"

She smiled. "I have that dark beer you always liked. Wiley makes sure he keeps it around just in case you show up unexpectedly, not that you ever do."

"I'm here now, am I not?" I said defensively.

The doc turned to face me. "And why? Because an old navy buddy asked you for help. You didn't come up here to see Wiley or me. We just happen to be here."

"Doc, I'm really not in the mood."

She turned away, opened the small refrigerator door and retrieved a bottle of dark beer. When she had brought it over to where I was seated, she said, "Sorry, but I just thought you should know, David, that it's very apparent you practice the out-of-sight-out-of-mind philosophy."

I took a deep swallow from the bottle. "Okay, so what brought that up?"

Virginia sat in a chair across from me. Her dark eyes looked troubled. "Oh, I don't know. Maybe I'm getting old. Or maybe I'm suffering from empty-nest syndrome."

"I'm not your child, Doc."

Her eyes turned sour. "Damn you, David. Do you have to be my child for me to worry about you?"

I felt a sudden anger. "Damn it, what is it with women? Why am I the target for every maternal instinct in Atlanta?" Then, when I suddenly realized what had occurred, "You talked to Mickie, didn't you." It was a statement.

Virginia slowly nodded her head. "Yes, and she tells me that she's uneasy about this new case you're on."

"Wiley's on it, too. Shouldn't you be worried about him instead of me?"

She smiled. "Wiley doesn't have a death wish."

"And I do? Is that what you're saying?"

The doc shrugged. "Yes, sometimes you do."

"Do you plan on sending me a bill for this session, or is it on the house?" There was unintentional sarcasm in my voice.

Virginia leaned back and folded her hands across her lap. "David, it doesn't take a psychiatrist to see what's inside you. You've been stretched too thinly these last few years, and the whole painful mess with Joan Marie took its toll."

"But I'm all over that now," I said, although I didn't believe it.

As perceptive as ever, the doc responded with, "Are you? Are you really?" When I didn't reply, she went on. "I don't think you are. If you were, you would be married now."

"To whom?" I tried to make it sound light, but I didn't do a very good job.

"David, I don't have to think very hard to come up with one very good prospect ... Mary Elizabeth. Do I have to remind you that Philip Michael needs his father?"

I took another deep pull from the bottle. "Mary Elizabeth is married, Doc."

Her eyes clouded. "Oh. I'm sorry. I didn't know."

I shrugged. "Better for her and better for our son. Hell, what kid needs a father who is gone all the time?"

"Better a father who is gone than no father at all."

I felt the anger welling up inside me. I finished the beer, giving myself time to get my irritation under control. Then I said, "If it's all the same to you, Doc, I'd just as soon drop it."

She acted as though she hadn't heard me. "All right, so Mary Elizabeth found someone else. There are others."

"No, there aren't."

"Yes, David, there are. Mickie comes to mind."

I looked at her incredulously. "Mickie? Whatever put that in your mind?" Then, "Oh. She told you about last night."

Virginia slowly nodded. "Yes, she told me, and she also told me that it was an accident and how she didn't want it to happen again. What she didn't tell me is both of you needed the closeness." Then, after a moment, she added, "And she didn't have to tell me it was good for you both."

I felt my cheeks burning hotly. "Do we have to discuss my sex life?"

She smiled. "No, we don't. But we do have to settle one thing."

"And what's that?" I asked.

"That you'll stop fighting it."

"It?" I asked innocently.

She gave me a motherly look. "Yes *it*, David. Love. I want you to promise me you'll accept the fact Joan Marie is gone and she'll never come back. It wasn't your fault."

"Hell, Doc, I know that."

Her eyes were dark pools of concern. "I don't think you do, David. I think you keep expecting her to come home. I think subconsciously you expect to walk onto your boat and find her waiting there patiently."

I laughed, but it came out sounding hollow. "Why in the world would I ever want that?"

Doc Virginia looked down at her hands. It appeared to me she was going through some inner dilemma, weighing her professional knowledge against her love for me as a friend. When she looked back up at me, I could see she had decided to let me have it with both barrels. Instinctively, I braced myself for her words. "David, whether you realize it or not, you operate on ego and adrenaline, and those two don't mix well. When you were stalking your prey back in those wars you fought, it helped make you good at what you did. But even as it made you good, it also made you vulnerable. You teetered on the edge. One false step and you would have gone over."

I interrupted her. "What does all that have to do with Joan Marie?" I asked, a little too much venom in my voice.

She gave me another of her motherly looks, only this one was tempered with a smile. "When you were playing your war games, you had a vent for all that adrenaline, and because you were good at what you were doing, your ego was well fed. When Joan Marie told you she didn't love you anymore, and your marriage was over, the animal within you wanted to lash out at her, to defend your position, but you couldn't. If you had slapped her, or kicked her, or screamed at her, it would have been a vent. But you didn't do any of those. You couldn't. And because you couldn't, there was no way to burn up all that adrenaline. So frustration set in, and your ego took a beating, a beating from which it has never recovered. If she came back, it would give you the opportunity to throw her out, as you think she threw you out." She watched me carefully for a second, then said, "Or perhaps you might even take her back."

I opened my mouth and let out a laugh, but as I did, I could feel my hands begin to sweat. Maybe the doc was right. Maybe I didn't want to admit it to myself. And if I couldn't do that, then I certainly couldn't admit it to her. So I said, "Well, Doc, this is one time you are one hundred percent wrong. I wouldn't have her back, even if she wanted to come back. You have to trust someone in order to love them, and I stopped trusting her a long, long time ago."

She shook her head sadly. "David, don't you see, we aren't talking about Joan Marie the person; we're talking about Joan Marie the memory. You were so blind to her, and what she was doing, that you stopped seeing her in reality long before she left. And from that moment, she became a dream. She existed in your subconscious as the Joan Marie you had married; not the Joan Marie who walked out on you. And you are so damn logical you can't accept the fact that she would turn her back on you, but instead of being angry at her, you've been angry with yourself. You tell yourself it was you who failed; not she. You tell yourself that had you chosen any other career, she would still be by your side. For some odd reason, you have this thing inside you that says the failure of your marriage is a direct reflection on your capability as a man. You failed at love, so you certainly can't be successful in anything as mundane as life."

She paused for a moment. I took the opportunity to say, "Hey, I was a damn good cop, and I'm a damn good private detective. And as far as women are concerned, I haven't had any problems."

Her brown eyes clouded. I thought she would cry. But, Doctor Virginia Frazier isn't the crying type, especially when she has her sights set on repairing crack in someone's self-image. "David, you were a good cop. But why?" When I didn't respond, she answered her own question. "Because you took chances, most of which were dangerous. And, yes, you are a good private investigator. You run headlong into situations which would get most men — or women — killed, and you somehow manage to come out reasonably unscathed. None of us would ever accuse you of being cowardly."

I think she paused, giving me a chance to defend myself, but I didn't. "And how about your lady friends? Yes, you are a ladies man, and yes you have more opportunities than most men. But don't you see, they're all indicative of your problem."

I felt anger well up inside me. "Doc, just who the hell are you to say something like that to me? Problem? I don't have a problem! What I have is friends who stick their noses into my business!"

Her eyes lowered for a second, then came back up to mine and held firmly. "All right, so I'm sticking my nose into your business. I wouldn't be doing it, David, if I didn't care about you." There must have been fire in my eyes, because she went on quickly, "I promise this is almost over. I'm a doctor, trained to see problems, even when my patients don't even know they exist — or don't want to admit they exist."

"Okay, so what do you see?"

"I see a man who is allowing a painful memory to destroy his life."

"And this memory that's ruining my chances for happiness, you think it's Joan Marie?"

Virginia nodded slowly. "Yes. You have all this pent up guilt about what happened, and you are letting it destroy your future. The memory — and what it's doing to you — has become your penitence, David. You wear it around your neck for all to see. And every time you start to get close to another woman, you allow that memory — and the pain of that separation — to come between you and the new woman." She gave me a look suddenly filled with strength and determination. "You have to stop beating yourself up this way, David. You understand that, don't you? You have to stop."

I started to object, but I didn't. I don't know why, except I knew the doc was right about the memory of Joan Marie, the inability to allow another woman to get close, and about me and the job. When Virginia had said I have a death wish, it had startled me. And with the shock came recognition; a realization that I *did* have a death wish. I didn't contemplate suicide, but I did accept death as a normal part of life a little too easily. My philosophy was when it came, it came, and there was nothing I could do to prevent it. So I took chances, and some of them *were* reckless.

I looked over at her. She looked so intense I had to smile. "If I promise to do better, can I have another beer?"

Then she smiled, too. "Yes, you can have another beer."

I came back with two cold bottles and handed her one of them. I opened my own and took a long swallow, gaining a little time and distance from her words. I noticed that she was watching me, her own bottle left unopened, so I sat down on the sofa. "You touched a few nerves there, Doc."

"I know I did."

"Trouble is, you are probably more right than even you know. Maybe if ... "

She cut me off. "Maybe if nothing. Joan Marie was a lovely lady who was spoiled rotten. I'm going to tell you something about that dear lady, something you may not want to hear, but you'll damn well sit there and listen to me." I answered her by taking another swallow from the bottle. "Did you ever wonder why she kept having children, even when it was easy enough not to?"

I shrugged. "Because she wanted a large family."

"That may be what she told you, but the truth is, she kept having kids because she thought it would make you give up your career in the navy and take her back home. She thought you would take off the uniform and put on an expensive suit and tie, and become a yes-man for her father. She wanted to be back in society, surrounded by her parents' friends, with all the glitter that comes with that sort of life."

"Hell, Doc, I couldn't live like that."

She nodded. "And Joan Marie knew it, only she wouldn't admit it to herself, and she wouldn't give up her desire to be back on the veranda, sipping mint juleps, talking about the weather and tennis and golf with *her* friends. So she stuck it out until you retired, hoping you would take her back home. Only you traded one uniform for another, and it destroyed her dreams. She couldn't take that, so she left."

"You make it sound as if it was my fault."

"It wasn't your fault, and it wasn't her fault. David Michael MacGruder was destined for adventure. You are one of those special individuals who has to be in the fight. Take the danger away, and you would start to deteriorate. Joan Marie wanted a stable, happy home filled with little girls in white dresses, tea parties, and afternoon bridge games. And she wanted her husband to be at her side, smiling at her friends, ever ready to respond to her smallest whim. That isn't the David Michael MacGruder I know, and it wasn't the David Michael MacGruder Joan Marie married. See, you didn't change. You remained the same man you always were. And Joan Marie couldn't change to suit the life she would have been forced to live."

I suddenly saw what she had been trying to tell me, but I wanted to hear it from her. "David, you and Joan Marie just were not meant for each other. There was nothing either of you could have done to make it work, not if you wished to regain your sanity. You spent a long time with a beautiful lady who was still a child. The good thing is, you had four sweet and intelligent daughters who love you, even though you may think differently. Remember whose children they are — yours. And we both know you have more than a little trouble expressing your emotions." She fell silent.

"Doc, you have a nasty habit of hitting below the belt."

She laughed. "So Wiley has told me a few times."

"Can I ask you a question?"

"Sure," she said.

"What brought all this up?" I asked, finishing the bottle of beer.

Virginia smiled, her eyes crinkling at the corners. "I got to thinking about our conversation about Wiley. Since our move up here, I've done a lot of soul-searching. In my way, I've done the same thing to Wiley that Joan Marie tried to do to you. I've been feeling very smug at how I maneuvered Wiley out of Lauderdale and up here into that prison cell of an office. I admit, I like seeing him go off to work in the morning wearing a suit and tie. I admit that a part of me is pleased at being married to a man who is successful, a man who is equal to me, the great psychiatrist." She gave me a sad smile. "See, David, I'm just as human as you are." I could tell there was more so I kept still. "That's why I asked you to get Wiley out of that office. I was watching him die, and I can't do that. But I also laid a lot of guilt on you about how you are the wanderer, and how Wiley is stuck in that office. That wasn't fair — and it wasn't true." The good doctor paused for emphasis. "That's really what tonight was about."

Virginia arose and stood before me. "You okay?"

I gave her a smile. "The wounds aren't bad and the scars won't show." Then I nodded. "I'm okay."

"Want another beer?" When I didn't respond immediately, she said, "One is usually my limit, but this afternoon I'm going to have two. As long as I'm at the refrigerator, it won't be any trouble getting another for you."

"All right, but I'm not having any more after this one." I heard the refrigerator door close and then watched as the doc stopped in the doorway.

The dark brown eyes in that lovely, ebony face stared incredulously out at me. "Did I hear you correctly? Is David MacGruder really going to stop at three beers?"

"Yes, doctor, I am."

She tilted her head slightly, her eyes laughing at me. "So what's the occasion?"

"For your information, I have a date."

She brought the bottle over to me. "Oh? Mickie?"

"No." I shook my head. "You don't know her. Matter of fact, I don't know her. I just met her this morning."

She sat close to me on the sofa, her right hand touching my left arm. "Do I get a name, or am I going to be forced to refer to her as *that woman*?"

I raised my eyebrows in mock concern. "Doc, I don't want to be the topic of your gossip."

"David, for goodness sake, I have to tell Wiley something. He'll wonder why you aren't here when he gets home."

I laughed softly. "Virginia, I hope you and Wiley have more to do when he gets home than talk about me."

The doc had began to blush. "Of course ... " she stammered. "Well, I mean ... "

I laughed. "Okay, so I wasn't asking for a script." I took her beer and twisted the top off, handing it back to her.

"So take a swallow and think up a good reason why I should tell you my lady friend's name."

She didn't wait. "Because I care about you. Because every time I get near you, I have this overwhelming desire to mother you. And before you protest, I have the right. I've known you for thirty years. You and Wiley and I have been more like family than friends." She paused long enough to take a sip from the bottle of beer. "And, damn it, David, there are times when you need a mother. So, what is her name?"

"Her name is Brenda Carlisle. She's an agent with the Georgia Bureau of Investigation. And just so you won't get the wrong idea, it's a business dinner."

Her eyes widened. "Business?"

I didn't have a good explanation as to why I was taking a GBI agent out to dinner, so I fished the black leather case from my pocket and handed it to the doc.

Virginia opened the case and stared at the badge and the identification card. When she looked up at me, her eyes were full of questions. "What's this?"

"A badge," I responded.

She set her jaw and said, "I can see that, David. What I mean is, why do you have it?" Then, almost without hesitation, she said, "It has something to do with the case, doesn't it?"

I nodded. "Agent Carlisle thought the badge and the ID might make my investigation a little easier. People tend to answer questions more quickly if the one asking is an official cop."

She handed the leather case back to me. "What's this all about?"

I shook my head. "Hey, Doc, you know the score. When I signed the papers making me a member of that elite group, I gave up the right to discuss the case."

She watched me for a few seconds. Then, "I know that.
What I was asking was why would the GBI put you on their
payroll as a special agent?"

I laughed. "Well, in this case, their payroll isn't going
to be dented too much."

She shook her head at me. "Stop being evasive,
David."

I took a pull from the bottle. "Ben was my friend. I
found him. He didn't die easily, and he knew it was
coming. He was murdered by someone whom he trusted
enough to go out on that ledge with. They were talking —
just as you and I are talking — and that person slipped
around behind Ben and pushed him off that ledge.
Whoever did that to him was an animal, and that kind of
animal doesn't deserve to live. And I plan to find that
person, and make sure whoever it is doesn't get the chance
to do the same thing to another person."

"You can't take the law into your own hands, David."

I flipped the case open, exposing the badge. "I can
now."

"But ... "

I cut her off. "I think Agent Carlisle knew I wouldn't
sit back and watch as the authorities botch this one. She
did some checking and found out I'm pretty good at what I
do, and I think she figures if the killer is to be caught, it'll
take someone like me to do it."

"And if the killer is really good, your Agent Carlisle
won't have the blood of one of her cronies on her hands.
David MacGruder, full-time private investigator, part-time
special agent. If you get killed, it won't mean anything to
the GBI."

I tried to look hurt. "Doc, I'm taking my boss to dinner.
Have you forgotten that this is David *God's-gift-to-women*
MacGruder you're talking to? How can you sit there and
say that my death won't mean anything to her?"

She looked as though she was going to protest, but she gave me a wan smile and asked, "You like this woman?"

I shrugged. "I don't know her well enough to decide."

She nodded thoughtfully. "But you are attracted to her?"

"Is that a question or a statement of fact?"

"Both," she said.

"All right. I like the way she looks. She's an attractive lady and something about her makes me feel I want to get to know her better."

There was a sudden relaxation in the doc's eyes. "Good, then you finish your beer, get on upstairs and make yourself presentable. And if you find out you really care for this lady, then I expect you to invite her here so Wiley and I can meet her."

I chuckled. "All right, mother Frazier."

I finished the beer, and stood to leave. Her hand touched my arm. "David?"

"Yes?"

"Thanks."

"For what?"

"For a lot of things. Mostly for being yourself."

I leaned down and kissed Virginia on the cheek. When I straightened, I said, "You're very welcome, doctor."

Chapter Nine

Late-afternoon traffic is always a pain and Atlanta is one of those cities that makes you wish mass transit really worked. It was 6:45 when I arrived at Brenda Carlisle's address, and I was feeling the tension of fighting the traffic all the was to Kennessaw. It was one of those mock-Tudor houses with white-painted stucco and lumber stained brown crisscrossing the stucco facade. The area was affluent, but not rich, houses built for the newcomers, the young executive crowd who had yet to have their two and one-third children. To say I felt out-of-place was putting in mildly. I was never meant for suburbia, and that neighborhood was as suburban as it gets. But still, I was here to see a beautiful woman, even if on the pretext of business. So I squared my shoulders and sucked in my paunch.

As I knocked at her door, I patted my coat where I had placed the report. My shoulders ached and my head was pounding, and I needed a stiff drink. The tautness in my shoulders and the throbbing in my head stopped when the door was opened.

Brenda Carlisle was standing, framed in the doorway, smiling out at me. She was wearing a red, cotton dress. Spaghetti straps held the red material high on her body, but not so high as to hide the deep cleft of firm female cleavage. Her shoulders were sun browned. The skirt of the dress hung full down to her knees. She wore white leather sandals on her feet. The lack of three-inch heels did not diminish her. She was still a large, luscious and lovely girl.

I must have been staring because when I looked at her face, she was smiling at me, evidently enjoying my admiration. "You always leer at your dates?" she asked barely able to contain an impudent chuckle.

"I didn't realize I was leering."

She nodded curtly. "And ogling," she said.

"Should I apologize?" I asked.

She let the chuckle escape. It was a good laugh, light and full of fun. "Not if you don't want to find out what they taught me in hand-to-hand combat."

I made a very obvious and overly gratuitous bow. "I wouldn't want that," I said.

She stepped back into the doorway. "I hope you don't mind. I made a reservation at a restaurant not far from here. The food is good, the service is passable, and it's quiet." She looked down at her watch. "The reservations are for eight, so if you like, we'll have a drink here first."

I stepped into the doorway. "Be a good way to start the celebration."

She closed the door and turned to me. "Celebration?" she asked. "I thought this was going to be strictly business. I didn't know we were celebrating anything."

I gave her my best wolf-smile. "Oh yeah? So why the party dress?"

She laughed again, and her eyes sparkled, the lights dancing in them. Her laugh sounded like crystal clinking together. "I guess I do look like I'm going to the prom." She put her hands on her hips and turned a half-turn to her left, then to her right. "You think this is too much?"

I shook my head. "I like it."

She motioned me to follow her. "I don't date. Generally speaking, the men I meet at work resent a female cop. Men I meet outside of work inevitably ask me what I

104

do. When I tell them I work for the GBI, they either run like scared jack rabbits, or have those silly sexual fantasies about sleeping with a cop." She turned abruptly to face me so quickly that I almost ran into her. "Was I too abrupt?" she asked, her eyes searching mine.

I shook my head. "Remember, I was a cop, too. I've seen my share of groupies."

She surveyed me closely, then smiled. "I just bet you have." Then she was off and I was following her into a large living room, comfortably furnished and tastefully decorated. She motioned me onto a large, overstuffed sofa. "What'll it be? I've got just about everything."

"Dark rum?" She smiled, and I said, "On the rocks."

When she brought the drinks, she took a seat in a matching overstuffed chair across a glass-topped coffee table from the sofa. "So, Special Agent MacGruder, did you finish the report?"

I handed her the report and sat back in the sofa, sipping at my drink as she read it. Her eyes were a mirror of her mind as she read the description of what I had done, seen and heard the prior morning. When she finished reading my words, she looked up at me. "You do this very well."

"Thanks," I said.

She looked down at the form, then back up at me. "The car and the truck, you remember any of the license numbers?"

"Only that they were both Georgia plates. The truck had one of those two-toned plates, with Georgia spelled with a peach instead of an *oh*. The other was personalized, but I don't recall what it said."

She watched me for a few seconds. "The scuff marks you saw, did you obliterate them in any way?"

"No, of course not. I was a cop, remember?"

She held her hand up. "I wasn't accusing you of anything."

"Then why the question?"

She thought for a moment before she answered. "None of the other reports described them as detailed as you did."

I took a long pull from the glass. "Agent Carlisle ... "

"Brenda," she cut in.

"All right, Brenda, I learned a long time ago the first cop on the scene is usually the one who collects the best evidence. That makes me alert. Maybe the officers were too busy with other things to pay attention to that ledge."

"Maybe." It sounded as though she was not even aware she had spoken the word.

I hurried on. "When I heard the cry ... "

She interrupted me again. "You didn't use the word *cry* in your report."

I was thoughtful for a moment. "It wasn't really a cry; more like a loud moan; like someone was surprised at something that had happened."

"All right," she said.

"I heard the sound, then I heard what sounded like pebbles falling, then I heard ... "

"What did you hear?"

I shook my head. "Listen, I've been there before. I know the sound of a body falling against something hard. It's as unmistakable as the call of a bird. I knew what it meant. I didn't even have to guess. I knew what I would find when I went down that ledge."

She watched me for a few seconds, her eyes a mixture of concern and concentration. Then she folded the form and, leaning forward, placed it on the glass top of the table that separated us. "It must have been hard on you, finding him that way."

"It was," I said simply.

"Can I ask you a question?" Her eyes were soft, but I could see the professional hardness behind them.

"Sure," I said.

"Why did you go down there?"

I looked at her doubtfully, as though I had not heard her correctly. "Why did I go down there?"

She nodded. "Yes, why?"

"Because he might have still been alive. Maybe I could have helped him."

"Mr. MacGruder ... "

"Dave." It was my turn to remind her that I had a first name.

She smiled. "Dave, most people would have run away from there."

"I'm not most people, Brenda."

Her eye softened. "I'm beginning to see that." She glanced down at her watch and then up at me. "Finish your drink and we'll get going."

I did as I was told and she took the empty glasses. When we were standing at her front door, she turned to me, her eyes searching mine. "The questions were not accusations, even if that's how they sounded."

"Then what were they?"

She tilted her head and shrugged. "I don't know. Maybe I was just curious. I'm a cop, and cops are naturally curious about things that are out of the ordinary."

"I'm a cop, too."

She watched me for a second, her eyes intently on mine, her stare curiously soft. "I know that." Then she gave me a smile. "Was I too professional?"

I shook my head. "No, I guess not."

Her face went solemn. "I do that sometimes, get too professional, I mean."

"Is that what makes the boys flee?"

She laughed softly. "I think it is." Then, "Are you going to flee?"

"No," I said. "And I'm too old to have fantasies of leather and guns and nightsticks and handcuffs."

Her face brightened. "I think you and I are about to become good friends, Dave."

"I think that would be very nice indeed, Brenda."

She opened the door and I followed her out into the warm, summer evening.

We were seated on bar stools, watery drinks in front of us, talking easily as we awaited the call from the hostess, signaling that our table was ready.

"So tell me why there isn't a marital partner in your life," I said stupidly.

She laughed. "Where did that come from?" Before I had time to answer, she went on with, "MacGruder, you of all people should know cops don't make good spouses."

"Except to other cops," I argued.

Her eyes narrowed, but her voice did not hold an edge as she said, "That would depend on who the spouse-cop was."

I was thoughtful for a moment, sipping my drink. "Yes, I suppose it would at that. Mr. Macho Cop would make a lousy husband. He would try to outgun you, and I suspect that wouldn't work."

She laughed. "No, it wouldn't."

"And Mr. Badge Heavy would offend your sense of propriety."

Again the laugh, soft and gentle as breeze. "He would."

"So what kind of cop would make you happy?" I asked, sounding too obviously unconcerned and uncaring.

"A cop like my father." A cloud passed through her eyes, but was gone almost before I recognized the pain behind it. "Kind, gentle, loving, soft in ways that most men can't even understand." Then she added, "But always the professional."

I watched her for a few seconds. "That's a pretty big pair of shoes to fill." I said, smiling gently at her.

She turned her eyes from mine. "I guess they are, at that." Then she tilted her eyes back in my direction. "Think I'm too particular?"

I sat my drink on the bar and turned in my stool to face her. "I think you're smart." I said, and left it at that.

Her eyes widened, but before she could respond, the hostess came to where we were seated and told us our table was ready.

When we got to the table, there were two candle and a rose. "Your idea?" I asked.

Brenda laughed gently, "No," she started to answer, then said, "Well, maybe it was. I happened to mention to Benito that I was bringing a man, so maybe he got the wrong impression."

"Well, I happen to like candles, so maybe ... we should just sit down and take advantage of ... Benito's efforts."

We sat and the waitress came, took our orders, and left us to low conversation and fresh drinks. In the minutes we had, I filled her in on what Wiley had told me about Gloria and Ben. She listened intently, asking questions only when I paused. I found myself extremely aware of just how feminine Brenda was, even when she was being a cop. I found myself watching her as she, in turn, listened to me. And somewhere between the first sip of the new drink and the soup, I felt a warm glow begin to spread through me like a warm bath on a cold evening. I was beginning to notice that the cleavage was deep and that the breasts were ample, and that the lips were warm and appeared to be full and soft, and that the eyes watched me in a peculiarly daring manner. Silently I warned myself to be careful around this extraordinary woman.

She ate with an appetite that was close to voracious. I found myself enjoying watching her eat. There was nothing self-conscious about her while sating her hunger. She knew I was watching, and yet she acted as though I was not. Throughout the meal, she would take a bite, chew, swallow, sip her wine, and ask me some obscure and innocuous question about something Wiley had said, or something I had mentioned in my report.

All-in-all, it was a memorable meal. When the coffee was served, I found myself wishing the dinner was not coming to a close. I prolonged it as long as possible, telling her what I hoped were funny stories about my boat, *The Other Woman*, and about adventures she and I had shared.

When we had stretched the after-dinner coffee past 10:30, I motioned for the waitress. She dutifully came with the check. I handed her the plastic money I hate to use, but which identifies a person as one of the acceptable ones, and told her that Brenda and I would be in the bar.

After the check was paid, and two drinks had gone down a little too easily, I escorted Brenda from the restaurant and out to my unmarked sedan.

The drive to her house was also all too short. When I was parked in her driveway, and had switched the engine off, Brenda turned in the seat to face me. "It was a nice evening, Dave."

"I hope that means you'd like another one just like it."

In response, she leaned across the car, her face upturned for a kiss. Her kips were warm and soft, and parted slightly as our lips touched. I could taste her lipstick and my brain screamed for the kiss to continue. But as I let my hand rest on her shoulder, Brenda tensed, breaking the embrace. I could see the hazy sparkle in her eyes as she said, "Is it the alcohol or the company?"

"I hope it's the company."

She laughed gently and moved closer on the seat. "Could we do that once more just so I can be sure?"

This time there was more pressure, more warmth, an age old question and a searching for an answer. My right arm slipped around her, and when her arms encircled me, my left arm trailed lightly over her back. I could feel the muscles tense as her lips hungrily pressed against mine.

When the kiss ended and was followed by other gentle kisses to her nose, her eyes, her brow, and her neck, she murmured, "Oh, damn it, I wish I could invite you in."

I kissed her lips again. "You can," I whispered.

She pushed away from me, her eyes full on mine. "No," she said adamantly. "I can't."

I smiled at her in the darkness. "All right. You can't." Then I kissed her again and felt her reluctance melting away. She moved closer and my hand cupped a warm breast. I felt her subconscious response to my touch. She tensed, suddenly stiff and aware. Then she relaxed, her mouth against mine, her lips hungrily open. At the precise moment when I knew I could have pushed her back in the seat, I let our lips part. "No one can justly accuse MacGruder of ever taking advantage of a woman." I thought of Mickie and subconsciously kicked myself. Somehow, I tried to convinced myself, this was different. And I knew it was, so I kissed her softly on the lips and sat back in the seat. "Maybe I should walk you to the door."

She sat back breathlessly, and whispered, "Maybe you should."

There are times when human beings ignore all suggestion of morality and appropriateness. As I climbed from the car, I knew what it was like to shut off the finely purring motor. I could feel the sexual shock of premature shutdown. I walked awkwardly to the passenger door of the car, opened it and stepped aside as Brenda came up from the seat. I was acutely aware of the natural forces which were being a little too slow to subside as I escorted this beautiful woman toward the front door of her home.

When she had opened it and stood in the doorway, a luscious female creature awaiting the final kiss of the evening, a cold, uncaring creature took hold of me. I pressed myself to her and crushed my lips against her own. She moaned into my mouth as I caressed her. I could feel the dams close to breaking and I inwardly cheered myself toward certain success.

There is a moment when the animal instinct takes control and the conscious mind ceases to govern those forces that rein in the procreative beast. I knew, as absolutely as I knew my own name, that moment was rapidly and certainly approaching. As I held her, pressing myself against her, mentally and emotionally — and sexually — aware of her soon-to-be total and unquestionable acquiescence, something inside me clicked. A small but very determined voice told me to relax my embrace, and I obeyed. I gathered all my strength and gently pushed Brenda to arm's length. I kissed her eyes and whispered, "I guess you can tell I want you," I said in a voice that was coarse with need.

I felt her shudder against me, and then saw her smile at me in the darkness. She nodded and said, "I want you, too."

Even as she spoke the words, I could feel some veiled reluctance buried deep within her that told me this was not the time or the place. It was probably that reluctance my subconscious sensed, and perhaps that is why the voice told me to end the vigil. I released her, my hands slipping down her arms until I was holding her hands. My eyes looked into hers. "That was pretty close," I said.

She managed a smile. "Yes, it was."

I kissed her lips again. "Next time, I might not accept that you can't ask me in."

She leaned against me, her face resting on my chest. "I know. Next time — if there is a next time — I may not be able to let you leave."

I cupped her chin with my hand and tilted her face up to mine. "Then, sweet, beautiful lady, let's hope there is a next time."

Chapter Ten

I awoke to the sound of a knock on the bedroom door. I glanced at my watch. It was only six. "Yeah?" I called.

"Hey partner, we need to get an early start on it. Virginia has the coffee on and the eggs are about to go into the frying pan."

"Do I have time for a shower?" I asked.

"Yes, you have time for a shower, a shave, and a one-mile run — provided you make it snappy."

I grunted at him through the closed door and dragged myself from the bed. I plodded into the bath and dropped tee-shirt and drawers on the floor. I turned the tap to full cold and stepped into the stinging spray. I stood there, letting the cold water slowly bring me back to life. For a passing moment, I thought of Brenda, but shook the thought from my mind.

I finished the shower and shaved, slapped some lotion on my face, picked up my underwear and went back into the bedroom. I found a white shirt that Virginia had laundered, dried and pressed to perfection, and wondered vaguely when she had found the time. I smiled appreciatively and slipped into it. I had gray slacks and a blue blazer, and a burgundy striped tie. When the tie was knotted, I slipped into oxblood, tasseled loafers. I surveyed myself in the full-length mirror on the closet door and gave a nod of approval. I looked just like every other corporate executive in America — save for the sun browned face and the deep creases at the corners of my eyes.

Breakfast was a hurried affair, quiet for the most part except for the occasional compliment given the cook. When the repast was completed, Wiley curtly informed me both of us would be going to the office that morning. His look told me not to ask questions, so I kept quiet.

He and I walked out the front door into the early morning. I got into my state vehicle and Wiley got into his car.

As I followed him south and into greater Atlanta, I found myself strangely homesick for *The Other Woman*. I had never been, was not, and could never be a nine-to-five man. My life was patterned and I liked it just the way it was, no matter what Doctor Virginia Frazier thought. Subconsciously I wondered if I was making excuses.

For some reason I was surprised to see Beaufort Maldin wasn't on the security desk when we arrived. A happy blonde in the starched and pressed uniform smiled at us as we entered, and I wondered absently why I had been surprised. Didn't Beaufort deserve a few hours at home with his family — presuming he actually had a family?

I took the corporate badge from the guard and pushed the thoughts of Beaufort and his presumed family from my mind. Wiley and I rode up in the elevator in silence. I wasn't surprised Mickie was not at her desk, which made me think of Beaufort and his supposed family again. Why was I so intent on the certainty that he would have a family? Maybe the doc's words were having more effect on me than I thought they could have.

When we had crossed the foyer and had entered Wiley's office, I noticed someone had arranged two chairs facing a roll-around stand that held a television and a video cassette player. Wiley motioned me toward a seat and said, "Sit down. I have something I want you to see."

Wiley busied himself at the television while I sat back in the chair. He placed a videotape in the slot, turned the

116

power switch to on, adjusted the sound, then took the chair beside the one in which I was seated.

"Home movies?" I asked.

"Just watch."

I turned my head back to the TV in time to see the words *A Time To Kneel* flash across the screen. In the next frame, the words *Starring Glory O'Riley and Peter D. Long* were painted in bold red letters. There were other names, but I wasn't interested.

When the movie began, a petite, buxom female who just happened to be naked and reclining spread-eagle on a bed smiled into the camera and began doing some very unladylike things to herself, all the while making sounds of pleasure. This went on for about five minutes until the sound of a doorbell could be heard on the tape. The female smiled again and winked at the camera, arose and padded out of the room. In the next frame, she came back into the room, accompanied by a male. The female immediately began unfastening his belt and unzipping his trousers, while telling the male what she was going to do to him. When he was exposed and she dropped to her knees, I said, "Not exactly my style, Wiley."

"Not mine either," he said as he flicked the remote control to off.

"So why the smut?"

"I thought you might want to see Ben's wife in action."

I turned to him. "That was Gloria Spence?"

He nodded. "In the flesh — if you'll excuse the pun."

"I don't. Where'd you get that?"

Wiley shrugged. "I bought it in a pit on Fourteenth Street in DC. Seems she has quite a name in the business. This one is one of about a hundred they had on the shelf." He chuckled to himself. "They even had dolls in her likeness. Gloria Spence Guron — alias Glory O'Riley — is — or was — quite a name in that circuit. The shopkeeper where I bought this told me she had been there many times autographing full-body nudes for everyone who bought one of her movies. Told me she was his best drawer."

"Okay, so now we both have seen her in action. Maybe it's time I went out and met her in person."

Wiley arose and went to the video player. He hit the rewind button and stood there until the machine clicked to a stop. He punched the eject button and removed the tape. When he turned the TV and the video player off, Wiley said, "Now I want to see where Ben was killed." As we walked from the office, Wiley dropped the tape into the waste basket.

As we drove out to Tallulah Gorge that morning, a strange heaviness hung about the car. The pictures of the naked female kept dancing through my mind, and I had the feeling that I had somehow intruded on a private part of the now-dead Ben Guron's life, a part he had hoped no one would ever see. I felt glum and somehow soiled even though it was bright and sunny and the summer sun was beating down on the car in which we were riding. Several times Wiley made small jokes about the GBI sedan I was driving. We both knew it was only nervous conversation. Like me, Wiley had no eagerness to see where a comrade had been murdered.

We arrived early enough so we were alone at the iron rail above where Ben had died. The area was not cordoned off so I presumed the county had done its work and had removed the tapes securing the area. Wiley followed me down the precipice and onto the rock outcropping. As we stood on the rock cleft, I turned to Wiley and said, "Somehow I can't believe he's dead."

He nodded. "I know what you mean. It's hard to accept a friend has gone."

"No, Wiley, it's more than that. You and I — and Ben — we lived with death for a lot of years. There were so many times when I didn't know if we would make it out, I don't even try to count them. But to die like this ... to die at the hands of someone you never suspected would kill you..."

Wiley interrupted me. "So you think it was someone he knew and trusted?"

I nodded in his direction. "That's exactly what I think."

Wiley's eyes were dark as they peered at me. "Any ideas who it might have been?"

I turned to him. "Follow me," I directed. We inched our way down the slope until we reached the second outcropping. The footprints I had seen were partially obliterated, but the ribbed soles of the second pair could still easily be seen. I knelt down beside them. "Look at these."

Wiley crouched down beside me and studied the prints in the sand. "Ribbed, just like any climber or hiker would use."

I nodded slowly. "What else do you see?" I asked.

His eyes stared down at the marks in the sand, then turned up to look at me. "These foot-prints are pretty small." When I smiled, he went on. "You make it a man with very small feet?"

"Or?"

"Or a woman," he said.

I gave him a rueful smile. "Exactly, Detective Frazier."

A wan smile crossed his mouth. "Special Agent MacGruder, you have someone in mind?"

I eased myself down on the rock and lit a cigarette. When Wiley was settled down beside me, I said, "What I have in mind is that Ben may have gotten himself involved with a woman who was not exactly what he thought she was."

119

Wiley's brows furrowed. "Dave, I didn't find anything out about this Gloria Spence that would suggest she could commit murder. She might be a little rough around the edges, but prostitution and pornography aren't the same thing as murder."

"But the prints, Wiley, don't they suggest a woman to you?"

He shook his head. "Maybe, but how many women are there around here? And how do you know that he didn't have other enemies?

I gave him an incredulous look. "Who hated him enough to kill him?"

He shrugged. "Why not? If this thing he was into took someone's money — a woman's — and that someone didn't like it, why couldn't she be the murderer?"

I cut my eyes across at him. "Or a man with small feet?"

"Why not?" he asked.

"Because it just doesn't fit, that's why." I took a long drag from my cigarette and let the smoke trail from my nostrils. Okay, let's look at it from another point of view. Let's make the assumption that Gloria Spence Guron is as clean as new-fallen snow. The picture falls apart right there."

Wiley gave me a critical look. "What's your exception?"

"The fact she was a prostitute and was into blue movies."

"That doesn't make her a killer."

I took another drag from the butt and crushed it against the rock face, rolled it between my fingers until all the tobacco was gone and rolled the paper into a small ball. I held the rolled paper up between my thumb and forefinger. "No more than this paper causes cancer."

"It doesn't, Dave."

"But the tobacco it holds does, so that makes it equally guilty. Without the paper, there can be no cigarette."

He shook his head. "All right, so we both have decided that cigarettes can kill. What does that have to do with Gloria Spence?"

"No paper, no cigarette. No tobacco, no cigarette. You take either of them out and what remains is not harmful. It's just paper or shredded tobacco."

"So which is Gloria? The paper or the tobacco?" Wiley asked, his eyes crinkling at the corners.

I angrily thumbed the paper into the chasm. "You aren't listening, pal. She's neither. Pornography in itself isn't dangerous. All it does is allow some sick person to accomplish what he — or she — might not be able to accomplish without it. The problem with porno is what it replaces — and maybe that's not so bad, either, if the people who watch it know what they are seeing isn't real. If they know the people up there on the screen are just going through the motions, then maybe porno isn't so bad. But it's the ones who think that the women — or men — up there on the screen represent normal human beings who are dangerous. They see a male and female coupling in ways every-day people never do, and they think that's the way it's supposed to be. Or they see some teenage girl — or some female who could pass for a teenage girl — wearing a cheerleaders outfit, jumping around, begging for some male stud to do her, and they think every teenage girl wants an adult male in her bed. That's the poison of pornography, Wiley. That's the cancer the cigarette causes."

Wiley cocked his eyes over toward me, but he remained silent while I was thoughtful. "Gloria Spence Guron was the paper that held the tobacco in place. Without her — or males and females like her — the scum that produce that trash could never make a cent. And if there was no money in it, the so-called producers wouldn't film naked bodies thrashing around on a bed. The Glorias and the producers cause the cancer."

"Okay, so you get no argument from me, but it still doesn't make her a murderer."

I turned my face to him and shrugged. "No, I guess it doesn't. Somehow, though, I can't separate her from the deviants who kill just for the sake of killing. Wiley, perversion is perversion, whether it's sexual perversion or sadistic perversion. Cold-blooded murder is the purest form of sadistic perversion."

"So you're saying because she was in porno flicks, she's a pervert?" When I didn't respond, he went on. "Okay, so maybe she had a wild streak in her, but that was a long time ago."

I nodded. "It was that, all right. Still doesn't change anything in my mind, though."

Wiley gave me a sad look. "Dave, it sounds as though you've already tried and convicted her, and you don't even know her."

"I know what I saw on that television screen this morning, Wiley, and in my mind that scene makes her something less than human. A person who could do what she was doing isn't exactly what I picture as being pure."

"So maybe she changed."

"Maybe she has." Then, "And maybe she hasn't. Maybe the same thing that drove her to make that movie, drove her to do other things."

"But where's the proof? Where the evidence that says Gloria Spence Guron killed her husband? Where, Dave?"

I shrugged again. "It's here somewhere."

"But you have none now."

I turned to him and stared at him squarely. "I have the footprint."

He gave me a wan smile. "Okay, so that's something. Now all you have to do is prove that a print that is no longer here is the print of one Gloria Guron, loving wife of the deceased." He gave a rueful chuckle. "Good luck, Special Agent MacGruder. You have an impossible task in front of you."

We crawled back up the steep path until we reached the overlook. Wiley leaned against the rail and looked over the precipice down into the gorge. "It's beautiful, isn't it?"

I was standing a few feet from the safety rail and could not see down into the canyon, but said, "Yes, it is."

"Ben called you out here to talk and for some reason, was killed. Maybe he was killed to keep him from talking. You see it the same way as I do." It wasn't a question.

"Ben wanted to talk about Gorge Development, and someone didn't want him to do any talking."

"Which means?" Wiley asked rhetorically.

"Which means he had something on the corporation that would close its doors and put some — or all — the corporate officers in jail."

"Ben was a corporate officer, Dave." Wiley's voice was soothing.

I nodded. "I know. Maybe what he had to tell me would have put him behind the same bars as the rest of them, but we'll never know now, will we? So he's dead now and he can't talk. If he was doing something wrong — and I can't believe he was — whoever pushed him over the edge did it to shut him up. Maybe whoever it was saw it as just punishment for his betrayal, only he never got a chance to betray anyone. In my mind, that makes this the worst kind of murder. A drug deal goes sour, and one pusher kills another pusher, I see it as ridding the streets of one more piece of scum. Someone gets angry with someone else and kills them outright, it's wrong but you can understand what provoked the killer. But to kill someone because they might talk to another about something you don't want discussed ranks with the useless killings that take place in robberies because the victim might be able to identify the perpetrator, or the rape-murders, or the gang war retaliations, or stupid gang initiation murders. They all share one thing in common — they're atrocities, abomination on the face of humanity, and they have to be stopped."

Wiley cleared his throat. "Easy, Dave. You sound like a one-man crusade against crime."

I took a moment before responding. "Anything wrong with one man getting angry because our system allows that sort of thing to happen?"

He shook his head slowly. "Not unless that one man carries a badge and is sworn to uphold the law."

I felt my shoulders sag. "So what am I supposed to do? Make an arrest and watch the courts release the guilty?"

"You're supposed to do your job, Dave. Nothing more and nothing less. You're supposed to protect, not destroy."

I pulled the leather case from my pocket and flipped it open. I stared down at the badge that made me one of the official cops. It wasn't ornate. It wasn't even pretty; just a piece of metal shaped like a shield. I closed the case and looked up at Wiley. "All right. So I handle this the right way." I returned the case to my rear pocket and turned toward the car.

Wiley's voice stopped me. "I knew you would, partner."

I turned back to him. "Did you?"

He nodded. "Yes."

I shrugged and gave him a smile. "That makes one of us."

Chapter Eleven

As I drove the state vehicle south toward Harlanwood, Wiley sat quietly on the passenger side. From time-to-time as we crossed a high knoll, the radio would squawk. Somehow, it was like old times, being back in a squad car, a Sheriff's Department patrol vehicle. I glanced over at Wiley to see if he was feeling the same thing. His face was ashen and his eyes were sad. "You okay?" I asked.

He turned pained eyes at me. "Yeah. I was just remembering Captain Guron. He was an okay guy. Back when we had all that racial crap on the ships, he was skipper of one of the carriers. Bunch of brothers thought they could take over the mess decks and force him into listening to their grievances. He was from the old book. His ship was run clean and neat, and the sailors were not black or white or red or yellow, or brown; they were just sailors; all the same. He was an impartial son-of-a-bitch; hard as nails, but fair. To leave the bridge and go down to where they were would have meant he was giving in to mutineers — which is what they were — so he sent the marines in to cordon off the area, turned the ship around, and headed back into port. When he got there and they had the ship tied up, he unloaded the whole lot. When they were all gone, he untied the ship and headed back out to complete the mission." He paused and looked at me. "You ever hear that story?"

"No," I said.

"So you never heard what all that got him?" When I shook my head, my eyes on the highway, Wiley said, "It got him relieved of command, and destroyed his career. I broke him, Dave. He was never the same after that. Up until that point, he was strong and forceful. When the E Ring Ballerinas took that ship from him, they killed him. I the Navy had backed him, maybe he wouldn't have ended up married to someone like Gloria."

The car fell silent, but the air was heavy. I knew Wiley had something more to say so I kept still, watching the roadway in front of the car. When he finally spoke, his voice was stronger. "I think it was the old Captain Guron who called you. I think he was making a stand. In his way he was saying *This is wrong and I won't put up with it*."

"And it got him killed," I added after a moment.

"But he died standing up for what he believed, and that's something."

I nodded. "Yes, I suppose it is."

When we drove into the limits of Harlanwood, I stopped at gas station and filled the car with gas. While the attendant cleaned the windshield and checked under the hood, I glanced around the packed sand lot. When he was finished, I handed him a twenty and he made changed. When I took the folded bills from him, I asked, "Can you give me directions to the police department?"

He eyed me with a certain dislike. "You a state cop?" His words were almost snarled.

Other memories of being a street cop flooded back. I gave him a friendly smile. "Matter of fact ... You have a problem with that?"

The attendant curled an upper lip, exposing rotten teeth. "Yeah, I got a problem with that. You want to make something of it?"

The smile never left my face. "You work here?"

His face went through a quick change from open hostility to animal wariness. "I own this place. Why?" The sneer came back.

I shrugged. "Oh, nothing really, except that it appears there has been a lot of gas and oil — and other petroleum products — dumped on the ground here for years. I make a call to the folks in the environmental protection office, they'll come over here, take some samples, and probably close you down. Maybe you'll only have to pay a few thousand in fines, and dig up a few hundred yards of fill. Maybe they'll find a leak in one of your tanks. Fine goes up and you get closed down for a lot longer." I smiled at him again. "You were going to tell me where the police department is?"

This time he gave me very precise directions, only he acted like it hurt him to talk. As I drove out of the station, I noticed him watching us leave.

"What was that all about?" Asked Wiley.

"Just a slight alteration of opinion." I had no trouble finding the Harlanwood Police Department building. It sat on a rise on Main Street, which also happened to be Highway 441. When I parked the car, I said, "We're going to play this like we are on official business. Don't tell them you aren't GBI unless they ask for identification. If they do, you're a special investigator for ... for the state looking into discrepancies pertaining to land fraud and fraudulent misrepresentation."

He laughed. "Am I suppose to remember all that?"

"Okay, so play it by ear. I don't want these locals thinking we're cutting in on their territory. We may need them later. I want to talk to this Officer Ryan and all we're after today is filler."

We went into the air conditioned office. I was not surprised to find it was very professional. A uniformed female officer looked up and smiled at me as I approached

127

her desk. "May I help you, sir?" She had a thick southern accent that made her pronounce the word as *sah*.

I showed her my credentials and said, "I'm MacGruder. This is Frazier." I motioned over my shoulder at Wiley. "We're here to talk to someone about the murder that took place up at Tallulah Gorge."

The officer leaned forward in her chair, batted blue eyes at me and said, "You're name's MacGruder?" She said it a *Magruda*. When I nodded, she said, "I heard there was someone up there from the GBI. That was you?"

"In the flesh." I leaned down and looked at her name tag. "Officer Paulk, Mr. Frazier and I are hear to talk to Officer Ryan. Is he on duty?"

She nodded. "He's one of our dispatchers. Maybe you and Mr. Frazier could take a seat and I'll see if I can get him out of the radio room."

I gave her a big smile. "You do that."

Wiley and I took a seat on the wooden bench that had been placed against the front wall of the office. After a minute, Officer Paulk returned. "If y'all will just follow me." She turned and I noticed she filled out her uniform trousers very well, and very femininely.

Officer Paulk led Wiley and me into an office off the main room. As we entered the door, I noticed a plaque with the words *Captain Robert R. Kilborn, Supervisor* painted on it nailed to the door. I turned and gave Wiley a wink.

A large, balding man of about fifty was seated behind a desk. He turned steel-blue eyes up at us as we entered. When he spoke, his voice matched his eyes. "Thanks, Annie Sue. You can leave us now." When the door closed behind her, he said, "What's this all about?"

I took out my identification and flipped the case open toward him. "I'm Special Agent ... "

He cut me off. "I don't give a crap who you are. I want to know just what the hell you state boys are doing here?"

He had not offered us a chair, so we stood in front of his desk while he glared up at us. It was easy to see he wanted to be inhospitable. I quelled a spike of anger and smiled down at him. I didn't have to return the favor. "Captain, we are here on official business. A man was killed up at Tallulah Gorge ... "

He cut me off again. "Don't you think I'm aware of that? His name was Guron."

I nodded. "Benjamin Guron."

He leaned back and folded his arms across his chest. "All right, so this Guron got pushed over the ledge and he died. He got himself killed in Habersham County, and that makes the murder the sheriff's problem — not the GBI's."

I felt anger turning my face red, but I controlled it. "We're here for two reasons, Kilborn. First, Tallulah Gorge is a state park. That makes any crime committed there our problem."

Kilborn swallowed back angry venom. "And the second reason?" He asked, his voice cold.

"Ben Guron lived here."

"So you think that you can waltz in here and we'll just open our files to you?"

"Something like that," I said.

He snarled at me. "It doesn't work that way, MacGruder. I don't know where you got your training, but there are rules. You ever hear of going through channels? I never got a call that you were coming. That makes this visit an intrusion. I advise the two of you to go back to Atlanta and file the proper paperwork before you stick your noses back into this department."

I placed my hands on Kilborn's desk and looked him straight in the eyes. "If I didn't know better, Captain, I'd think you were trying to hide something."

He made a great effort at controlling his temper. It took him almost a minute, but he managed it very well. "I don't have to even talk to you, Agent ..."

"Make that Special Agent," I cut-in.

His face reddened. "I don't know a Special Agent from shit, MacGruder, and as far as I'm concerned, that's exactly what the bunch of you up there in Atlanta are. You come over here thinking all you have to do is wave that state badge and all of us will jump. Well I don't jump for nobody. I don't hold to what Gloria and her husband did to her grandparents, but she's been a model citizen since she came here, and I won't have her riled by the likes of you. Now whether her husband's death is within the states jurisdiction or not, I don't know. That's the sheriff's problem, not mine. You want to talk about the murder, you head on over to Helen. I'm sure Sheriff Bolls will be more than happy to talk your ears off. You come back to Harlanwood, you make damn sure you got the proper papers filed." Then, after a moment, he added, "And don't come until you get the official invitation from this department. Do I make myself clear?"

I stood. "Yes, Captain. You make yourself perfectly clear." I turned to Wiley. "Mr. Frazier, I think we caught Captain Kilborn at a very inopportune time. Why don't we just leave him to his work?"

Wiley smiled. "Of course, Special Agent MacGruder."

Over my shoulder I called, "Thanks for your time, Captain, and if we can ever be of any assistance to your department, just let us know." I slammed the door before he could respond.

On our way out, I stopped at Officer Paulk's desk. "Is he always that pleasant?"

She giggled. "Sometimes he's a lot worse."

130

"Mr. Frazier and I have been on the road most of the day. Is there someplace where we can get a cold beer and a bite to eat?"

"There's a couple of good restaurants here in town. Most of the cops here go to the Harlanwood Restaurant. It's four doors down on the left." She looked down at her watch. "Y'all want to go on down, shift change is in fifteen minutes. I'll bring Billy Ryan down with me."

I smiled at her. "You do that and I'll buy you a beer." Then I asked, "Kilborn make the roll calls down at the Harlanwood Restaurant?"

She shook her pretty head. "He doesn't even drink."

I nodded. "See you in fifteen minutes then."

Cop bars have a certain feeling to them. It isn't the dress, although if you look closely you can see the bulge of snub-nosed service revolvers or short barrelled automatics beneath nylon wind breakers. The feel is more a tenseness, a reluctance to welcome outsiders. A hushed silence always fell when an unknown person walks through the door. And then there is the high pitch of anxious laughter which barely conceals the pent-up frustrations which hang heavily amid the smells of stale beer and cigarette smoke and nervous perspiration.

The Harlanwood Restaurant must have been a family oriented establishment before the cops took it as their own retreat. But once marked as a place where cops spent a few moments — or hours — relieving and reliving their work day, it was not a place where families would want to spend their evening.

Wiley and I took a rear booth and smiled into the blank and suspicious stares. When the waitress came, I ordered a beer and a menu. Wiley ordered a cup of coffee. When the waitress asked him if he wanted a menu, he shook his head.

The eyes were turned away and the den of conversation began to rise, but the wariness was still there. The waitress brought the beer and the coffee, and Wiley and I sat quietly for a while, me sipping at the frosted glass and Wiley stirring two teaspoons of sugar into the steaming cup of black liquid.

Wiley had finished his coffee when Officer Paulk came in. A neatly dressed man followed her through the door. She gave her eyes a moment to adjust, then she smiled and waved in our direction. She came to our table, stopping briefly to greet other off-duty officers and to bark an order in the direction of the waitress.

I made room for her on my side of the table while Wiley slid further into the booth to make room for the man. "This is Billy Ryan," Officer Paulk said.

I leaned across the table and shook Ryan's hand. "I'm Dave MacGruder and that big ugly dude beside you is Wiley Frazier."

Ryan shook Wiley's hand. "I talk to you on the phone?" When Wiley nodded, Ryan turned back to me. "Annie Sue tells me that this has something to do with that killing up at the gorge."

I nodded. "It does. She also tell you that your captain politely threw us out of his office?"

Ryan laughed. "She said something about that, only she didn't use the word politely."

"Then you understand that we don't have your department's permission to speak to you?"

It was Annie Sue Paulk who spoke. "It's off-duty time now, and Captain Kilborn isn't around. The way I see it — and me and Billy talked about it on the way over so I know it's the way he thinks too — a murder happens and it's our duty to help find the killer."

I smiled at her, then to Ryan, I said, "You were very helpful on the phone with Wiley. What I need from you is clarification on a few points."

He nodded earnestly. "Anything I can do to help," he said.

"You told Wiley the people here won't have anything to do with Gloria Spence Guron."

Ryan nodded. "The Spence's are good folks. They been here for a hundred years — maybe longer. Old Mrs. Spence — Gloria's grandma — taught me in Sunday School. She's as good as they come, Agent MacGruder."

"Let's make it Dave."

"Okay. Anyway, Dave, when Gloria came back and bought their home out from under them, it didn't sit too well with the folks around here."

"The Spence's run into problems?"

He shrugged. "The way I heard it — and this is pure hearsay you understand — somebody down at city hall was in on changing the zoning where their house stands. That don't happen too often, and never like it was done here."

When I raised my eye brows, Annie Sue cut in. "Sometimes people will want to open a small business in their home, and if it's zoned residential, the zoning board has to change it to business. See? But it's always done because the family who lives there wants it done."

Ryan took up the story. "In this case, the old Spence's, they didn't have no intention of opening a business in their home, but the board rezoned it business. That made the property value go up. They was living on a fixed income, so the increase in taxes was too much for them. They fell behind on the taxes, and just before the auction, in steps Gloria and — or at least a dummy corporation she set up — buys the property. Only it was done kind of shady like in a closed bid. Bought it for maybe forty percent of it's value. The city got most of what she paid, and the Spence's were out on their ears. So she moves her husband in and the property gets rezoned residential again. The old couple ended up in a home, and not a nice one."

"This sale, in order to get it done that way, she had to have help from inside city hall."

Ryan nodded. "That's the way it would seem, all right."

I looked at him. "Ask you a question?"

He narrowed his eyes. "Something tells me you're about to ask if Captain Kilborn has any connection with the city zoning commission." When I nodded, he said, "His wife — Kate — is the chairman."

"Explains why he's so touchy about having us here."

"That don't mean he's involved in the murder," Annie Sue interjected.

"No, it doesn't." I changed the subject by asking Ryan, "But you said that Ben Guron was okay?"

Annie Sue answered me. "The word is that he paid to get the Spence's out of that home, set them up in a small house down in Demorest, and sent them money each month. That was all done hush-hush though, and I don't have any real proof, except that one day they were in that old folks home, and the next day they had that house."

"Maybe it was Gloria who did it." Wiley interjected.

Ryan cut his eyes over at Wiley. "Not that one. I doubt if she'd bury them if they died. Nobody knows why she hates that old couple so much, but every one knows she does."

"Okay, so tell me about Cleetice Dubois."

Annie Sue shivered visibly. "That's one man I wouldn't want to meet alone."

"Why?" I asked.

"Because he gives me the creeps. I was working patrol just after I got out of the academy, and I stopped him for speeding. While I was writing the ticket, he kept staring at me. It was like he was trying to figure out how I'd be … "

A red hue crept up her cheeks. "When I handed him the ticket to sign, he gave me a smile that made me go cold. He told me that if I'd tear up the ticket, he'd take me in the back seat of his car and show me what a real man was. I told him to sign the ticket and get on his way. So while he's signing, he started telling me what he liked for women to do to him." Her face reddened even more. "I'm not a prude, but some of the things he said to me made me sick. I actually felt like he was going to do something to me right there on the side of the road."

Wiley asked, "What did you do?"

"I got the hell out of there as soon as I could."

Ryan asked, "You didn't report it?"

Annie Sue shook her head. "What was I going to say? I stopped a man and he made a pass at me, and it scared the hell out of me? Sure, and as soon as I reported it, I could kiss my job goodbye. Billy, sometimes you are about as dumb as you look."

Unconsciously, I placed my hand over Annie Sue's. "You did the right thing. A lot of cops are killed because they forget to get scared in situations like that." Then to Ryan, "This Cleetice, he ever been in trouble?"

"Not anything that would put him behind bars. He has this thing about young girls."

"And young boys," added Annie Sue.

I shook my head. "Okay, so he's not what the rest of us think is respectable. Is there anything else that might help us?"

Billy looked sick. "I told Mr. Frazier ... Wiley that he moved in with Gloria and her husband right after they came here. People talk about how Cleet and Gloria were carrying on right there in that house. One of the officers found them parked up a deserted road, and you can figure what they was doing, but other than that, the two of them were discreet. They got this maid — make that had.

Bertha Wilkes is her name and I hear she quit this morning Anyway, she told some folks that since her husband died Gloria and Cleet sleep in the same bedroom. Bertha said the two of them prance around through that old house almost naked, and she caught them in the act yesterday. That's why she quit."

"That's gossip. We can't go on that," I said.

Annie Sue spoke up. "It isn't gossip. Bertha's daughter is a matron at the city jail, and they don't gossip. That's where we got that. Either of them says something, you can believe it."

Billy Ryan looked down at his watch. "Hey, I got to run. Wife's parents are coming over tonight, and it wouldn't do for me to be late." He arose. "If there's anything else I can do, just let me know."

Both Wiley and I said thanks and watched him leave. Wiley looked over at me, then at Annie Sue, and got up making excuses about calling his office. When he was gone, I noticed that my hand was still atop Annie Sue's. A voice screamed in my brain, and used the word lecher. I removed my hand from hers. "I owe you a beer," I said.

She shook her head. "I don't really drink, and when I do, one is my limit." She turned to me, her blue eyes serious. "What you said earlier, that thing about cops getting killed because they forget to be scared, did you mean that?"

"Of course I meant it."

Her eyes softened and I felt the warmth of her hand slip over mine. "You've been a cop a long time." It was a statement, and when I nodded, she said, "I bet you could teach me a lot."

"About being a cop?"

She narrowed her eyes and smiled sweetly, demurely and more than a little coquettishly. "And about other things."

136

I felt my ego go up ten points on the scale. She was nubile and ripe, her feminine attributes straining against the cotton of her blouse. Back in the police station, I had seen the twitch of her rump as she walked away from me. The sway of hips had been unintentionally intentional, but it was still there, and it was all woman. But still, there's something about having a kid make a very obvious pass that throws a danger switch in my brain, even if the kid is all female-woman. I took a deep breath and pulled my hand from beneath hers. I thought to myself, *Here you go again, MacGruder*, as I patted her hand in a very fatherly way, and asked, "Annie Sue, how old are you?"

She blushed. "Twenty-four. Why?"

I gave her a fatherly smile. "Because I have a daughter older than you."

Her eyes went wide. "You do?"

I nodded. "I do. And as pleasant as the thoughts are — and as flattered as I am that you are offering — taking you on your first trip down that particular lane is not something I wish to do. And the last thing I wish to think about is some over-the-hill cop teaching one of my girls something they should be learning from a man their own age."

Her eyes went down and she mumbled, "Is it that obvious?" Then she said, "I'm so damned embarrassed."

I reached over and cupped her chin, turning her face toward mine. "Kiddo, it isn't something to be embarrassed about. I think you should be very proud of the fact that you have scruples."

She tried to smile, but it didn't work very well. "I got this thing that tells me to hold on to it until I meet the right guy, and we get married. Trouble is, I'm afraid that I'll never meet him."

I gave her my best fatherly smile. "You will, and when you do, you'll be glad you waited for him."

This time the smile worked. "Maybe I will, at that."
Then she leaned up and kissed me on the cheek, in a ver
girl child- ladylike way. "Thanks." She got up and left.

Wiley returned, sat across from me and gave me
wink. "You get something set up for yourself?"

"Shut up." I said.

Wiley's eyes widened. "What did I say?"

I looked at him for a long moment, then shrugged
"Nothing. I guess I suddenly feel very old."

In a voice that was both understanding and comforting
Wiley said, "Welcome to the real world, Dave."

Chapter Twelve

We drove back into Atlanta just in time to catch the last dregs of the rush hour traffic. I dropped Wiley at his office, promising to keep in touch. I found one of those telephones attached to a pole and dialed Brenda's number. I let it ring eight times, and just as I was about to hang up, I heard her voice answer. "Yes?"

"Brenda, it's MacGruder."

I could hear the smile in her voice when she said, "The renegade agent finally checks in. Is it all right if I ask what you've been up to?"

"I'll give you a complete report if you'll have dinner with me." There were a few too many seconds of silence, so I said, "If the notice is too short, I promise you I'll understand." Then, when she still didn't speak, "And if you've got other plans ... "

"David, will you please shut up? I was in the shower when you called, and I'm standing here in my bath robe sopping wet. My hair is a mess and I have clothes piled two feet high all over the laundry room."

"Oh. Well, we can make it another time," I said dejectedly.

I heard her laugh. "I wasn't going to let you off. I was trying to figure out how I could make myself presentable."

I breathed an audible sigh of relief. "I was afraid ... "

She cut me off. "You come on over, but we'll have dinner here, if that's all right. I have a pot of Brunswick stew on the stove. It's my grandmother's recipe, and it's out-of-this-world. One bowl and you'll be mine forever."

"Is that a promise?" The words were out before realized what I was saying.

She laughed again, only lighter. "Better be careful wha you say, Special Agent MacGruder. I have a degree in law and I know when I hear an implied contract."

It was my turn to laugh. "I'll pick up a bottle of wine on the way."

"No need," she said. "I have plenty here. You jus bring a large appetite, and a good memory. I want to hea everything that went on today over in Harlanwood."

"Something tells me you already know."

"Isn't it funny how quickly someone can pick up phone and make a call, especially when they have a beef."

I let her comment pass. "I'll be there in fifteen minutes."

"Not if you want to get in the door, you won't. It'll take me at least thirty minutes to make myself presentable."

"See you in thirty minutes, Brenda."

I stood outside her door and waited for her to open it When she did, I felt my heart race. She had pulled he shoulder length hair back, and tied it in a pert and sassy pony tail. Her face was bare of any makeup, except for light coating of pale pink lipstick. The lack of makeup enhanced her strong features rather than detracting from them. Her eyes were big and brown and bright, and her smile was welcoming. She was wearing blue shorts and white pull-over shirt. Her feet were bare.

At first I had thought there was nothing fragile abou her, but now I saw that beneath the feminine muscle was soft flesh and subtle warmth. Her waist was small beneath the firm expanse of breast. Her hips were smoothly curved and sensually accented the slight roundness of tummy When I had first seen her, the clothes she had been wearing

140

suggested big boned woman. Now, I saw that there was nothing masculine about this five-foot-eleven inch female.

She stood in the doorway, framed by the light coming from inside the foyer and I had the sudden urge to drop all my inhibitions. She must have sensed it because she stepped back away from the door and motioned me in saying, "I don't know about you, but I'm starving. Why don't you just come on in so we can go try my grandmother's recipe?"

She had set up a couple of TV trays in front of the sofa. When I sat down, she poured a glass of white wine for me. Then she poured one for herself, went off into the kitchen, and returned carrying two steaming bowls. She sat one in front of me, stood back and watched as I tasted the stew. It was just as good as she had promised it would be. My smile of appreciation relaxed her and she took a seat beside me.

She ate like she had not eaten in weeks, with an appetite that matched my own. I found myself enjoying this female person. I gave several seconds to watching her eat, but after the first succulent bite of the Brunswick stew, I was only interested in finishing the first bowl of stew so I could have a second helping.

Between the two of us, we managed to finish the whole pot. We made small talk over cups of coffee. Somewhere between the second cup and the second rum-on-the-rocks, Brenda managed to turn my attention toward my visit to Harlanwood. She kept steering me back in that direction every time I would wander. She got it all out of me, including a detailed explanation why I took Wiley in with me. She made me go over it two or three times, and she was full of questions. When I had finished, she told me that Captain Kilborn had called her supervisor. She told me that she had run interference for me, and she thought that most of the rough edges had been smoothed.

When I asked her if she knew anything about Kilborn she shook her head. "Only that he's been over there a long time, and he's got a pretty good reputation as a cop. A few years ago, he made a name for himself by cracking a really sticky murder case. The way I hear it, he's a professional. Why do you ask?"

I shrugged and narrowed my eyes at her. "I think he's afraid things will come out that might leave some stains on his good reputation. It's my guess his wife was the one who fixed the rezoning for Gloria. Kilborn acted a little too brusk today. It was more than hurt feelings because I didn't inform him that I was paying his department a visit. I'm not saying he had anything to do with fixing the zoning commission vote directly, but I am saying that he's probably covering up for his wife." I paused and drained the glass I had been holding.

Brenda brought me another drink, and a glass of white wine for herself. She took a small sip and asked, "You don't think he's mixed up in this murder, do you?"

I shook my head. "No, but I think he's indirectly involved in Gloria's plot to ruin her grandparents — but only by association."

"How could that be?" Brenda asked.

I leaned back and closed my eyes. "Brenda, a dirty cop is the worst of the breed. He exudes corruption, but he's not equipped with camouflage so he's easily spotted. Kilborn is an ass, but he doesn't strike me as being dirty, not in the normal sense. I got the feeling that he was trying to protect something — or someone." I paused. "This is how it appears to me, Brenda. Kilborn's wife is the chairman of the zoning board. When Gloria plotted against her grandparents, she needed someone on the inside so the revenge would work. Without the rezoning and the subsequent rise in the property taxes, the old couple would still be in that house. So Gloria — or Cleetice Dubois —

approaches Kilborn's wife and convinces her that it would be in her best interest to play along with them."

"But why would she agree to that?"

"Money is always a pretty good vote getter." I saw she wasn't too keen on that idea, so I said, "No, I don't buy that either. Something Annie Sue Paulk said today makes me think this Cleet Dubois might have given Commissioner Kilborn a very good reason to play along."

Brenda's brows raised. "Paulk? She's the cop, isn't she?"

I nodded. "From the way she spoke of him, I think Cleet is capable of coaxing a lonely woman into the woods. After that, he would have the leverage he — and Gloria — would need to force Mrs. Kilborn to vote their way."

"So you think it's blackmail?"

"I think that's a pretty good possibility."

"These are the days of peaceful co-existence between law enforcement agencies, David. A small town police department can't afford all the modern technologies. They have to depend on the larger agencies for assistance, so I guess it doesn't make sense that Kilborn would raise such a fuss over your being there unless he had something to hide." Brenda watched me for a few seconds, her eyes dark with thought. "All right, so let's assume that they had something on Kilborn's wife. How can we prove it? And what does it have to do with the murder?"

I gave her a confused look. "Maybe nothing at all. My gut tells me the only way Kilborn is involved is he happens to be married to the woman who runs the zoning commission."

"And if he knows she was bribed ... "

"Or coerced," I cut in.

Brenda nodded her head slowly. "Same thing either way. Whether she fixed the rezoning because she had to or because she wanted to doesn't make it right. And if

Kilborn knew what she did and hasn't taken any action o_
his knowledge, he's as guilty as she is."

Brenda was right and I knew it. A cop has to uphol_
the law, or he's worse than the criminal. If my guess wa_
right about Kilborn's wife — and I was pretty certain that
was right — and Kilborn knew what was going on, he wa_
bound by his oath to stop it and bring the guilty parties t_
justice. But, it's a whole lot easier when the bad guys — o_
gals — don't sleep next to you every night.

I shook my head and exhaled loudly. "The problen_
with this thing, Brenda, is it's too neat, too tightly woven_
It's fixed all the way up and back down so well the onl_
way we're ever going to get enough evidence on Gloria is i_
someone breaks down. The corporation is a hoax — or s_
close to it that most people couldn't tell the difference.
think Ben got too close and saw it was all a ruse, and that'
why he was murdered."

Brenda looked thoughtful for a few seconds, then said
"So let's see what we have." She held her right hand up an_
touched each finger with the index finger of her left hand a_
she spoke. "We know Gloria has a dirty past, and we knov
she is ruthless. She would have to be to put he_
grandparents out on the street. But is she capable o_
murder?" She went on quickly before I could speak. "An_
we know that Gorge Investment and Developmen_
Corporation is a scam. So it's logical to assume that all th_
senior partners are in on the scam. That gives us Glori_
Guron, Marvin Dubois and Cleetice Dubois. Those are ou_
prime suspects. Do you agree?"

I looked at her for a moment before I spoke. "You'r_
forgetting the foot print."

"No I'm not. Maybe Gloria pushed her husband off tha_
cliff — remember I said maybe — but I don't think sh_
made the decision it was time for him to die on her own."

"So what we have is a conspiracy. Is that what your saying?" I asked her.

"David, we don't have enough evidence on any of them at this point to pin it down, but I think it's safer to assume that they are all equally involved."

"Ah," I said. "Your telling me to be careful who I lean on."

Brenda smiled at me. "Exactly," she said. "You start leaning on the wrong person trying to get them to break down, and you'll have all three on you so fast you'll never know what hit you."

"And you wouldn't like that?"

Her face reddened slightly. "No, but I wouldn't like any of our agents to get ... " She let the words trailed off.

"Listen, lady, the last thing I want is to get myself killed, and I can be very careful when the need arises. So you can stop worrying about me." I took a sip of my drink. "But I think I was right about cutting someone out of the pack. As air tight as this whole thing seems, it's my guess that like a house of cards, it'll come toppling down very easily. What I have to do is figure out the best direction to approach it — and who to approach."

Brenda's eyes narrowed. "Maybe this thing with Kilborn's wife is the weakest link."

I paused and scratched my chin, and gave her a smile. "That's how I had it figured, too."

She sipped at her wine thoughtfully. When she looked up at me, her eyes were intense. "So why don't you tell me what you plan to do next?"

I shrugged. "I was going to go in and play the role of the financier, try to get on the inside, but I doubt if that'll work now. What I'll probably do is go back over and see if I can talk to Kilborn's wife."

She laughed sourly. "That won't be easy."

"I know, but if I have to, I'll let Kilborn know that we know what went on."

"And if he doesn't give in?"

I shrugged again. "I think he will, but if he doesn't then I'll just use my authority."

"And Gloria Guron?"

"She'll keep. As a matter of fact, it might be better to give her — and the Dubois brothers — some time. Let them think they are in the clear."

"What happens if you lean on Kilborn's wife and she goes running to them for protection?"

I gave her a smile that I hoped conveyed confidence. "I'm a special agent for the GBI, Ms. Carlisle. We are thoroughly trained to handle ourselves in those kinds of situations."

Her eyes darkened. "But this Cleetice Dubois, you said he was dangerous."

I shrugged it off. "I said the cops over in Harlanwood think he's a loose cannon."

She shook her head. "It's the same damn thing, David. If he's dangerous, then I don't think you should go in there alone. Maybe you could take your friend back in with you."

I shook my head. "That won't work."

"Then what about me?"

I turned my head toward her. "That might make getting to Kilborn's wife easier. She might talk to you quicker than to me." Then I let my voice grow firm. "But Brenda, if she breaks down, the rest is mine."

I could see the cold defiance in her eyes. "MacGruder, you seem to forget who's in charge here. If this thing backfires, it won't be you who has to answer the questions. So I'm in it all the way. No grandstand plays. Understand?"

"Brenda, if it goes like we hope, and Kilborn's wife talks, then the next step will be to get at Gloria or one of the Dubois'. That has to be a one-man show, and you know it."

Her eyes flashed. "Sounds like you're saying you may have to sleep with this Gloria Guron."

I felt my face flush. "That isn't what I'm saying, and you know it."

This time when her eyes flashed, there was more humor than anger. "But if that's what it takes?"

I shrugged. "I suppose I've done worse in my life."

I was going to add something about sleeping with Gloria Guron not being on my list of top ten-million most desired ways of spending two-and-a-half minutes, but Brenda cut me off. "All right, so maybe I'll have to sleep with one of the Dubois brothers."

I turned my eyes quickly toward her. "Brenda, that's the dumbest thing I've ever heard. This isn't some drug store detective novel where the hero — or the heroine — use their sexual prowess to wheedle a confession out of the bad guy. A man has been killed, and we don't know who did it. Maybe if was Gloria, or maybe it was Cleetice Dubois. But whoever it was, that same person might kill again. I don't want you in the middle of that. You understand?"

Her eyes flashed angrily at me. "And you think I want you in the middle?" Then the anger passed, and Brenda looked at me skeptically. "I am well aware this is not a game. I hope you are, too." Then her eyes softened, but when she spoke, she forced herself to sound like the boss. "All the same, I don't like the idea of you going in alone. I'm going over there with you, and I don't want any arguments about it."

I leaned over, my face an inch from her's. "Am I suppose to get the idea you're worried about me?" I gave in to the impulse and kissed the tip of her nose. "Don't answer. I would rather think that's what it is."

She smiled. "I guess I am worried. I like you, MacGruder. I like you a lot, and I don't want you getting yourself killed before I get tired of you."

"Hey, we had all that wonderful Brunswick stew and now we're sitting here on the floor having a drink together. Let's not get all mushy."

The red returned to her face. "I wasn't being mushy, damn it. I mean it wasn't like I said I was falling in love with you." Then, after a moment, her eyes looking down at her hands, "Which I think I am."

"Whoa," I said. "Back up there, lady. Did I hear you say what I think you said?"

She raised her eyes to mine and I thought I saw a quick flash of fear. "If you heard me say that I think I'm falling in love with you, then yes, you heard what I said."

"Little early for love, isn't it?"

She gave me a hard stare, then a smile caught at the edges of her mouth. "Maybe for some people it is, but not for me. I'm a fairly intelligent lady, MacGruder, so I'm smart enough to recognize what's going on inside me."

I sat my almost empty glass on the coffee table and pushed myself up. When I was standing, I said, "Maybe it's time I went out the front door and down the road."

"Why?" She asked, her eyes staring up at me.

"To give you some time to think."

She raised herself and stood in front of me. "Think about what I just said, you mean?" When I nodded, she asked "What is there to think about? I'm well over thirty and that makes me a grown woman. If I want to fall in love with a man, I can do it."

"But you don't know anything about this man, lady. I could be the worst thing that ever happened to you."

She smiled. "I know that. But you can also be the best thing that ever happened to me, can't you?"

"I won't argue with you, Brenda. Like you said, you're a grown up woman, but maybe you're mistaking what you feel."

Her nostrils flared and her eyes went hot. "Damn you, MacGruder, I know the difference between love and lust."

I stepped closer to her and took her in my arms, placing my mouth over hers. When our lips touched, she tensed and I felt her body stiffen against mine. Then I felt her relax, and she returned my kiss.

It lasted only a few seconds, but when we parted, I could see the blurry softness in her eyes. I had the same silly reaction to her. I let my arms drop away from her as I said, "I won't deny that there's something there, Brenda. I like you, too, and maybe it's more than that. I don't know. What I do know is what I felt when I kissed you is nice — very nice. It made me think of soft sheets and warm bodies, and it's a little too soon for that."

Her eyes flashed hotly again, but then she surprised me by laughing. "Mr. Ruff-and-tumble has principles. I was right about you."

"Right about me?"

She nodded and moved herself close to me, her arms around my neck. "Something told me that you wouldn't take advantage of this poor, innocent little girl."

I looked down into her eyes. "Don't press you luck, lady. I'm not made of iron. You're close enough so I can feel how warm you are — and how soft — and I can smell your perfume. Your lips felt nice against mine and I want to kiss you again."

She brought her face close enough so that when she spoke, I could feel her lips brushing against mine. "Then why don't you shut up and kiss me?"

149

There are times when a man should do what the lady asks him to do, and that was one of those times. The kiss was longer, hotter, more frantic, and more passionate. When it ended, we were both breathless. She did not move away from me, and it was getting harder to hide the fact that I was reacting to her nearness.

It took all the will power I could muster, but I managed to disentangle myself and step back. "Brenda, if we do that again, there won't be any way of stopping what comes next."

"I know," she said in a small voice, her eyes glittering.

I sighed, turned and walked to the foyer. When I was standing in the open doorway, I leaned against the jamb and said, "I want to get an early start in the morning, so I'll be here at seven."

She smiled at me and I saw humor in her eyes. "I suppose I should thank you for protecting my virtue."

I leaned toward her and kissed her softly on the lips. "Lady, the last thing I want right now is for you to thank me for not doing something I want to do."

As I was walking toward my car, I heard her say, "All the same, thank you."

It was one hell of a long and painful ride back to Wiley's.

Chapter Thirteen

Brenda and I were traveling east on I-85 by 7:30. Most of the traffic, except for two or three thousand semi-trucks, was heading into Atlanta. I kept the state sedan at the posted speed limit, give or take four or five miles per hour.

Brenda seemed reticent as we drove out of the city. I figured she had the am-I-glad-I-didn't-screw-up-my-life morning after doldrums, so I gave her some space. I limited my conversation to an occasional curse word when an eighteen wheeler tried to inch me closer to the shoulder of the four lane than I thought was reasonably safe.

When I took the I-985 exit and we were headed into the rolling foothills of the Smokey's, Brenda turned in the seat and looked over at me. "David, I have to ask you something."

"Ask away," I said, not taking my eyes from the roadway.

"Did I make a complete fool of myself last night?"

Her question had come out of left field so fast that I didn't have time to prepare a stock answer. "What are you talking about?" I asked.

I cut my eyes over in time to see her blush. "You know damn well what I'm talking about," she said.

There are times when the gentleman of our species must enjoy the discomfort of the lady who is ill-at-ease, but who feels it her right to explain an indiscretion so that the gentleman will not think it a normal thing for the lady to do. I could have told her it was not her fault. I could have said I found her very attractive — which I did — and that I forced her to the edge. I could have said that as the man, felt her weakness and took advantage of it. And I coul have told her I felt like a total fool for not completing th liaison. I could have said all of that — and maybe I shoul have, but I didn't. I simply shook my head and said, "No don't."

She gave me an exasperated look. "I'm talking abou the way I threw myself at you last night. You must thin I'm some kind of animal the way I went at you." Sh blushed again and firmed her jaw. "I know how it feels t check the biological clock and see it ticking its way down but I assure you I haven't set my sights on you, and yo aren't in any danger from me."

I took my foot off the accelerator and let the car slo down enough so that I could pull onto the shoulder of th road. When it was stopped, I turned to Brenda. "Mayb we had better get something straight right now. I don't fee like I'm in any kind of danger where you are concerne and I never thought anything about being sighted on."

She gave a nervously embarrassed laugh. "I must hav been something to see last night. I was ready to lead yo off to my bed. I wish I could blame it on the wine, but can't." Another laugh, only this time there was somethin in it besides the nervousness. "You must have had a reall good laugh over that. Have you told your friend about ho the female cop threw herself at you and how you turned he down flat?"

I could hear the faint edges of anger in her voice "Brenda, what in hell's name is this all about?"

She brought her eyes up to mine. They were cold wit anger. "It's about rejection, MacGruder."

"If you think for one minute that it was easy for me t leave you last night, you have another thought coming. told you last night, I'm not made of steel. If I hadn't lef when I did, you wouldn't have gotten the chance to lead me off to your bed. But I did leave ... "

She cut me off. "Yes you did."

I felt the far off pangs of what I thought was anger approaching, so I naturally became defensive. "All right, so I left. So what?"

"So what? You bastard! I threw myself at you and you just walked out the door. How do you think that made me feel?"

When it drew close enough for me to recognize, I noted that it wasn't anger I had seen. It was self-reproach, so I held my hands up in surrender. "You win. I don't know how I could have been so thoughtless. There I was, ready to frolic you right there in your living room with no fanfare, no silly romance, no dumb preliminaries. I was ready to rip your cloths off, jump on and go for the count. And that's damn well what I wanted to do — and came very close to doing. But I found myself liking you. I found myself wanting something a little more memorable than a romp on the living room carpet. Somewhere after the first kiss, I started feeling light headed and giddy, and suddenly I didn't want a one night stand. I stupidly thought that it should be slow and warm and loving, and it wouldn't have been that way last night I assure you." Then the anger welled up inside me and I blasted her. "Maybe I should have stayed. I could have been the brightly colored gamecock and we could have played all night. Along about day break, I could have jumped out of your bed and into your shower, and then gone running out the door feeling like I had taken something that wasn't mine to take. And when I was gone, you could have washed the smells of me away. Is that what you want?" I didn't give her time to answer. "Lady, if you think you're feeling lousy because nothing happened last night, just give some thought to how you'd be feeling if something had happened and it was just fun and games."

I pulled the car into gear and jammed my foot down on the accelerator. The sedan leapt into the outside lane, narrowly missing a rusted old Japanese import. I caught sight of the driver, and thought I could hear a few four letter expletives.

We had not travelled more than a few miles when I felt Brenda's warm hand touch my arm. "Guess I was being little silly back there."

I cut my eyes over to her. "Not silly. Just mixed up."

"I suppose that's it." Then after a few moments, "David?"

"Yes?"

"Have you ever had a partner who is in love with you?"

I shook my head. "No, I can't say I ever have."

Her voice was almost a whisper when she said, "You have one now."

I took a deep breath and let it out slowly. "You ever had a partner who was in love with you?" Out of the corner of my eye I saw her shake her head. "Well, guess you and I are in the same boat. Next question is just what the hell are we going to do about it?"

She slid across the seat and let her hand rest gently on my arm. "Since I've never been in this predicament, I don't know what we'll do about it. Guess we'll start by being honest."

Her fingers caressing my arm were having a strange erotic effect on me. I smiled to myself. To Brenda I said, "Good a way as any to start a relationship."

She took a deep breath and spoke softly. "I'm not a virgin," she said.

I almost laughed but I held it in. "I didn't know that was a prerequisite."

Brenda smiled and said, "It isn't, but I wanted you to know."

"Okay, so I know. I'm not a virgin either, so we're still equal."

After a few seconds, she said, "I've never been married."

"I'm one up on you there, girl. I have been. I have four beautiful daughters to prove it, if I ever needed the proof. I also have the scars."

An awkward minute passed before she spoke. "What was she like? Your wife I mean."

I gave myself a full ten seconds before I answered her. "She was a sweet Georgia Belle who thought I was fun and excitement, only I wasn't. She out classed me by a mile. I think we both knew the marriage was a mistake, only we kept trying to keep it together, until there was nothing left. One day I stopped going home. When I did go back, she was gone. End of a marriage." Before she could ask anything else about my defunct marriage, I asked, "It's obvious that there was almost a Mr. Right in your life. What was he like?"

Brenda laughed softly and rested her head on my shoulder. "He was a silly college boy who romanced me into the back seat of his car and out of my bloomers. We both shed the obligatory tears and promised that it would never happen again, but the next time we parked, into the back seat we went. I thought he loved me — hell, I *thought* I loved him — but along came Spring break, and when the next session opened, he didn't show up. I must have written him a hundred letters, and I never got a reply. A few months later, I got a very short note from his mother telling me that he was married. She said that if I really cared for him, I should leave him alone. God was I heart broken. I must have cried for a month. I pulled myself out of it by getting into the books. I finished college with one of the highest grade point averages in the school."

"So that was your only love?"

I heard her giggle. "David, a gentleman doesn't ask lady such things. But I'll answer you anyway. No, h wasn't my only love." She raised her head and looked me. "Does that matter?"

"Does what matter?"

"That I'm used merchandise, even if only slightly."

It was my turn to laugh. "I wasn't asking about tha You're a very beautiful lady, and I figured you would hav had more beaus than you could count."

She shrugged and shook her head. "No, not by an stretch of the imagination. I guess it all goes with the job."

"What?" I asked.

"The fact that I'm a loner. I'm too intense, at least that what most of them say — the ones who take time to offe any excuses. See, I really like what I do and I'm damn good at it. Most of the men I date — when I date — want woman just like their mother, and I'm not like anyone' mother. I'm too tall and too big. I think I scare them off."

I lifted my arm and put it around her shoulders, pullin her closer. "Well, I know one man who won't be scare off."

She rested against me quietly for a while. Then, "Don' commit too soon, David. You never know how you'll fee in a month, or even a week. Anyway, I'm enjoying th newness of this."

"No more morning after blues?" I asked.

I felt her shake her head against my shoulder. "No None."

"Feel better?" I asked. When she nodded, I said "Good. Now we both feel better."

We drove in silence for the last few miles. When w drove into Harlanwood, I steered the car to the Polic Department, parked and switched the engine off. I turne in the seat to face Brenda. "When we get inside, follow m lead."

"Is that your way of telling me to let you do the talking?"

I shook my head. "No, but Kilborn is a hard nut. I've had one go around with him, and I got the distinct impression that he didn't like me very much. Matter of fact, he got damned angry the last time we talked. If he reacts the same way this time, maybe we can use his anger to our advantage."

Brenda's eyes narrowed. "Are you telling me you are going to purposefully make him mad?"

"That's exactly what I am saying. And when I do, you can step in and take over."

"Good cop, bad cop, is that what this is?"

I nodded. "Something like that."

"Suppose it doesn't work?"

I pulled the release and the door swung open. As I stepped from the car, I said, "We threaten to arrest her. He'll cave, I promise you."

I heard her ask, "And if he doesn't?"

I walked around to the passenger side, and when Brenda got out, I said, "Then we go question Kate Kilborn, whether the good Captain likes it or not."

Officer Annie Sue Paulk's eyes lit up when she saw us. Her smile was warm and friendly. "I didn't expect to see you this soon." Her smile faded as she turned her gaze to Brenda.

I made the introductions. "Officer Paulk, meet Agent Brenda Carlisle, Georgia Bureau of Investigation.".

The ladies did not shake hands. Annie Sue turned her eyes to me. "You here to see the captain?"

I nodded. "If he can fit us into his busy schedule."

A smile crept across Annie Sue's face. "You going to piss him off the way you did the last time you were here, I just might find some excuse not to let you see him."

"I promise to go easy on him," I said.

Standing, she said, "In that case ..."

She lead us back to Kilborn's office. When she started to knock, I gently grabbed her hand. "If you don't mind, Ms. Carlisle and I would just as soon surprise Captain Kilborn."

Annie Sue looked from me to Brenda and then back at me. Finally she shrugged and walked back down the hallway. When she had gone through the door to the squad room, I knocked. When I heard the "Come in," I opened the door.

As soon as Kilborn saw me, he jumped to his feet. could see his hands ball into fists at his sides and it was exactly the physical reaction I had expected. I switched my gaze to his face.

It's hard to describe the reaction Kilborn gave us when we walked through the door. The word surprise comes to mind. Bewilderment, too, but also anger — cold, fuming, murderous anger. He had them all down pretty well, so that his face cycled from one to the other, and then to the third — and then back to the first — in such a rapid change that I had to be very alert to catch them all.

I did catch all the inflections, though, and catching them, I was quick to react in my own way. "Kilborn, Agent Carlisle and I are here to get this thing settled. We know your wife is involved with Gloria Guron and the Dubois' and suspect she's tied in with Gorge Investment and Development Corporation. Ben Guron was killed by someone. We think his murder has something to do with Gorge Investment and Development Corporation, and that means the suspects are Gloria Guron, Cleetice Dubois, Marvin Dubois, and anyone else who is involved with them, and if your wife is on their payroll, she's a prime suspect." I gave him three seconds for all that to sink in and then I went on. "Now, do we talk to her here, or do we talk to her at your home?"

Kilborn's face contorted into what I thought was cold-blooded anger, but after a moment, I saw that it wasn't anger at all. It was fear. I had struck an exposed nerve. As I watched him, he crumpled into his seat. He looked older than he had when we first entered one minute before. His face turned ashen and he slumped over, his head coming to rest on a stack of papers that were on the top of his desk. For a moment, I thought that he had fainted, but then I heard what sounded like deep, guttural sobs. Then he started to shake, and I knew that he was broken.

Breaking a human is not a pretty thing. It isn't something to be proud of. Most of us spend our lives on the edge, our psyche bound by merely a thread. Only a few ever have the thread severed. Those poor souls spend months, years trying to patch the tear. Some never manage to find the shreds and spend the remainder of their lives lost in some timeless dimension, oblivious to who they are, and to the world they once inhabited.

I looked over at Brenda and I saw the pain in her eyes. When she saw me watching her, she shook her head slowly, and I motioned her toward Kilborn. She moved around the desk and knelt beside his chair, her hand resting on his arm.

Kilborn lifted his head, and turned wet eyes to Brenda. "Kate had nothing to do with Guron's murder."

"But she is involved with Gloria Guron." Brenda's voice was soothing."

"She didn't know what she was getting into. They used her. He ... " Kilborn let his voice trail off.

"He? Who is *he*?" I asked.

Kilborn turned his head and looked at me. He watched me for a full minute and I could see that he was fighting to regain control. He straightened himself and squared his shoulders. When he spoke his voice was hard. "You have no right to question me."

Brenda stood. "Captain Kilborn, it isn't too late. If yo
cooperate with our investigation, I promise you that we'
do everything we can to keep it quiet."

"And if I don't cooperate?"

Brenda shrugged and moved back around the desk unt
she was standing at my side. "Then we'll be forced to tak
your wife back to Atlanta with us. We can hold her as
material witness, but you already know that, don't you."

I saw his shoulders droop again, and I said, "Kilbori
up to now, Agent Carlisle and I have played it easy. W
don't want this thing to get out of hand, but if you fight u
on this, we'll come down on you with everything we have
That isn't a threat, it's a promise. You understand me?"

His eyes went askew, and he slowly nodded his head
"All right. What is it you want to know?"

Brenda took the lead. "We don't want anything from
you. We want to talk to your wife."

Kilborn's eyes were pleading. "I can tell yo
everything you want to know. My wife ... "

Brenda cut him off. "Her name is Kate, isn't it?"

Kilborn nodded. "They got to her — to Kate. Glori.
and Cleet Dubois, they took advantage of her. My wif
isn't well and they found a way to make her do whateve
they wanted."

"How?" I interrupted.

"How?" His eyes flashed in my direction. "They jus
did, that's all."

I shook my head. "Not good enough, Kilborn. You tel
us what we want to know, or all bets are off. You hav
exactly ten seconds to start talking or we go get your wif
and haul her in. Is that what you want?"

For a brief second I thought I had gone too far
Kilborn's eyes narrowed and his knuckles went white as hi
hands balled into fists. Then I saw the light fade from hi

eyes and he relaxed. "All right. What is it you want to know?"

There are times when it is best to lay back and let things happen. This was not one of those times. I squared my shoulders and looked him straight in the eye. As I spoke I shook my head. "What we want to know, you can't tell us." He started to speak but I cut him off. "Maybe you can fill in some of the back ground, but your wife is the only person who can tell us what we need to know. So here's the only deal you are going to get. You pick up the phone and call your wife. You tell her Agent Carlisle and I are going to your house to talk to her, and we want her to talk openly. We don't want any run-around, and we don't want any half truths. If she tells us everything, we'll do everything we can to keep her out of it. If either of us gets any idea she's holding back, your wife goes to Atlanta with us. You hear what I am saying, Kilborn?"

His eyes were pained but he managed to nod. "You have to understand that Kate isn't well. This has all been a strain on her. You have to promise that you won't be too hard on her."

I said, "Kilborn, your wife is at least guilty of complicity. Neither Agent Carlisle or I have to promise you anything."

I saw his knuckles go white again. Brenda must have seen his reaction, too, because she interjected, "Captain, Special Agent MacGruder and I aren't here to arrest your wife. That's the last thing we want to do. We know she had nothing to do with the death of Ben Guron, and it's his murderer's we are after. If she can help us put them behind bars, nothing will happen to her. I promise you."

Kilborn looked from Brenda to me, and then back to Brenda. Then he nodded, picked up the receiver and spoke into the mouth piece. "Get my wife on the phone," he said.

161

Chapter Fourteen

Kate Kilborn was standing on the front porch waiting for Brenda and me. We got out of the car and walked toward the front steps, and I could see the strain in her face. I felt a sudden tug at my heart when I thought about the additional worry Brenda and I were about to cause this woman.

Kate Kilborn was nothing like I would have imagined. She was small, almost petite, with dark wavy hair that was cut short. Her eyes were dark brown and her face was neatly chiseled. She was in her mid-fifties, and was teetering on that half-step between matronly-striking and middle-aged attractive, but leaned more toward striking. It was the eyes. They were alive, fluid, effervescent, so that you felt you could see into her mind.

But there was also a fragility about her that made me want to run to her side, to put my arm around her shoulders to support her. As we walked from the car to the front steps, I saw what it was. There was a certain dark-stained-pallor about her face. I knew at once what it was, even if I had not seen the frail, skin stretched, bone protruding look. There was a monster within her, eating away at her insides, and the monster's name was cancer.

I was the first to take her hand. "Mrs. Kilborn, I'm David MacGruder and this is Brenda Carlisle. We need to ask you a few questions."

Her hand was fragile and limp in mine. "Yes, of course you do." I let go of her hand. "Agent Carlisle and I are investigating a murder, Mrs. Kilborn, and we think you may be able to help us."

Her face went pale, but Kate Kilborn was a trooper. She steadied her chin and said, "You're from the Georgia Bureau of Investigation. Bobby told me to expect you." She pulled the screen door open and held it for us. Her eyes held a strength that made me feel even more that I was intruding on her last days. "It will be more comfortable for us inside."

When Brenda and I were seated on the couch, Kate Kilborn asked, "Can I get you anything? Coffee?" When Brenda and I said no, Kate seated herself on an overstuffed chair across the table from the couch. When she looked over at me, her eyes darkened and she smiled sadly. "Bobby doesn't deserve what I did to him. He's always been here for me, and it wasn't right that I should have brought all this down on him, not with my ... " Her eyes saddened, but then she smiled. "Did he tell you that I'm dying?"

I felt Brenda shudder even though there was a foot separating us. I took the lead. "Your husband told us you aren't well."

The brown eyes flashed a satiric mirth. "Bobby hasn't accepted it yet, but I guess he'll have too before long." She gave us a smile. "You see, they tell me it's almost over now. I was in the hospital, but they sent me home. Better that I should die here, I suppose." She looked from Brenda to me, and I saw the resolve in her eyes. She knew what was coming, and she had accepted it as her fate. "Bobby didn't tell me much. He sounded funny over the telephone, as though he was afraid of where this might lead. All he said was that you wanted to know about Cleet Dubois." Then she added, "And his cousin Gloria."

"Mrs. Kilborn," I began.

The smile flashed again. "Please call me Kate."

I nodded. "Kate, we'll make this as easy on you as we can."

Kate Kilborn laughed, and I couldn't help but smile. "David — it is David, isn't it?" When I nodded, she went on, "David, there is absolutely nothing you can do that will make this easier for me. What I did was terrible — for me and for Bobby. If things had been reversed, I don't think I would have been able to accept it. But Bobby did, and he has been right here by my side ever since. It hasn't been easy for him knowing what I did, especially as he found out just after they told me that I was terminal." She paused for a moment, her eyes going vacant. A pained expression crossed her face, but she pulled herself together. "I'm sorry. Sometimes the pain comes, but it isn't too bad."

I suddenly wanted to end this. I didn't have the desire to sit on this woman's couch, in her home, and put her through any more misery. I turned my eyes toward Brenda and I saw the beginnings of tears at the corners of her eyes. I forced myself to be hard. "We have to know."

Kate Kilborn straightened her shoulders and smiled. "I knew I would have to talk about it someday. Now is as good a time as any." She looked at us both. "I was on the city commission when Gloria Guron petitioned to have the property her grandparents owned re-zoned. Of course, we were all against it. I grew up here — most of the commission did — and we all knew the Spences from the time we were children. The first vote was against the re-zoning."

"But the property was re-zoned," Brenda said.

Kate Kilborn nodded her head. Her eyes were sad. "I'm afraid that was my fault. Things got out of hand, and I had to cast my vote in support of them — Gloria Guron and Cleet Dubois."

I cut in. "You said things got out of hand. What kind of things?"

Kate Kilborn's eyes went sad. "I'm so ashamed of what I did." She looked at Brenda and I could see Kate' shoulders sag. "Bobby and I have been married for thirty years, and I never did anything like that before." Then she made a noble effort to raise her shoulders. "One day I was a happily married woman and Bobby and I were pillars of the community. The next day I was in bed with Cleet Dubois, wondering what in heaven had come over me. All the time I spent with Cleet Dubois, I knew it was wrong But I couldn't seem to help myself. When he would call, told myself that I wouldn't let it happen again. But it was no use. He would call and I would go to him. I forced myself to believe that he loved me, that it was more than just another sordid affair. But that's all it was. And then the re-zoning thing came up, and when I voted against it Gloria came to visit me. She knew all about the affair, and she threatened to tell Bobby. I stood up to her and I told her she could tell Bobby anything she liked, but it wouldn' make me change my vote. I was so high-and-mighty Then she showed me the pictures. I felt so ill when I saw the first one that I never looked at the rest. I could have told Bobby about my affair — I did tell him — but telling him about it was one thing. Having him see pictures of me with another man was something else. I couldn't do that to him. So I changed my vote. And when I changed my vote the rest of the commission did the same." She sat back in her chair, her face gray and exhausted.

Brenda spoke up. "Kate, after your ... after the last vote on the zoning change, did you and Cleet ... have you ... "

I could see that Brenda was having a lot of trouble asking the obvious question, so I stepped in and asked "Have you had anything more to do with either Cleetic Dubois or Gloria Guron?"

There was a slight darkening of her face, but then Kate Kilborn shook her head. "No. I haven't seen or heard from either of them again."

I continued. "Do you know of anything else that could help us?"

Kate tilted her head slightly, her eyes watching mine. "If you are asking if I know anything about a murder, the answer is no. But ... " She let her words trail off.

Brenda cut in. "But what, Kate?"

Kate Kilborn looked over at Brenda. "It isn't anything, you understand. It's just a feeling I have."

"Go on," I prompted.

"Well, I mean there were times when Cleet and I were .. together, he would say things to me — terrible things. At first I thought that it was just his way of ... of ... "

"Yes?" I asked.

Kate's face reddened and she drooped her head against her chest, her hands nervously twitching in her lap. "We would be making love," she shivered, "And he would say things about how he wanted to hurt me. He never did, you understand — hurt me, I mean, not really, at least not enough to leave any marks. But sometimes when he talked about it, he would do things just to prove that he wasn't just talking." Her eyes clouded. "And there was something very exciting about it all ... at first. Then it wasn't exciting at all, but I couldn't seem to help myself. I would be with him, and for days afterward I would hurt so badly that I would have to stay in bed." Her eyes cleared and she shook her head slowly. "It all seems like a nightmare now. How could I have done such a thing?" She had not directed the question at anyone in particular. She lowered her eyes and fell silent.

After a minute, Brenda asked, "Was there anything else?"

Kate Kilborn raised her head and spoke. "When Gloria came here to talk to me about .. about changing my vote she said Cleet could persuade me to do what she was asking. She told me he had ways of making death seem better than living in the hell he could create for me." She paused, and then in a voice almost too quiet for us to hear she went on. "I knew that Cleet could hurt me more than he ever had, and I could never tell anyone about it. So even if I had not already told Gloria that I would change my vote, hearing her say all that would have made me do anything she wanted. But I had already agreed to help her. All she had to do was show me those pictures. I would have done anything to keep Bobby from knowing. I think she enjoyed frightening me — and I was frightened. In that way, Gloria and Cleet are very much alike. They both enjoy hurting people."

The impact of what Kate had told us weighed heavily and we said nothing. It was Kate who finally broke the silence. She squared her shoulders and raised her chin in defiant strength that caused me to flinch. "I suppose you'll have to make a record of what I've told you."

Brenda stood, walked over and knelt in front of the chair where Kate Kilborn was seated. "Kate," she said, "It's over. What you did was silly, and maybe stupid, but it isn't anything we care about. You — and your husband — won't hear from us again." Brenda leaned forward and placed her arms around the dying woman's shoulders. "I'm sorry about all this."

Kate Kilborn looked into Brenda's eyes. A smile of gratitude creased her face. "Thank you," she said. I stood and we left her. She was still sitting in that overstuffed chair, her hands clasped in her lap as I pulled the front door closed.

I made the turn onto US 441 and drove south. There was a motel that looked clean and empty. "This one be all right with you?"

"What?" Brenda asked.

"Is this motel okay?"

She came out of her reverie. "Oh," she said. "Well, yes, I suppose so."

I pulled up into an empty spot and switched the car's engine off. I turned in the seat to face her and asked, "You okay?"

Brenda gave me a nod. "I hate this job sometimes."

"It's like that. Most of the time it's bad guys. Putting them away only does the rest of the populace good. When you have to play it hard with a nice person who got caught in the middle, it leaves a sour taste in your mouth."

"It's more than a sour taste, David. I feel as though I intruded on her secrets, and it was a terrible secret to force her to tell us."

I reached across and took her hand. "But now that she's told it, she's out."

I felt her shudder. "Is she? She's dying and she has to live with what she did. We shouldn't have gone there. We should have talked to her husband, and left it at that."

I squared myself in the seat until I was facing her. "You and I both know we couldn't do that. Maybe what Kate told us didn't have anything to do with the murder, but we had to hear it from her. It wouldn't have meant much coming from her husband."

Brenda's eyes were pools of sadness. "But that doesn't make what we did right, does it?" she asked.

"No, it doesn't, and it doesn't make it any easier to live with knowing that we had to do it, but we had to all the same." I gave it a moment, then asked, "You know we did, don't you?"

Her eyes fixed on mine, but the sadness was still there. "Yes, I guess we did."

I pulled her hand to my lips and kissed her knuckles. "Will you be all right while I get us a couple of rooms?"

She nodded. "I'm okay. It's just that there are times when I feel so dirty." She took a deep breath and let the corners of her mouth turn upward. "I guess I just need to be reminded that what I do is necessary."

I opened the car door, but before I got out, I turned back to Brenda and said, "What you do is not only necessary but important."

I got us a couple of rooms on the ground floor. We had dinner at a cafe about a block north of the motel. I noticed Brenda had a few too many drinks with — and after — dinner, but I kept my mouth shut. I held her hand as we walked back to the motel.

When I walked her to her room, I don't know what made me do it, but I reached out and took her in my arms and kissed her deeply. She did not pull away from me even when I pressed my lips tighter against hers. When relaxed and stepped back from her, I saw that her lids were lowered and her eyes danced. I wondered if it was the power of my kiss, or the effects of the booze. "Was I too far out of line?" I asked her.

She smiled and shook her head. "I think I wanted that as much as you did."

I took the key from her and she stepped aside as opened her door. "It's still early," she whispered. "If know you, you've got a bottle stashed in your room. You go get it and we'll have a nightcap." She gave me a mischievous smile. "Give the lady ten minutes to shower and get into something sexy."

I went to my room and retrieved the bottle of dark rum had buried in my canvas bag. When I got back to her door, he was leaning against the doorjamb, wearing a flimsy yellow thing that tried miserably to cover her voluptuous body, but failed. Brenda was giving me a slightly drunken smile. She stepped to one side and I came through the door. I went across the room and put the bottle on the table. Then I came back to her, stopped and turned as she closed the door. "Can I ask why?"

"Why what?" She asked.

"Why you wanted me to kiss you," I said.

She gave me a crooked little smile. "I think I wanted to know if last night was real, or if I've been single too long to know the difference between reality and fantasy."

I moved closer to her, taking her in my arms. "And?" I asked.

She melted against me, her arms reaching around my neck. "And, my heart pounded, my breath quickened, and my knees went wobbly." She turned her head a little, brushing her lips against mine. "No heroics tonight, MacGruder. I'm not in the mood."

Then she came to me. Her lips were sweet and her kiss was warm. It took only about three seconds of the second kiss to make my heart start pounding and my breath to come in quick, shallow gasps; another second and my knees threatened to buckle beneath my weight. I had been right the first time. There really wasn't anything fragile about Brenda Carlisle, nothing that mattered anyway.

My arms found their way around her and my hands clasped at the small of her back. I caught the scent of soap and tasted the freshness of her lips. I felt myself reacting to her, and began the battle with the male beast that lurks deep in the hidden dark confined recesses of my being.

I think I must have been losing the battle, and Brenda must have sensed it, because she pushed away from me and leaned back against my hands, her eyes watching mine.

171

She spoke in a hoarse whisper. "Maybe we'd better put this on the back burner for a while."

I eyed her. "Does this mean it's time for the drink?"

She laughed. "Or a cold shower."

"For you or for me?" I asked, giving her my most impish smile.

She opened her eyes widely in innocence. "For both of us. Didn't you know?" Then she added, "You get the cold shower in your room and I get to cool off in here all by myself."

I kissed her quickly on the tip of the nose, and released her. "If it's all the same to you, I'll skip the cold shower."

"Oh?" she asked mockingly. "I wouldn't have figured you for the hot water type."

"I'm not. It's just that if I am going to lose, I want to do it like a man."

"Silently suffering?"

I nodded. "And when the smoke has cleared, I'll crawl off somewhere and lick my wounds."

She placed her hand on my cheek, and I felt her reserve melt. Her hand was warm. "I don't think that will be necessary."

I took a long, deep breath and let it out slowly. "Brenda, my ego tells me to pick you up and carry you over to that bed before you have the opportunity to rethink what you just said."

She laughed softly. "As I told you, I'm well over thirty, MacGruder, and I don't make offers very often — almost never in fact. When I do, I don't retract them." She leaned toward me and kissed me softly again. I could feel her warm breath on my face when she said, "But let's be very slow and careful about this. Okay? I want to know beforehand if it's for sex or for ... " She didn't complete her thought, but I knew what she meant.

172

I took her in my arms and held her tightly as I kissed her. There was nothing gentle about the kiss, from either side. I could feel her responding almost immediately. Her lips were pliant and willing. When my hands touched her, she tensed for a moment, then relaxed, allowing me to slip the flimsy material she was wearing off of her shoulders until it caught at her waist. When my hand cupped the warm flesh of her breast, she stiffened. Her breath caught in a long shudder. Then she was pressing her flesh against my hand.

I kissed the tip of her breast and felt her hands stroking my hair. I felt her responding and I lost myself in the wonders of her. She gently pushed me away, stood, and reached her hand out to mine. There were no words, just a warm, inviting smile on her lips. She led me over to the bed. I sat on the edge and watch her slip the nightgown to the floor. She wore black panties beneath them. When she hooked her thumbs in the waistband and pushed them down, she was watching me closely. Naked, she slipped into the bed, and turned so that she could watch me undress.

It was times like those I cursed myself for allowing the paunch to develop, and for shunning a tan, but somehow her eyes said she didn't see the paunch, or the expanse of white male flesh.

When I crawled into the bed beside her, she reached out and hugged me close to her. In the next moment, the light was out, and I was caressing warm female flesh, tasting the erotic flavors, smelling the sensuous aromas. She pulled me and rolled onto her back, carrying me with her, until I felt the warm slipperiness of her against me.

She moved herself, and I felt her hips arch up to meet me, opening for me, willing me to enter, wanting me to be with her in this ultimate physical closeness. It was a slow, nerve-bending glide from warm touch to complete

173

enclosure. She called out to me, whimpering softly against my neck, holding me within her. Then she began to move away from me, only to move back until we were one person, one body, one soul, one entity longing for release.

I can not recall when I sailed into that oblivion of sexual wantonness. Nor do I know whether she sailed off with me, before me, or lagged behind. All I know is that she cooed and coaxed, and whispered that she wanted me to love her.

I was somewhere off there in that darkness that surrounds that oblivion when I heard a male voice not too unlike my own tell the female that he loved her, that he was enjoying her more than he had ever known was possible. A few moments, hours, or an eternity afterward, I heard the voice again, and somehow I knew that it was my voice, and that I was telling Brenda that I loved her more than she could ever love me, that I would be there for her that night and for all nights to follow. And then it was another time, another place, when I felt the heated pulsations of her body and I knew that it was time, not just for her, but for me also.

There is a moment when the orchestra works itself up for the grand finale, when the bass drums boom and the trumpets blare and the strings swell in harmonious notes. It is at that moment when the listener's heart synchronizes with the beat of the drum. And that is how it was with Brenda and me. At the moment of crescendo, we were together, bodies entwined, loins attached, and heart sounding the beat of the perpetual drum of love.

We drifted off into a drowsy slumber, my body curled against hers. At some moment, I felt her snuggle her bottom against me, and sensing that I was aware of her nakedness, and responding, she moved ever so slightly so that I was inside her again. And, coupled, we fell into a deep sleep.

174

The dawn broke bright and sunny. I was standing in the doorway to the motel room having a first smoke of the day when I felt arms encircle me. I smiled. "Morning Brenda."

She cuddled to my back. "Morning yourself."

I turned around and took her in my arms. "I trust you slept well."

"Like a baby," she cooed.

She had turned her face up to me as she spoke, and I couldn't resist giving her a quick kiss. "Hungry?" I asked her.

"Famished. I think I could eat a horse."

I stepped back far enough to see she was wearing only a towel. "If you can force yourself to put on something a little more substantial, we'll go out and find someplace that serves horse meat."

She smiled up at me, turned and headed back into the room and toward the bath.

I had already tucked my canvas bag into the trunk of the state vehicle when Brenda came out of her room. She was wearing stretch denims and a white blouse, and light blue canvas sneakers. She looked pretty and clean, and not very much like a professional state investigator. When I told her as much, she wrinkled her nose and asked, "And just what am I supposed to look like?"

I shrugged. "The words *stodgy*, *frumpy* and *mousy* come to mind."

She shook her head, tossing her bag into the trunk. "Not my style, MacGruder. You see, I'm one of the new breed. I can be good at what I do, and still be a woman."

I reached over and patted her bottom. "That you can, lady."

It was one of those roadside diners that advertised home cooking, but horse meat wasn't on the menu. Brenda downed three eggs, at least a pound of bacon, and a half dozen pancakes. All I could manage was a scoop of scrambled eggs six inches deep, four biscuits, two helpings of grits, and four links of country sausage. Somewhere in the middle of the meal, Brenda and I decided that we wouldn't discuss the case until after we were back on the road to Atlanta. So we ate. Needless to say, when the meal was over and we were enjoying the last of our coffee, both Brenda and I were content.

When I turned southwest on Rte 23 at Cornelia, Brenda was busily scribbling notes on her pad. "Writing a book?" asked her.

"No, smarty. I'm outlining our conversation with Kate Kilborn. It's for my report."

"Thought we weren't going to involve her."

"We aren't," she said. "But I have to account for my — our — time. I'll sketch what she said, but I'll leave her name out of it."

"And if someone — such as the state's attorney — asks who gave you the information?"

"Then I'll go into a tirade about protecting an informant." She gave me a triumphant smile and went back to scribbling.

After a few minutes, I said, "She really didn't tell us anything we didn't already know."

Brenda clipped her pen to one of the pages of her notepad, closed the small book, slipped it back into her purse, and turned in the seat to face me. "That is a problem." She emphasized the word *is*. "All she did was tie Gloria and Cleet into extortion, and that doesn't help our case any."

"But it does give us a reason to arrest them."

Brenda sighed audibly. "Only if we drag that poor woman into court and put her on the witness stand, and

David, I can't do that. Kate Kilborn has suffered enough already."

I nodded. "Well, at least we know what our two prime suspects are capable of."

From the corner of my eye, I saw Brenda shake her head. "Blackmail, extortion, and possibly mayhem, but we have nothing to prove either of them committed the murder. And footprints in the sand aren't sufficient to convict, David."

"So we'll just have to get them to confess." I had said it so matter-of-factly it stunned me. Somewhere in my mind I had decided it would be easy for me to get a confession. I suppose small, limited minds work that way.

"So what do we do now?" Brenda asked.

I shrugged, pressing the accelerator to pass a slower vehicle. "I think it's time I talked with Gloria Guron."

"And I get to talk to Cleet Dubois?" There was a slight irony in her voice.

I didn't like it, but I knew it would come down to that. "You're the boss," I said, and let it go.

Chapter Fifteen

Mickie Norton gave me a skeptical look when I stepped from the elevator. I walked across the reception area and stopped at the side of her desk. "Miss me?" I asked.

The green eyes flashed. "No more than I'd miss being run over by a truck. You could have called."

I leaned over and rested my elbows on her desk, my face an inch from hers. I leaned forward enough so that I could place a kiss on the tip of her nose. "Don't be angry, Mickie. Anyway, I thought we had all *that* taken care of."

Her eyes went wide. "I wasn't talking about *that*. You are a partner in this company, you know, even if you are out playing cop. When Wiley asks where you are, it would be nice if I knew. It would make me look more like the professional administrative assistant I am trying to be." Then she said, "MacGruder, sometimes you can be such an ass."

I nodded. "I may be a heel, but I'm still the MacGruder half of this company. That makes me the boss, and it isn't nice to call the boss names."

She fixed a cold-eyed stare on me. "But honesty is always the best policy, so it's my duty to remind you every now and then just how dumb you are." She said it spitefully, but I saw the green eyes had a sparkle creeping into them.

I pushed myself upright. "Hitting below the belt isn't fair, or didn't they teach you that in secretarial school?"

"What they taught me was to listen quietly, tak[e] dictation masterfully, and keep my damn knees very clos[e] together." Then after a moment, "David?"

"Yes love?"

"This woman — this Brenda Carlisle — is she right f[or] you?"

"How did you know ... " But even as I spoke th[e] words, I knew the answer. "You and Virginia have bee[n] talking, haven't you." I didn't mean it as a question.

Her face went bland. "Well, yes we have. She calls t[o] check up on Wiley, and when she called this morning, yo[ur] name came up. We just don't want you to make anothe[r] mistake, that's all."

I straightened. "Why is my love life so important to th[e] two of you? First you give her a blow-by-blow descriptio[n] of our little scene the other night, and now she tells yo[u] about Brenda. If I didn't know any better, I'd think you ar[e] jealous."

"David, that isn't fair. But I suppose you have a right t[o] *hit below-the-belt*, too."

I felt an uneasiness welling up inside me — a[n] apprehension I could not explain. I narrowed my eye[s.] "I'm a grown man, Mickie, and whether you know it or no[t,] I'm not stupid — a little on the thick side at times, and I ca[n] be a little dumb when it comes to females — but I know th[e] ropes. I've been down the road a few times."

She smiled at me condescendingly. "Yes, you have a[t] that, and you've made some pretty blunders, too. All I'[m] asking is that you be very careful this time. Give yoursel[f] some time to get to know this woman. You have no ide[a] what she wants — or needs — or what she's after. Don'[t] get involved if you aren't willing to see it all the wa[y] through to the end. If you really care about her, relax an[d] let it happen."

180

The apprehension suddenly turned to anger. "Just who the hell are you to be giving me advice? You're a great one to be talking to me about relaxing. As I recall, you're the one who came to me the other night just to make sure you're okay. A broad who doubts herself shouldn't be giving advice."

I saw her eyes sadden and her face go pale. I wanted to kick myself for that remark, or at least find a very large hole that I could crawl into. Maybe I didn't understand why I had lashed out at her, but I had, and I was sorry for it. But knowing Mickie, I wasn't about to make it better, so I stood there like the idiot I was.

The seconds of silence grew heavy until I took a deep breath and let it out slowly. "Listen kid, I'm sorry about that, but you will admit that it isn't any of your business." I just had to remind her that being nosey wasn't an admirable trait, notwithstanding the fact it was a necessity in our line of work. Her green eyes were a mixture of anger, hurt and sadness. They told me that I had said too much, and I decided to get back to business. A tactical retreat in the face of an overwhelming enemy was sometimes the best course. I gave it three more seconds. "Wiley in his office?" I asked.

She turned her back on me and said over her shoulder, 'Go on in. I'm sure he'll be glad to see you."

Wiley was seated behind his desk when I went through the door. His face broke into a wide grin and he said, "All hail the wandering knight."

I slumped into one of the chairs in front of his desk. "Funny, Wiley."

His eyes opened wide. "Oh? So what's got into you? You lost your sense of humor?"

"No," I said, shaking my head, "I haven't lost my damn sense of humor."

He shook his head and gave me a knowing look. "Okay, so we'll let it pass. My ears are open, partner, so give me what you've got on the case."

So I did. I told him about the interview Brenda and I had with Kate Kilborn. I finished it up with, "Now all we have to do is keep her out of it."

He nodded. "I can see where that might be best for her, but only if you can get enough on the Dubois clan to convict them."

He was right. He knew it and I knew it, of course. Nobility is great when it's an affordable alternative. This was one of those times when I prayed the pricetag of my noble efforts wouldn't include allowing Gloria and her kin to slip free. I simply said, "We don't have another choice, Wiley. It's our only recourse."

"Doesn't make it any easier to get something on Gloria Guron — or her cousin." There are times when Wiley Frazier can read my mind. Or maybe it's just that he and I think alike. Either way, he verbalized my thoughts by saying, "It would be a terrible thing if you had to let them walk because you can't bring this Kilborn woman into the case."

"That won't happen," I said with conviction.

"Sounds as though you have a plan," Wiley said.

I shrugged. "I wish it was that easy. Problem is, not only do I not have a plan, I don't even know where to begin."

He laughed. "That's never slowed you down before."

I couldn't help but smile. "No, I guess it hasn't."

Wiley's smile faded. "I know you too well to accept that you haven't got some kind of strategy worked out."

I gave him a nod. "Okay, so maybe now that I think about it, it doesn't sound like much of a plan."

"Why don't you try it on me and let me be the judge?"

I took a deep breath. "If I expect to get anything on Gloria — or Cleet Dubois — I have to go into the enemy's camp."

Wiley's eyes clouded. "Sounds dangerous to me, given the fact that Gloria may have already killed one person, and this Dubois is not someone I'd trust in the hen house."

"You see a better way of hanging the murder rap on them?"

Wiley thought a moment, then shrugged. "No, I don't." He watched me for a few seconds, then said, "Okay, so now that we have that settled, maybe it would help if you talked about what's really bothering you."

I raised my eyes, about to protest. Then I shrugged. All right, you asked for it. It's all these women. Seems every place I go, one of them is trying to mother me. First it's Virginia giving me advice I don't want or need. And now it's Mickie. Am I wearing a sign that says I'm a total foul-up, so messed up that I need someone to watch out for me?"

"And is that so bad?" he asked.

I gave it a second or two, and said, "No, I guess not."

"David, this has nothing to do with Virginia or Mickie." Good old Wiley. Even though I had known Wiley for most of my life, there were times his wisdom surprised me.

I sighed. "No, I guess it doesn't, now that you mention it."

Wiley leaned back in his chair, clasped his hands over his stomach and closed his eyes. "I'm listening."

"Buddy, I think maybe I'm a little too aware of how screwed up I am. I had a talk with our girl out there. She has been talking to Virginia, and the two of them have decided that I have this fear about lasting relationships."

They big brown eyes opened a crack, and the gruff voice boomed, "So what else is new?"

183

"So I care for this GBI agent, and I guess I'm afraid I'll foul it up just like I've fouled up all my other relationships.

Wiley sat upright, his bulging arms crossed on his desk. "Dave, so what if you do screw it up. Is that so terrible? Partner, you and I, we know each other pretty damn well. More than that, we are friends and have been for most of our adult lives. So your marriage didn't work out. So what? And so what if you haven't made it stick with another woman? Can you sit there and tell me you'd change anything given the opportunity?" He shook his head. "You wouldn't do it differently if you had the chance, no more than I would give up one second of my time with Virginia. There are a few who don't fit the mold, and you're one of them."

I interrupted. "Wiley, there has to be a reason why I'm still looking."

He nodded. "Dave, there are worst things. You could still be married to Joan Marie, and the two of you could be hating every minute of it. As far as the hunt goes, part you're still looking because you haven't met the right woman." Then he added, "Or the right woman hasn't met you."

I was about to protest when what he said began to make sense. "And maybe Brenda is the right woman?"

He nodded. "Maybe she is or maybe she isn't. Either way, what you should do is enjoy what the two of you have. If it turns out to be a lark, no harm done. If it turns out to be something more, the two of you will have some really great stories to tell your grandchildren."

He waited for me to respond. When I didn't, Wiley said, "I know there's something else, so I'm still listening."

"I ruffled some feathers out there, now I have to go out and unruffle them, and I don't know how I'm going to do it."

"Oh, so you stepped on Mickie's toes," he said knowingly. "Well, as great as she — and she's the best — our Mickie can carry a grudge." He paused long enough to chuckle happily at my dilemma. "I don't envy you one bit, partner. But, if you made her mad, don't ask me to help you get out of it."

I breathed loudly. "If that's all it was, I wouldn't be so uptight about it. What I did was crack that delicate china, and now I have to patch it back up before it breaks into a thousand pieces."

Wiley leaned back in his chair again. "Like I said, don't ask me to come to your aid."

"Thanks buddy." I stood. "Wish me luck."

He laughed. "I'd be helping you more if I offered you an escape route."

"Right," I said, and walked out of his office.

Mickie did not turn to look at me as I entered her office, but I wasn't surprised. I had seen her angry before, so I was ready for her ire. I stopped in front of her desk. "Do any good if I said that I was the biggest jerk on the face of this planet?" Silence. "I'm sorry, kiddo. I shouldn't have said what I said. I didn't mean it." Still nothing but the big chill. I rested my back-side on the corner of her desk. "Maybe if I hung a target on the spot where you should kick me?" I saw her shoulders move and I knew that I was getting to her. "So I lashed out when I should have kept my big mouth shut, doesn't mean that I meant what I said."

"But you did say something, and what you said touched a nerve." She did not turn to look at me.

I knelt and forced her swivel chair around. When she was facing me, I said, "Mickie, you and I, we have something too good to spoil. What I said wasn't fair, and if I hurt you, I'm sorry. If I could take it back, I would. But I can't take it back. I said it, and there is nothing I can do to

erase what I said. I know that. I am asking you to forgiv
me for opening my big mouth."

Her eyes searched mine, and then they softened
"David, you big lug, don't you know that I could never sta
angry with you for long?"

I took her hand. "So I'm forgiven?"

She smiled, but there was a hint of sadness. "Of cours
you are."

"But?" I asked.

She bent her head to the side. "But what you said wa
true. I did seduce you, and I did it for my own purposes.
She pulled her hand free from mine and touched her finger
to my lips. "Don't try to be noble, David. What I did, I di
for me, not you, and you were right to remind me of it
Funny thing is, what you said didn't hurt me. What hur
was facing the fact that I had used you."

I leaned forward and hugged her close to me. "Mickie
show me a human who doesn't use another huma
sometime, and I'll show you someone who is totally alon
in this world. I won't debate whether you used me, or
used you. Maybe we used each other, but it doesn't reall
seem to matter right now. What does matter is that the tw
of us had a moment that was soft and pleasurable, and fo
whatever reason it happened, I'm glad it did." I leaned bacl
away from her, my hands on her shoulders. "You and me
kiddo, we're pals, and pals do things and say things. That'
life, and that's what it's all about." I leaned to her and
touched my lips against hers. When I leaned back, her eye
were soft. "You know, don't you, there is a person insid
me who feels very close to you, and who wanted the othe
night to be the beginning of something." She nodde
slowly, her eyes intently watching mine, but she did no
speak. "But we both know the fair Irish lady with the gree
eyes and the red hair could never be happy witl
MacGruder."

"And MacGruder could never be happy with this Irish girl, either," she added.

I smiled a rueful smile. "He wishes he could be, Mickie. He really does."

She leaned forward and pressed her warm mouth against mine, letting the heat of her lips convey the certainty of what we both knew. When she let the kiss lapse, she leaned into my arms, her lips against my ear. "And the lady wishes it could happen, too." When she leaned away from me, there were tears in her eyes. "So what do we do now, MacGruder?"

I shrugged. "I guess we stay friends."

"But without any of that other stuff," she said.

I nodded. "It only confuses the issue."

"And who needs to be confused," she said. Then the mischievousness flashed back into her eyes. "Still, you know where I live, and friends can always help sometimes."

"Like when friends need to be held?" I asked, giving her a roguish look of my own.

She laughed. "I had something a little more personal in mind."

I opened my eyes widely. "That sounds a little like good old Tom is out of the picture."

A melancholy smile turned the corners of her lips up. "Tom was much too gentle for me. I like my men more adventurous. My man has to be willing to take a chance once in a while." Then she added, "If you know what I mean."

"Baby, you keep that idea nestled safely in the back of your mind. You never know when I'll come knocking." I stood, leaned down and kissed her cheek. When I straightened up, I said, "Thanks."

She smiled. "Anytime, MacGruder." Then, "David?"

"Yes?"

"This lady friend of yours, is she special?" I waited moment before I nodded. Mickie smiled. "Good," sl said.

As the elevator door closed, I got the distinct impression that Mickie had already dismissed the idea tha I might come knocking at her door.

I found Brenda pounding away at her computer keyboard As I entered, she turned, gave me a smile and went back t her labors. I took a seat on the folding, metal chair and sa quietly until she pushed the keyboard away. "There," sh said. "All recorded, saved, and filed in case anyone want to know what we did in Harlanwood." She put on a ster face. "Oh, and Special Agent MacGruder, I filed you report, too, just in case you were wondering."

I returned her smile. "I wasn't, but thanks all the same.

The smile faded and she said, "I suppose you hav something planned."

I gave her a small shrug and said, "I thought I might ru over and pay a visit to Gloria Guron."

Her eyes grew serious. "When?" she asked.

"I thought I might run over there tomorrow."

Her face grew serious. "But I'm not ready to go ove there again."

"I hadn't planned on you going over with me." I sav her eyes cloud, and I hurried on before she could protest "I need to see her alone."

"And if Dubois doesn't like your idea?"

"He won't have any choice in the matter."

Brenda's eyes grew narrow. "MacGruder, is ther something you haven't told me?"

"No, there isn't. I just get the feeling that Dubois isn' the brains. I think Gloria Guron is running the show, and i she is, then I want to get her alone so I can ask her a fev questions without her ape-man friend."

188

"David, do I have to remind you of what Kate Kilborn told us? If he's really into pain, you might give him the opportunity to inflict some on you. I wouldn't like that very much."

I ventured, "Are you saying that as my boss, or my girl?"

"I could be saying it as a human being who is worried about another human being." Then, after a moment, she said, "But now that you've asked, I'll tell you why I am saying it. I care about you, David, and I don't want you hurt."

I sat in the folding chair, a stupid puppy-love grin spread across my face, and said, "I care about you, too, Agent Carlisle, and if you'll give me the chance, I'll take you off somewhere private and show you." Then I did something very silly, and certainly against the directives that govern what an agent can and can't do to another agent; I got off the folding chair, took the three steps that separated me from Brenda, pulled her to her feet, and kissed her heavily, hotly, and passionately.

When I lost control, and my hands began wandering where they shouldn't have been, Brenda forced herself free, put a foot of space between us, and tucked her blouse back into the waistband of her skirt. "Damn it, MacGruder," she breathed. "The door is open."

"I can close it," I said teasingly.

She shook her head adamantly, but pressed herself against me for a moment before stepping back from me. The contact did not last long, just long enough for me to feel the nipples of her breasts made hard by the kiss. When I reached for her again, she stepped back another two inches and said, "MacGruder, I have to warn you that I hold a black belt in karate. You close that door and I'll be forced to make sure you'll have a few days when you'll only be able to think about whatever it is you have on your mind."

I ignore her words and pressed my palm against he breast. "And neither of us would like that very much."

She sighed and nodded, but gently pushed me away "No, neither of us would like that, so I guess there is onl one thing we can do about it." She pulled the bottor drawer of her desk open, retrieved her purse, fumble inside and came out with a key ring. On it was one key She handed it to me and said, "I have a lot of work to d and you are a distraction — a pleasant one, true enough but a distraction nonetheless. So will you please get th hell out of here." Then, cautiously eyeing the ope doorway, she came into my arms. The kiss was short, but held promise. "Make yourself at home. The rum is behin the bar in the family room. If you like, you can use th shower in my room. It's the first door at the top of th stairs. Clean towels are in the linen closet in the bath." Sh touched her fingers to her lips and made a sweepin downward motion, and it struck me as a very sexy thing t do. "I'll be home by a little after six — no later tha seven."

I drove out to Powder Springs and let myself into Wiley and Virginia's home, and retrieved a fresh change o clothes. As I was about to leave, I saw the handwritte note on the table beside the front door.

David,

Before you ask, yes I talked to Mickie. I also talked t Wiley and my ears are still ringing. Someday you'll have t tell me exactly what you said that got him so worked up Anyway, I'm not trying to be your mother, although you d need one at times. And you aren't my patient — eve though you need more help than you may realize. What am is your friend. I care about you, and you worry m

ometimes with your romances and your way of life. But
hat isn't why I'm writing this note.

What I want is for you to grow up. Don't you think it's
bout time? If you agree — and even if you don't — you
an leave me a note telling me whether you're going to be
ome tonight. And before you get all huffy with me, it's
ard to plan an evening not knowing whether a fond guest
s about to drop in. There's a pen on the desk. Just write
"Yes I'll be home" or "No I won't be home." That will do
icely.

Love,
Virginia

I smiled, then took up the pen and scribbled, "Thanks
for the gentle reminder that friends should show a little
concern once in a while. No, Miss Virginia, I won't be
staying the night with you. I have other plans. You and
Wiley enjoy the peace and solitude."

The neighborhood still looked uninviting. I pulled into the
driveway — careful to leave Brenda enough room to park
her car. I was carrying my canvas bag when I let myself
into the house through the front door. I do not like being in
someone else's domain when they aren't there, not even
when invited. I always feel as though I am intruding on
their secrets. And this was no exception.

I felt soiled from the trip, and figured as long as I was
intruding, I might just as well do it the right way. Brenda
had offered and I decided to take her up on the offer. I
trotted up the stairs two at a time, suddenly feeling very
youthful. Just as she had said, the doorway at the top of the
stairs was open and it was the master bedroom — Brenda's
private world. I had no desire to enter that particular room
unless and until invited to do so by the mistress of the
house. There were seven other doorways from which to

select. I ruled out two of them. These were narrow indicating closets. Yet another brilliant deduction by on of the world's great detectives. Of the remaining fiv doors, one was almost certainly a bathroom, so I set out t locate this room.

That particular door was in the wall at the end of th hallway, and it was the first one I checked. Chalk anothe one up to my intuitive and deductive powers. Problem wa: when I opened the door and went into the small room, was bare. It had the usual things: a sink, a tub-shower, toilet, and expensive towelry made for looks rather tha effectiveness. So it was either the bath in the maste bedroom, or go on through the other rooms until I found useable bath. As much as I had no desire to enter Brenda private domain without her being there, I opted for th former.

Brenda's bedroom was done in soft hues of beige an off white, with a vaulted ceiling expensively trimmed. Th bed was made and all the drawers were closed. There wa nothing left out to suggest that it was a male or a femal who inhabited this room. But there was a faint scent in th air of Brenda's perfume. I think I had a dumb smile on m face as I went through the room and into the bath.

I had been around a few times, and I chuckled t myself. I knew the bath would be a dead giveaway as t the occupant-user of the room. I had expected to see myriad perfumes, sprays, powders, lipsticks, and othe feminine things cast about the sink. I was wrong. It wa also neat and tidy, with no tell-tale bottles, boxes or tubes The toothbrush was neatly placed in the holder. Even th mirror was clean. The room screamed of organization. wasn't necessarily sterile, but it did lack the feeling o reality, and it was a little too defined for my tastes.

Where people live there is unavoidable clutter. Most o the time it's an organized sloppiness. When it is too clea ind too neatly arranged, it depicts a person who is wrapped a little too tightly. Keep everything in its rightful place and no one will ever suspect that the person inside is cracked and broken and ready to shatter into a thousand pieces.

That wasn't how I had perceived Brenda at all. To me she had been very alive, very real, and not on the verge of emotional collapse. Maybe I'm making too much of it, I thought. Maybe Brenda cleaned up this morning because she knew I would be here tonight. Yeah, that was it.

No, that wasn't it. If she had been expecting me, the key would have been on the desk, or in the drawer, not buried in her purse, and suddenly I was aware that I didn't know this woman at all. I had held her, kissed her, and subsequently made love to her, but I didn't know who she was or what made her tick.

Oh well, I thought, I came up here for a shower, and a little splashed water and steam on the mirror won't hurt this room at all.

I opened the linen door of the closet, and I had to smile. There on the floor, in the corner of the closet, in a pile next to the clothes hamper, were a cotton nightgown and white cotton panties. Draped over the edge of the hamper was a white bra. I remember noting that it was made of plain material with no frills and no lace. It had been made to perform a specific function, and it did not need any window dressing to complete its assigned task.

Even so, the clutter — as meager as it was — told me that Brenda was not a fragile china cup, teetering on the edge of the shelf, waiting to slip off and crush itself on the floor. I felt a sudden relief, or maybe it was elation. Either way, I knew that this fastidious woman who had suddenly come into my life just might really need me, if for no other reason than to teach her how to lean back and let go.

I showered, leaving the bath steamy, but no worse for wear. I found the rum, and mixed myself a stiff one. Then

193

I settled into one of the chairs in the family room, sipped my drink, and waited for my lady to come home.

I was on my third when she arrived, all tense muscle and strained nerves from her drive in the evening traffic. When she came over to me for the obligatory kiss, I think I surprised her by spinning her around and gently massaging her shoulders. It was working, too, until she suddenly stiffened, made some excuse about changing clothes, and sped out of the room.

At the time, I didn't think much of it, crediting her actions to weariness. I was soon to learn that it was more than that.

It took Brenda fifteen minutes to return to me. I had expected her to be dressed in finery, ready to go out for the dinner I had offered at some fine restaurant. When she walked into the room, the faded sweatsuit, tennis shoes and white cotton socks told me she had no intention of venturing out into the evening. I accepted it, though. An evening indoors with a beautiful woman — even one wearing clothing more appropriate to a gymnasium — was okay with me.

It was supposed to be one of those nice evenings where two people get to know one another, talking about nothing in particular, just things. After the heated scene at her office, I had expected Brenda to stay close during the evening, giving me little pats and touches of affection. But it wasn't that way at all. It wasn't even romantic, except for the fact that a man and a woman just happened to share a meal, a few glasses of wine, and an after dinner drink. All the while, however, she kept a certain distance from me. When the conversation drifted to us, she adeptly steered it off in another, less personal direction.

At one point, I said how pure the intimacies we had shared the night before had been. Brenda stiffened, grabbed my glass, and left me sitting on the couch, mouth pen, thoughts spinning in a hundred directions at one time, trying to figure out what I had said wrong.

At eleven, Brenda yawned, stretched, and made a vague remark about being a working girl and needing her beauty rest. Then she sat on the couch two feet away and stared at me. I got the distinct impression she was waiting for me to move on off toward the door, give her a quick peck on the cheek, and rush off into the night.

MacGruder may be a lot of things, but he sure isn't immune to subtle hints. I am as open to suggestion as any human, more so than some. But something told me to stay put, so I did. I picked up my half-finished drink, leaned back against the cushions of the couch, took a sip, and smiled innocently at Brenda.

It took about fifteen seconds for her face to redden and her eyes to go darting off, staring at unseen objects here-and-there in the room, and never once looking at me.

It was time to let her off the hook. "Okay, lady, I get the picture loud and clear. So relax. It'll take me another five minutes to finish this drink, and I'll be off." Then I added, "And out of your personal life, if that's what you want."

The eyes narrowed and came to rest on mine. The shoulders stiffened and the arms crossed over her chest. "Yes, well, it's been a long day and I really am tired. You understand how it is, don't you?" The eyes were plaintive, but there was a hint of something that I took to be fear behind them.

I took another sip from my glass, placed it on the coffee table, and turned to her. "All right, so why don't you tell me what this is all about."

The shoulders twitched and the eyes darted, but I just kept watching her, waiting it out. It took a full minute until she began to relax, then another half-minute until she was able to look at me. "I'm waiting," I said.

"David," she began. "Last night was good — no, it was great — but it was a mistake. I like you." Then after too long a pause, she added, "I like you a lot." I expected – no, I wanted to hear her use the word *love*. She hadn't, but I kept my mouth shut as she went on. "This whole thing is too much for me right now. I wasn't looking for relationship when we met, and I'm not looking for one now. I allowed last night to happen because ... " She paused again, then said, "Because you are a very charming man and a woman needs to be charmed once in a while. However, once in a while doesn't mean every night."

For a moment, I was taken by the surprise of her revelation. Then I began to see what she was actually trying to tell me. In her mind, the first night, she had offered and when I reluctantly said good-night, she felt rejected. The next morning we had talked it out, and like good little boy, I said it was all my fault. That night she had made another offer, and when I accepted, she had allowed herself to be used by me. Then when I went to her office that afternoon, I had taken her by surprise. The kiss had been a mistake, a reaction rather than sign of willingness. She had not had the time to adjust her defenses, and after I left, the fact that I — or any man — could break through her shield so easily gave her cause for thought.

After thinking about what had transpired, she saw herself as an object, and that didn't sit well with her. Now she was telling me that she wasn't my toy.

I had not before that moment thought of her as a toy, and I had no intention of using her, not then or later. If she wanted to be alone, that's what I wanted, too. "All right, Brenda. If that's what you want, I'll go." But at the moment I was about to arise from the couch, an animal impulse came over me. I reached over, took her by the shoulders, and pulled her to me. There was nothing gentle

196

bout the kiss. And there was nothing about it that could
e construed as sexual. She fought against me and I held
er, my lips bruising the flesh of her mouth.

I kept it up until I felt her begin to relax. First I felt it in
he muscles of her shoulders; then in her lips. Then she
melted and her arms went around me, and she moved as
lose to me as she could. From that moment, she was fire
nd heat, and it was she who clung to me.

When the kiss ended, she asked, "Why did you do
hat?"

I stroked her cheek. "I didn't want you having second
houghts about what happened last night. You and I made
ove. I didn't use you. I wanted you, and I think you
wanted me, but it was for something more than just a
exual pastime. If you sell what we had last night that
heaply, you'll be lying to yourself, and you'll be turning
omething that was good into something dirty, and I won't
llow you to do that."

She watched my eyes for a few seconds. Then, "You're
ight. I know that. This afternoon, when you came to the
ffice, I was ready to make love to you right there on the
pot. That isn't me, David. I'm not like that. Then after
you left, I kept thinking how silly I was being. I was afraid
you told me you loved me just to get me into bed, and that
made me feel cheap and dirty. My life is orderly because I
keep it that way. I felt so empty when my parents were
killed that I thought I would die. I wanted to die, but I
didn't. When I didn't die I promised myself that I would
never become so attached to anyone again. And I never
have, not until you came into my life. It scared the hell out
of me, and I tried to convince myself it was wrong. When I
left work this afternoon, I thought I knew what I had to do.
I was going to come home, be nice to you, but put you out
before anything happened."

"And the key?" I asked.

197

A pink hue spread across her cheeks. "I don't know. was confused about ... us. I wanted you to go away, but didn't want to lose you."

I touched her neck and I felt her shiver. "What do yo want now?" I asked her.

She pressed her face into my neck. "I don't ever war you to leave." Then she straightened herself. "Damn i MacGruder, I've fallen in love with you."

I laughed and pulled her to me. "Brenda, is that s bad?"

"No," she murmured, her lips close to my ear. "I gues it isn't." She moved back and stood, holding her hand ou to me. "Well, as long as I have decided to love you ... "

I took her hand and we went out of the room and up th stairs.

I had been asleep for a few hours when I felt her mov next to me. I felt her weight shift, then lift from the bed. drifted back off, and awoke when I felt her slipping bacl into the bed beside me. I opened my eyes to find he leaning her head on her hand, staring down at me "Something wrong?" I asked after a yawn.

"I was watching you sleep."

I slipped my arm beneath her and pulled her to me "I'm not asleep now."

She shifted against me and I felt soft down tickle m hip, then the pressure of her leg as it came to rest agains my thigh. I felt her hand move slowly over my stomach an then down. She giggled. "No, I guess you aren't at that."

I lifted gently and rolled her until she was resting on he back, me atop her. "Well, as long as we are botl completely aware that I'm no longer asleep ... " I move against her and heard her sigh softly.

Later — how long I don't know — as we breathe deeply and contentedly, lying side-by-side spoon fashion, remember thinking how perfectly we matched one another

hen I felt more than heard her deep breathing of sleep.
oon afterward, I, too, drifted off.

Chapter Sixteen

In the misty early morning fog, the air was warm and heavy. I rolled the window of the unmarked car down, and felt the weighty mugginess of the air. A few times I recalled visions of a sleeping Brenda. In her sleep she had kicked the covers down, exposing full, upturned breasts and gently curving hip. When I arose from the bed, careful not to awaken her, I noticed something that made me smile. While I had hurriedly undressed so that my pants, shirt, socks, shoes and underwear were piled in a clump at the side of the bed, strewn over the carpet of the bedroom were various pieces of female clothing. She had begun as she entered the door, dropping sweat-shirt, then sweat-pants as she plodded toward the bed. Then, discarded from the foot of the bed to where she finally came to rest, were panties and bra, still cotton and usefully unadorned. Dropped, and discarded hastily with her clothing, were any thoughts of tidiness.

I kept the speedometer at sixty as I drove east on I-85. When I turned north on I-985, I let the needle slip up to seventy. When I took the turn that led me onto US 441, I eased the car back down to sixty. I made Harlanwood by one-thirty.

I stopped at the same small store Wiley and I had stopped at on our visit to Harlanwood. The attendant I had cautioned was nowhere in sight. As I went toward the door, a gnarled old farmer nodded at me. He was wearing bib overalls and was chewing tobacco. He spat a long stream out onto the ground as I went inside. When I came

out, I said, "I'm looking for someone who lives aroun
here."

He turned faded old eyes up at me. "Who might tha
be?" he asked, his eyes warily looking in my direction.

"Fellow by the name of Dubois," I said.

He laughed, spat another stream of tobacco juice, an
said, "There's Dubois all around this part of Georgia, son
and they all got first names. Maybe if you can tell me thi
one's first name, I can tell you where to find him."

"His first name is Cleetice," I offered.

His face turned ashen. "You got business with tha
one?"

I shook my head. "No. Just want to have a few word
with him. You know him?"

He watched me for a few seconds, then a smile crease
his face. "That be Morgan Dubois' oldest boy. He's mea
as a snake, if'n he don't know you." Then he laughed an
said, "Mean as a snake if'n he does, too, now that I think o
it. You been invited up to his place, you ought to know
where it is. You ain't been invited, then if'n I was you, I'
stay away from that old boy."

I shrugged. "I just want to have a few words with him."

The old man's eyes were full of merriment. He wa
obviously enjoying our conversation. "Cleet Dubois, h
don't talk much. Might not be a good idea to offer hi
conversation if'n he don't want any."

I tucked my hands into my back pockets and gave hi
my best good-old-boy smile. "I'm not selling anything
Just want a few words with him, that's all."

"Like I already told you, son, Cleet don't talk to peopl
lessen he starts the conversation. You go up there to hi
place, you better be invited." Then his eyes narrowed
"What you wanting to talk to him about, anyway?"

"Friend of mine got killed up at the gorge. I heard tha
Cleet Dubois is in some kind of business up there, and

202

wanted to find out if he knew anything about my friend's death."

The old man looked at me intently. "I heard about a fellow that went over the edge. That be your friend?"

I nodded at him. "His name was Ben Guron. I understand he lived around here. Maybe you knew him?"

Another dark stream of liquid spattered the ground. Then, "Knew of him. Didn't know him personally, but folks said he was a nice enough sort. Sorry to hear about him getting killed that way." Then after a moment and another stream of tobacco juice, "You say you want to talk to Cleet Dubois about that?" He stood and tucked his hands into the pockets of his overalls. "If you're meaning to talk about your friend's death, I'd be careful if'n I was you."

"I just want to ask him a few questions," I said.

The old eyes looked me up and down. "You the law?" he asked.

I removed the wallet from my pocket and opened it so the old man could see the badge. "Georgia Bureau of Investigation," I said.

He looked at the badge, then at my face. He chewed on the tobacco for a few seconds, spat again, and laughed. "Son, you go out there, you better be real careful of that one. He's as likely as not to come right out of that house he lives in and kick your face in while he's smiling real friendly like. You look big enough to handle yourself right well, but that won't do you no good if he takes you unawares." He paused for a moment, surveying me. "You mind what I say, son."

"Rough customer?" I asked nonchalantly.

The old man laughed. "That ain't exactly the words I would'a used, but they fit all right." He grinned shrewdly. "Like I done told you, if Cleet comes out all smiling and

talking real nice like, you stand your guard or he'll be o
you before you know what happened."

"Thanks. I'll be careful," I promised.

He laughed again, slapping his thighs. "Sure wish
could be there to see it. Him having that little spit of
woman there will make him all cocky, kinda like a bantar
rooster. You know about them?" When I nodded, he wer
on with, "He'll be wanting to show off for her, and the wa
I hear it, she'll be all wide eyed and wet just watching hir
work on you."

I became alert. "This woman, you know her?"

He nodded slowly. "I know of her. You say you wa
friends with that man got himself killed?" When I noddec
he said, "Then you know her, too." When I raised m
eyebrows, he said, "She was his wife — that Guron fellah.
He furrowed his brow and tilted his head, thinking. Ther
after a moment, he said, "Think maybe her name's Gloria
She was a Spence fore she married that Guron, but he
mamma, she was a Dubois. Her and Cleet's daddy was firs
cousins. Her and that Guron fellah, they had a nice hous
here in town, but now that he's dead, she's living some wit
Cleet. You know what I mean?"

"I know," I nodded. "You know where Dubois lives?"

He spat again, wiped at a dark stream that splashed hi
chin, and sat back down. "You go out Highway 17 like yo
was going over to Taccoa, and you just keep right on goin
until you cross over into Stephens County. There's a hard
pack road just over the line. The county graveled it, bu
only so far as it turned back into Habersham County, but i
won't be hard for you to find. It'll be on your right about
mile after you cross over the county line. Cleet's house i
the only one on that road, but it's more than a mile after yo
make the turn." He paused for a moment, then added, "If
I was you, I'd park far enough down the road so's he don
hear your car, and I'd walk on up to the house quiet like."

I nodded, and said, "Thanks for the information."

As I was turning to leave, the old man asked, "You got gun?"

I stopped, turned to face him and pulled my sport coat ack to reveal the snub-nosed handgun I was carrying. His nouth opened in a toothless grin. "Be better if it was a hotgun," he said warningly, then guffawed, spat tobacco uice at the ground again and grinned his good-bye up at ne.

drove slowly up the graveled lane. When I caught a limpse of a house through the trees, I parked, got out, and valked the last half-mile. I did not purposely keep my teps quiet, but I didn't come crashing through the trees like ome bull elephant, either.

It was an old clapboard house built ten bricks off the round. The roof sagged and one of the front windows was racked. The paint had long since peeled away to reveal he pine boards, dried and cracked through the years. One f the brick tiers that supported the front porch leaned recariously to the right, as though any weight at all might ring it toppling down, the porch with it. The house looked leserted, time-worn, unloved, and uncared for, as though he person or persons who lived there had no extra money o waste on the nonsense of keeping the homestead abitable.

There was a new, red four-wheel drive truck, and it rased those thoughts from my head. The pickup was arked in the front yard only ten feet from the front porch. t was one of those Chevrolets advertised as able to go nywhere and last longer than any of the competition. This ne was already showing the signs of neglect that the house vas showing, and it brought back to memory another four-wheel drive truck I had seen in the pulloff at Tallulah Gorge.

An old N-series Ford tractor sat under a lean-to at th[e] right of the house, its hood and fenders rusted from th[e] same neglect as the house and truck. One of its rear tir[e] was flat, the rubber cracked. As I walked into the fro[nt] yard, I caught the sight of the rear fender of a blu[e] Mercedes-Benz parked at the rear of the house. It was ne[w] with only a light coating of dust marring its sheen. I cou[ld] just make out the plate. The words *Glory-Oh* we[re] embossed into the metal of the plate.

I made my way to a place behind the four-wheel driv[e] truck. "Hey inside! Dubois!" I called. The hous[e] remained silent so I called again, "Cleet Dubois!"

I stood there in my place behind the truck, hearing th[e] creaking of the floorboards of the house as someone bega[n] moving around. He came out onto the rickety front porc[h] after a few minutes carrying a very old and rusted shotgu[n.] Even so, I tucked myself farther behind the truck.

Cleet Dubois was massive. He stood about six inche[s] over six feet, and he must have weighed two-fifty, and a[ll] of it appeared to be solid muscle. He had dark eyes an[d] dark, wavy hair, and I remember thinking that he looke[d] like one of those rugged men women would find handsom[e.]

He came out as far as the edge of the porch, the shotg[un] carried by the forestock, resting comfortably and readily i[n] his big left hand. I got the impression that he could bring [it] to the ready with only a quick flinch. "You?" he called in [a] friendly, deep sing-song voice. "Who you want?"

I moved an inch to the right, making sure that only m[y] head was showing from the corner of the truck. "You Clee[t] Dubois?" I asked.

He moved lithely a few steps and leaned against one o[f] the rotting uprights of the porch. "Depends on who'[s] asking."

I held my badge and identification card far enough out for him to see it. "Name's MacGruder. I'm a special agent with the GBI and I want to ask you a few questions."

He had started to move away from the post, but stopped at the top of the steps and grinned at me. "You a cop and want to talk to me, boy, you come on up here and we'll sit in the shade." He spread his legs about eighteen inches apart and rested his right fist on his hip. The left one still held the shotgun.

I didn't move. "You and me, Dubois, we need to get something straight before we talk."

His mouth spread into a big grin. "What's that you say, boy? You and me, we got something to get straight?" He shifted the shotgun from his left hand to his right, and rested it over the crook of his right arm. "Now just what in the world might that be?"

"What we have to get straight is this, Dubois, I came up here to talk to you, and I came peacefully. I call you, and you come out carrying a shotgun." I stepped from behind the truck, the snub nose in my right hand feeling small and insignificant. "A man might get the idea you're not hospitable." I raised the revolver I was holding, silently praying that Dubois didn't decide to shoot first and ask questions later. "Now why don't you just put that thing down nice and easy." When he didn't, I said, "You start something and I'll be the one who finishes it."

His face turned into mock perplexity. "You don't want to be saying things like that to me, son. I ain't never hurt nobody that didn't deserve to be hurt." Then a good-old-boy grin spread across his face. "But just so you know that I'm not meaning you no harm ... " He leaned down and let the shotgun drop to the floor of the porch. "Now you can put that peashooter you got away, and you and me can have us a talk." He took the step down to the ground and walked toward me, the smile back on his face.

I slipped the snub nose back into my holster, but when he was three feet from me, I caught the change in his eye and slight tensing of his right leg. In that moment, as I mentally kicked myself for relaxing my guard, I twisted around, lifting my right foot in a sweeping arch, catching him in the left knee. As he started down, I caught him on the right side of the face with the back of my right hand, driving him into the ground.

He lay still for a few seconds, his eyes out of focus. Then he looked up at me. "Why'd you go and do that?"

"To get your attention," I said. "Did I succeed?"

He sat up and shook his head. "You had no call to do that. I never meant you no harm." He reached his hand out toward me. "Help me up."

A voice way back in the recesses of my mind was screaming for me to keep my distance, but my hand reached out. At the moment I felt his grip tighten on my hand, I knew that I had made a big mistake. I felt the grip tighten, and then I felt myself being pulled off-balance. I tried to roll, but it was too late.

Cleet Dubois pivoted himself up and over until he was resting comfortably on my chest, his knees pinning my arms to the dirt. "Now, son, you and me are going to play. I saw his meaty fist start down toward me, turned my head and caught a glancing blow off my skull. Even so, the pain rang through my brain and I saw stars for a second. The next blow caught me square on the right side of my chin, but I turned my head away from it so that the force was diminished from a ton of pressure to no more than nine hundred pounds or so.

As Cleet was cocking his right arm for the next blow, I pivoted my hips up and brought my feet high, encircled his head and dragged him backward. As I felt the back of his skull hit the ground, I pivoted, concentrating all my weight in my legs and feet. As he bounced off the ground,

208

eleased his head, brought my legs up, and pounded the eels of my shoes into his face. Then I rolled to the side nd came to my feet, kicked out and caught him in the left ar with the toe of my right shoe.

As soon as I was clear, he came rolling up to his feet, rouching and bouncing. He was fast and strong, and I still ad ringing in my ears from the blows to my skull. My irst thought was to put some distance between Cleet Dubois and myself, a defensive tactic that had served me vell through the years. When I had put ten feet of eparation between us, I swung around just in time to see im charging, head down, like a defensive tackle after a quarterback. I sidestepped him and brought my knee up nto his chin, raising his head two feet. Then I swiveled round and kicked him in the groin as he sailed past me.

He fell face first into the dirt, moaned loudly, tried to aise himself, then collapsed into the dust of the yard. watched him for a moment. When I was certain he was ut, I turned and walked toward the front of the house. I vanted to get that shotgun out of sight.

When I stepped up to the porch, I saw her. She was tanding on the porch, her eyes heavy lidded and veiled, her mouth opened slightly, one hand at her throat and the other esting on her hip.

Gloria Guron was a thirty-something little thing, not nore than five feet tall. She had hair the color of summer vheat and eyes the color of the late afternoon sky, a dark blue with specks of auburn. She was wearing a tee shirt she had tied tightly beneath the fullness of her breasts. Around her hips were pale pink bikini panties. She was vearing nothing else.

I stood there looking at her, my mouth agape. To say she was pretty was like saying a rose was nice. She was nore than pretty. She was elegant and sensuous, lithe and vanton. She exuded female sexuality from pouting lip to

209

smooth thigh. She was a vision of sexuality as she move out the door and came to stand in front of me; a fle moving, smooth, lusty female who radiated erotism wit her every move.

I suddenly felt intoxicated. My head swirled and m mouth went dry. Her face was finely chiseled and expert carved in bone and tissue and skin. Her eyes rose upwar at the outside corners in a vague, indefinite manner, the color adding to the mystique. Her nose was small an slightly upturned, and her mouth was narrow, yet full, he lower lips pouting downward in a demur way. Her ea were small and dainty, obscured by the gentle sweep of he hair as it flowed down and turned up at a neck that wa angled softly from her chin to her shoulders. She took deep breath and I could see that her breasts were not full all. They were small, and yet they were enticingly eviden Her waist was almost painfully slim, no more than twent inches. Her hips were neither wide nor narrow, but were c that particular size that said she was woman: soft, cuddl yet firm and active. Her legs were good and firm an muscular. She looked like a precisely made china do sturdy and yet somehow delicate and fragile and brittle the touch, and I got the feeling that she could be as soft as kitten or as fierce as a tigress.

I was totally awestruck by her, but then I looked int her eyes. In them, I saw a coldness, a shrewdness, calculating severity that her body belied. I knew that sh would be all breath and whispers and soft caresses, war touches and clinging embraces, but that would all be facade. The inner being was cruel and heartless an without mercy. Her lover would merely be just one mo target of opportunity. And I knew as certainly as I wa standing near her that once acquired, her target would b dead. She was a hungry jungle cat.

When she spoke, her voice was a breathless, husky whisper. "You kill Cleet?"

I shrugged up at her. "He won't be much good to you for a week or so, but he won't die. Are you Gloria Guron?"

She let the hand drop from her throat, trail across her right breast, and come to rest on her hip. "You may as well be taking my clothes off the way you're looking at me." Her eyes narrowed in a seductive way. "You enjoying the view?"

I gave her an obvious once over, and from my vantage point, there wasn't much hidden. A quick glance doesn't always show the imperfections. As my eyes slowly drifted from head to toe, I had time to see the damages that time, alcohol and debauchery had done. At a distance, she had seemed too perfect, too sensual, too much the epitome of female wantonness. When I stepped closer, I saw the creature in reality. The hair had been bleached once too often so that the ends had begun their slow deterioration. The face had begun to sag, if only slightly, and there were lines across the neck where the muscles had grown tired. My scrutiny showed the breasts that had first seemed full, then small and pert, were actually beginning that inevitable droop. The undershirt tied beneath cradled the spongy flesh and held it higher than gravity would allow if the material did not restrain their fall. The hands resting on her hips were tipped by fingernails which had been left to their own ends for too long, their cracking and peeling proof of their neglect. The panties were a size too small so that they failed to hide the meaty pudenda straining against them. Dark wisps of tangled hair protruded from the elastic edge of the panties. Her legs were not firm at all, but worn and tired, and the feet were stained by dirt.

I felt a sudden distaste, but I kept it hidden. When I tilted my eyes back up to her face, I smiled. "I like what I see just fine."

"Just who the hell are you?" she asked, taunting eye(s)
staring down at me.

I produced the badge. "David MacGruder."

She handled the situation well, never showing any sign
of wariness. "You a cop." It wasn't a question. When (I)
nodded, she asked, "So why'd you come here?"

"Ben asked me to come up here. He wanted my help.
Only I got here too late." Then I added, "I'm the one who
found him on that ledge."

I had expected some reaction. All I got was an uplifting
of one corner of her mouth. "Too bad about Ben." Then
her eyes darkened. "Help? What kind of help?"

I moved up on the steps and onto the porch, close
enough so that I could feel her heat and smell her perfume
tainted with the acrid smell of body odor. "I thought
maybe you could tell me."

Her eyes darted over toward where Dubois had fallen
but she didn't move away from me. "You better get on out
of here. Cleet comes to, he's likely as not to kill you."

I put my left hand on her right hand where it rested on
her hip. I squeezed gently, pulling her closer so that her
scantily clad body was touching mine. "When he comes to
he won't be in any shape to kill anybody."

Her eyes veiled again. "Except me if he sees us
talking." She let the corners of her mouth turn up and
shifted her weight forward. "And after he gets through
with me, he'll get you if he sees us this close."

I let my hand drop until it rested on her thigh. "(I've)
already put him down once, and I won't let him hurt you."

She threw her head back and laughed. "You don't know
Cleet Dubois like I do. He gets it in his mind to do
something, he does it, and there ain't nobody or nothing
that can stop him."

"Man gets this close to you, I don't expect he'd ever let
another man come between him and you. Anyway Gloria

212

ou and me, we have to talk about Ben." I took a breath nd leaned into her, letting my lips touch hers, but for only second.

She molded herself to me, then stiffened as our lips lost ontact. "All right," she breathed, "But not here, and surely ot now while he's laying out there in the yard." She raised er arms and draped them over my neck. "You're really omething. You know that?"

I smiled down into her face. "I've been told so a few mes."

She leaned her hips into me and moved them from side) side. "I ain't never seen nobody put him down the way ou did. Most men would run when they saw him come ut of this house the way he did, but not you. And then the vay you moved around, it was like you was some kind of a Greek god or something." She ran her arms down mine, ressing the flesh of my shoulders. "And so hard, too. Bet ou got other places that can make a person pass out like Cleet did, only not in the same way."

"Other people like you maybe?" I asked, kneading the lesh of her back.

"Um," she cooed. "Maybe. The way I feel right now, I ould be convinced to let you try. Watching the two of you to at it made me all warm and sticky inside."

"Maybe we could convince each other." I moved my ight hand around and cupped her breast. There are times vhen it becomes necessary to test the waters. If you are aced with an enemy you know little about, you spend ome time studying your foe, then you drop a few rounds n top of him to see how he will react. This seemed like ne of those times. Touching Gloria Guron in that intimate vay was not something I wished to do, but I had to see vhat she was made of, and how she would react. After a ew seconds of the touch, when I saw no reaction — neither positive nor negative — I gently pinched the soft flesh of her breast until I saw the first sparks of pain in her eyes.

She squeezed her eyes closed, but didn't pull away from me. She just stood there, half-closed eyes looking up at me, mouth slightly open, small pink tongue flicking out to lick at her lower lip. After a few seconds, she shuddered visibly, closed her eyes, and sighed. Her breath came in quick, shallow gulps, and it seemed as though it took great effort for her to ask, "How did you know I like it that way?"

"Guess I'm just intuitive about those kinds of things," I said.

As I relaxed the pressure, her eyes came open. "You got any more special games you like to play?"

"Might have a few," I said. "But if you really want to find out, you have to come talk to me."

She moved against my hand, which was still cupping her breast, and for a moment I was afraid she was going to come out of her tee shirt and panties right there on the front porch. Then she smiled and ran her hand up my back and pressed it against my neck. The next thing I knew, her lips were against mine and I was tasting stale cigarette smoke and cheap booze, and playing touchy-touchy with a tongue that was a little too quick for my appetite. She had meant the kiss to arouse me, but all it had done was solidify my distaste for this female. All the same, when she pulled her face from mine, I hid my revulsion and gave her a big toothed grin. "Okay, so you've got me convinced." Then I looked over at Dubois, then back at her. "Him laying out there doesn't bother me one bit, if it doesn't bother you."

She bit her lip, looking over at her unconscious lover. "Well, to tell the truth, making it here on the front porch would be all right, only I'd be watching over your shoulder for Cleet to come tearing up at us. I might enjoy some of it, but I couldn't get there knowing he might disturb us. S

ow about we go someplace else and have us this party."
hen her eyes became pools of wantonness as she asked,
You staying in town?"

I shook my head. "I'm staying over in Atlanta."

"That's even better. I have to go over there tomorrow.
ou know the East Point Inn?"

I shook my head. "No, but I can find it."

"I'll be there at noon. You have us a room and we'll
lk." She put enough emphasis on the word *talk* that I
new talking was not what she had on her mind. She
anced back over at Dubois. "He'll be coming to his
enses before long. You call me on my car phone at ten
night. I'll find an excuse to go down to where I live. My
umber is 555-1234. You remember that?" When I
odded, she said, "Now you better get on out of here while
ou still can. You stay too long and Cleet will come to,
nd sure as hell, he'll kill you."

"Would that bother you?" I asked.

She licked her lips. "It might, least until you and me
ad our time together." She gave me a crooked smile, then
ounded off the porch and ran over to where Cleetice
ubois was moaning loudly enough so that half the county
ould hear him. I shrugged and walked back down the
oad.

Chapter Seventeen

Atlanta is not all that hard to master, that is if you have good map. I did and I found the East Point Inn on my second pass through the city. It was on Main Street, a block or so out of the downtown area. I went in and registered. I got room number 1A on the ground floor. When I found the room and went in, I was pleased to find the room clean, spacious and nicely appointed with comfortable chairs and a king-sized bed. I gave a quick look at the recliners, and opted to sit on the bed, picked up the phone and dialed Brenda's number. She answered on the second ring. "It's MacGruder."

Her voice was expectant. "Where are you, David?"

"I'm in a motel room down in East Point," I told her.

There was a moment of silence before she said, "Are you coming here tonight?"

"I can," I said. "Or you can come here. Or we can meet at a restaurant and come back here after dinner."

I heard her laugh into the phone. "Meet a man in a motel room? That doesn't sound very professional to me."

"If anyone asks, you can tell them that it's business."

"Business? What on earth are you talking about?"

I took a deep breath and said, "I'm meeting Gloria Guron here at noon tomorrow."

"So you did talk to her," Brenda said.

"We did more than talk."

There was a plaintive edge on her voice when she asked, "What does that mean?"

"Let's just say that she has certain ideas about m[...]
Nothing substantial, you understand."

"Just what the hell went on over there?" The plainti[...]
quality turned into a nasty snarl.

I was getting a kick out of our conversation. "Mig[...]
say that I'm Gloria's new beau."

"Damn you, MacGruder! You didn't ... "

"No, of course I didn't," I interrupted. "I said I might b[...]
her new beau. I didn't say she was my girl. I'm talking [...]
the only girl I have, and I'm perfectly content to leave it [...]
that." Then after giving Brenda a few seconds to cal[...]
down, I asked, "Now are you coming here or am I comi[...]
there?"

"I'll meet you at Barber's. It's a restaurant about tw[...]
blocks north of where you are. I've had my dinner, but [...]
don't mind watching you eat."

"I'm guilty of having a greasy burger on the road," [...]
told her.

"Well, they have a great piano bar, so we can have [...]
drink."

"You need one?" I asked.

I heard her laugh softly. "Maybe I do at that. Anywa[...]
it will give you time to fill me in on what happened today."

"I could do that right here."

"No you can't, MacGruder. If I am going to meet yo[...]
at a motel, I don't want us discussing business when we ca[...]
be doing other things."

"Doll, I really like the way you think." Then, "I lov[...]
you."

"That sounds so nice, David, and the emotions ar[...]
returned tenfold. Give me an hour. Okay?" Then, "Wha[...]
should I bring?" she asked me.

I got a sudden mental image of cotton underwear. "G[...]
anything made of silk with lots of lace?"

"Well, now that you asked, I have a black number I've ever had the occasion to wear. Want me to bring it?"

"I think that would be superb," I said, the visions of cotton gone from my brain.

"Should I bring anything else?" I think she was beginning to enjoy herself.

"Just yourself."

"That I can certainly do," she said, and hung up.

I placed another call. This one was to Wiley's private line. When he answered, I said, "I need you to put out some feelers on Marvin Dubois."

"Marvin Dubois? Isn't he the president of that development company that Ben was VP of?"

I answered, "Yes, but doesn't it seem strange that we haven't heard anything about him?"

There was silence on the other end of the line. Then, "I'll make a few calls. Where can I reach you?"

I gave him the motel phone number and my room number. "If you get anything, call me back at ten-thirty sharp."

He didn't question my instructions. He merely said, "Be talking to you," and hung up.

I was sitting at a table off to the left of the piano when she came in. She was wearing a pantsuit, cut deep in the front. The V-neck revealed lots of warm, fleshy valleys, and the whole thing clung to her like a second skin. I noticed several masculine necks snapping around to watch her walk to my table.

"Had I known that you were going to come dressed that way, I would have told you to meet me in the parking lot of the motel." I moved around and pulled her chair out. As she sat, I kissed the side of her neck. "When forced, I can give the quickest reports you ever heard."

When I was seated across from her, she said, "I take a that to mean you approve."

I nodded and held my drink up. "Approve and toast th designer." I had asked the waitress — handing her a five a I did so — to be ready with a screwdriver heavily lade with vodka when my lady friend arrived. True to her wor she placed the frosty glass in front of Brenda at the precis moment of my toast, smiled and winked at me, and the strode off.

Brenda raised her glass. "My turn," she said. "To th man who has promised me nothing, but makes me feel lik today will always be." She took a dainty sip, made a face and sat her glass on the table. "What is this?" she asked.

"It's a screwdriver." I said, smiling the words at her.

"A what?"

"A wonderful mixture of vodka and orange juice."

She took another sip, scrunched up her face and put th glass down. "David, there's enough alcohol in this glass t sink a battleship."

"No," I told her. "There isn't that much, but there i enough."

"Enough to what?" Brenda asked me.

I smiled across the table at her. "Oh, enough to get yo pleasantly drunk."

I saw her eyes go soft and the edges of her mouth begi to turn up. "Why in the world would you want to get m drunk?"

I reached across, took her hand and brought it to m lips. "So that I can take advantage of you, of course."

She laughed softly, her eyes sparkling. "You don't nee to get me drunk to do that." Then she smiled at me, gentl pulled her hand free of mine, and pushed the glass away "All right, so now that we both know that I'm easy, tell m about your day."

So after taking another swallow from my glass, I did ust that. I told her about my short conversation with Cleet Dubois, but I did not tell her about the shotgun or give her ll the details of our confrontation. At the time, it seemed ne wise thing to do. I did tell her, however, that Dubois vas a nasty character, and I felt certain that he was capable f murder.

Then I told Brenda about my not-so-short conversation vith Gloria. Again I used discretion, and left out any descriptive adjectives. When I described Gloria Guron, 3renda's eyes opened wide, but she kept silent until I had inished.

"David, you make her sound like some kind of demon."

"She is, I assure you. From our brief encounter, I got he impression that she was as capable of murder as her cousin, although I don't think she killed Ben. But I do now that when you put the two of them together, you've got a volatile mix."

She watched me for a few seconds, and then said, "All ight, you've convinced me that they could have killed Ben Guron. Now all you have to do is get the evidence."

"That, my love, is what tomorrow is all about."

Her face tightened in jealousy, and perhaps a little distress. "So she's going to walk into your motel room and ell you all about how she and Dubois killed her husband. Right. If she's as hard as you make her sound, she's not going to tell you anything. As a matter of fact, I think she's etting you up."

I nodded at Brenda. "I think the same thing, that's why you are going to be sitting in a car in the parking lot. That vay, if it turns sour, you'll be close enough to come to my escue." I then asked, "You have a phone in your car?"

"Yes I do." Then, after a moment, she narrowed her eyes and asked, "And if I don't know when it turns sour?"

"Then you'll be the best looking lady at my funeral," said smiling at her.

"David, that isn't funny. I've had reservations about th[is] all along, and you aren't making me feel any better abo[ut] it."

I held my hand up, and tried to keep my ow[n] reservations out of my voice. "Brenda, I can handle this, s[o] stop worrying."

She reached across and took my hand. "David, will yo[u] listen to some reason?" When I didn't protest, she went o[n] "All right, let's see what we have. You went blundering o[ut] there and ended up pounding on Cleet Dubois. Then yo[u] talked with Gloria. How do you know that she didn't te[ll] him all about your little conversation? And you'r[e] assuming that she didn't kill her husband, but you don[t] really know who did kill him. It might have been Glori[a] and if it was, she's not going to admit it to a cop. Wha[t] she'll do is tell her boyfriend that you are getting a little to[o] close, and my bet is she'll send her goon-cousin after yo[u] And what if she tells Dubois that you forced her to play[?] Now he's got two scores to even. I think he'll enjoy kickin[g] your face in." She shuddered.

"And you won't like that?"

"Damn it, MacGruder, this is not the time for jokes."

I smiled. "It may have sounded like a joke, but I wa[s] actually fishing for a compliment."

Some of the tenseness left her face. "All right. No, [I] wouldn't like that at all. You already have enough scars o[n] that ugly face of yours, but I can live with a few more. It[s] the alternative I can't live with. You go playing it cozy an[d] these two nuts just might take you out. I've spent a lon[g] time looking for you, MacGruder, and I'm not anxious t[o] lose you now that I've found you."

I reached across and took her hand again. "Lady, tha[t] was the nicest thing anyone has ever said to me."

She gave me a crooked smile, and said, "And it ouldn't look very good on my record if I lost a special gent I forced my boss to hire."

She had me on that one, so I mentally scored one for ie boss lady. "There's something else, Brenda. Have you ot a line on Marvin Dubois?"

Her face turned serious. "Why are you asking?"

Her tone stunned me for a second, but I recovered and aid, "Sounds as though his name is *persona non grata* at iis table."

She shook her head. "It isn't that, necessarily." She aused and looked around the room. Then, her voice low, We've been trying to reach him — just to talk, you nderstand. The call went out — let's see — yes, a week efore your friend went over that cliff, but so far we haven't een able to locate him. It's all hush-hush. Only a few key idividuals know about it, so you have to keep it as onfidential information."

"Suppose we find him?" I asked.

She shrugged. "I don't think you will."

"Why not? We're pretty good at what we do. Maybe /e'll get lucky."

"MacGruder, some of the best investigators in the state aven't been able to locate him, so what makes you think ou can?"

I gave her my best smile. "We're professionals, and we pecialize in finding things that don't want to be found." hen, "But it sounds as though the GBI thinks he left the ountry."

She nodded slowly. "That's exactly what we think. 'en days before your friend was killed, Gorge Investment nd Development Corporation had bank accounts that held ver two million dollars."

"Now?" I asked, knowing even before she spoke what he answer would be.

"Zero. Someone cleaned out every account, and th[e] someone is probably Marvin Dubois. We think he took t[he] money and went somewhere far away."

I took a sip of my drink. "Brenda, try this on for siz[e]. It wasn't Marvin who cleaned out the account, it was Cle[e.] Ben found out about it, threatened to turn it over to t[he] cops, and got himself killed for his efforts."

She shook her head. "Won't work," she said. "It too[k] two signatures to withdraw the funds — Marvin Dubo[is] and Ben Guron's. Marvin Dubois disappeared a wee[k] before Guron was killed, and that spells out one thin[g,] Guron had to know what was going on." She paused, an[d] then went on. "David, if he knew about it, he was in on it."

I shook my head adamantly. "Brenda, I can't believ[e] that. Ben Guron was a good man. He was honest to [a] fault. He wouldn't have gotten himself involved in [a] scheme like that."

Her eyes softened. "But he got himself involved with [a] prostitute."

"Okay, so he made that one mistake, that doesn't mea[n] that he knew about the rest of it." I shook my head, tryin[g] to think of something to say that would convince he[r.] "What you are saying doesn't make sense, Brenda. If [he] did what you say, why was he killed?"

In her eyes I could see concern. "David, darling, mayb[e] your friend committed suicide. After all, there is no re[al] proof that he was killed, just a few footprints in the sand."

I felt the cold hand of anger touch my spine. "Brend[a,] why in the hell would Ben Guron commit suicide? He ha[d] it made."

Her face softened. "Perhaps when he found out th[at] Marvin Dubois left him high and dry, it was just too muc[h] for him to handle."

I shook my head slowly, my eyes watching her. "I can[']t] buy that. I knew Ben Guron. We served this damn countr[y]

224

ogether and we were friends. I would know if he was
apable of doing what you've said, and I say he couldn't do
."

Brenda looked at me. "All right David, I believe you."
hen her eyes glinted, and she said, "A while ago when you
ve're talking about finding Marvin Dubois, you used the
vord *we*. Who was the second person you were talking
bout?"

"Wiley, my partner. I spoke to him after I talked to you
onight, and I asked him to do some digging."

She winced. "Well, you just call him back and tell him
o dig very, very quietly."

I watched her for a moment, and then said, "I'll do what
ou ask and I won't ask why."

When we got to the motel, I glanced at my watch. It was
recisely ten o'clock. I placed a call to Gloria's car phone.
She answered with, "I'm so hot I could scream, and it's all
our fault, lover. You got the room?" she asked.

"Yeah, I got it. I'm in room 1A," I answered.

She panted into the phone, "If it wasn't so far, I'd come
here tonight and see if you're as good as I think you are."

For a moment, I was panicked, but I said, "Come on if
ou want."

I heard her laugh. "Can't, lover. You did a number on
Cleet when you kicked him, and I'm out getting some ice
or his ... jewels. But I'll be there at noon tomorrow. Bye
now."

I heard the phone go dead and replaced the receiver.

"She coming?" Brenda asked.

"Yeah," I nodded. "She'll be here at noon."

"And I'll be outside in a damn car, too far away to do
anything if it starts to go wrong."

I didn't feel like discussing it, so I picked up the small
valise she had brought and held it out to her. "I recall

something about a black frilly number. If it's all the same to you, I'd just as soon put tomorrow out of our minds for while."

She sat on the bed watching me for a few seconds, the said, "All right, David, if that's what you want." She stoo took the valise, and walked off toward the bath at the rea of the room. There was something in her step and th droop of her shoulders that told me she had some seriou reservations about my plan. I knew how she felt. I ha some reservations, too, but I hoped she didn't know it.

I sat on the edge of the bed and took out a cigarett Then before I could get it lit, Brenda came out of th bathroom, her face clean, but still wearing the whi pantsuit. She came over and stood in front of me. "Davi promise me you won't do anything stupid tomorrow."

"Stupid? Me?" I pasted a look of mock indignation o my face and said, "I'll have you know that I'm the be detective in our Florida office."

She looked at me, trepidation streaking through he eyes. "David, I happen to know you're the *only* detective i your Florida office, so that statement doesn't exactly fill m with confidence."

I shrugged. "Okay, so I was making light of it. Wha are you really worried about?"

She sat beside me and took my right hand in her "What I said earlier I meant. I don't want to lose you." Sh squeezed my hand. "Before you tell me how careful you'r going to be, let me say something. I get the feeling tha you take chances when you don't have to, and that scare me. You try to play it that way tomorrow, and I'll be th only widow wearing black who was never married to th dead man. I don't want that, MacGruder. I want you we and healthy for a long, long time." She reached up with he free hand and rested it against my cheek. "Am I makin any sense to you?"

"Yes, I'm afraid you are, but Brenda, you have to understand that this is not one of your cut-and-dried investigations. One or both of those people killed my friend, and I can't let them get away with that, not even if I put my life on the line."

She let her hand drop from my cheek and pulled her other hand free. "Then it's nothing more than a vendetta to you."

"No, but even if it was, is that so bad? You've already said that we'll never get them into court, that our only recourse is a confession, and we both know what the chances for that are. Anyway, isn't our whole penal system built around revenge?"

"Yes," she interrupted me. "But it's an organized, legal revenge. A trial court and a jury of twelve; that's as fair as can get."

I laughed. "Brenda, the whole world has seen just how fair our system really is. We don't fool anyone except ourselves. You happen to be poor, black, and living in a ghetto, it doesn't matter if you are guilty as hell, or innocent as a new baby, you're going to jail. On the other hand, if you are rich, and can afford the best lawyers money can buy, you're going to get off, even if you're as guilty as sin, and even if the jury is convinced of your guilt. So don't talk to me about how great our system is. It stinks."

"All right, so it isn't perfect. Is there a better system in the world? Is there another country in the world where a person at least has the opportunity to prove their innocence? Suppose Gloria Guron — or Cleet Dubois, for that matter — had nothing to do with Ben Guron's death, how right will you be to play judge and jury, convicting them, sentencing them, and then carrying out that sentence?"

I shook my head. "They aren't innocent. They did it and I'll prove they did."

"All right, so bring me the proof and I'll make sure the get what they deserve," she said pleadingly.

"Agent Carlisle, you're forgetting about the tw million dollars. Those two can buy some pretty good leg help with that much money."

Her eyes narrowed. "You're forgetting that Marvi Dubois is missing. If that money is anywhere, my bet that he has it."

"But if Gloria and his brother have it, what then?"

She looked perplexed for a moment. "David, I'm swor to uphold the law — and so are you. You take the law your own hands and no matter how you try to justify yo actions, it's murder, and that makes you no better tha Gloria Guron and Cleet Dubois."

I was about to tell her I wasn't going to back down, tha I wasn't going to give them the opportunity to escap justice, but the phone rang just in time to save me from another argument. Before I picked it up, I eyed Brend She took the hint and scampered off into the bathroom "MacGruder," I said into the mouthpiece.

"Dave, it's Wiley. Nothing on Marvin Dubois. On day he was there. The next he was gone, and nobod knows anything — not his maid, not his secretary and no his wife."

"So he skipped," I said dejectedly.

"Not unless he decided to go without even a change clothes. His wife told one of my — our — operative Dubois didn't take anything. She says that there's nothin missing."

I took a deep breath and let it out before I spoke "There's nothing unusual in that, Wiley. Lots of me decide to walk out, and never leave a trace."

"There's more," he said. "His wife told my man that he husband is a diabetic. He is insulin dependent. That mean that he has to take two shots a day. His wife says that if h

228

ere to miss one, he would die. She said he took one shot
t nine in the morning, just before he went to his office.
he second shot he took at nine at night. She said that he
ad a kit that he took with him when he traveled, and she
aid that he didn't have the travel kit with him. She said he
ever forgot his travel kit. Our operative said she was
damant about that."

"So she thinks something happened to him?" I asked.

A short pause. Then, "The operative said she didn't
eem to care one way or the other. He said that when he
sked her if she had reported Dubois missing, she laughed
nd said there was no way she would ever do that. She
vent on to say that she was happy that he was gone, and
hat she wouldn't be missing him, one way or the other."

I gave it a few seconds, then asked, "You have anything
lse?"

"That's it," he said.

"Thanks, Wiley." I thought about asking him to drive
lown and give Brenda some company while I met with
Gloria Dubois. But instead, I told him, "I'll check in with
ou tomorrow," and I hung up.

I leaned back against the headboard of the bed, lit the
igarette I had been toying with, and gave some thought to
vhat Wiley had told me. It was a good possibility —
lmost a certainty — that Marvin Dubois was dead. Okay,
o that left just Gloria and Cleet as suspects. That
mproved the odds a little, but not much. I took a draw
rom the cigarette and tried to put together some kind of
olan that would at least give me a fifty-fifty chance. I
lidn't come up with one.

I hated to admit it, but Brenda was right. No matter
1ow I looked at it, all I really wanted was revenge —
MacGruder at his finest. Damn the system if MacGruder
lecided someone was guilty. I only hoped that I was right. .

Brenda came out of the bath, wearing the black sil thing she had told me about, and I forgot about everythin except her. A few times during the next breathless hour, think she tried to ask me about the phone call I ha received from Wiley. I somehow managed to divert he attentions. In the end, I think she was grateful that I ha and I know I was.

Chapter Eighteen

I awoke some time after four in the morning. The curtain that had been drawn over the window gaped in the middle, so that light from a lamp outside the room cast a soft glow over the bed. Brenda was sleeping soundly next to me, the black material she was wearing gathered around her waist. She was sprawled on the bed, her left leg pulled up at the knee, and draped over my hips. In the dim light, I could see the misty darkness of down at the point above where her legs joined her hips. I got a sudden and almost uncontrollable urge to touch her, but after a long and hard-fought battle within myself, I resisted. I turned a little so I could look at her face, and she started, drew her knees up, then relaxed and cuddled closer to me.

It had been a long time since I had felt this close to a woman, too long. I was facing a dangerous situation, yet all I wanted to do was watch her as she slept. In the short time I had known this woman, she had managed to etch herself into my mind so profoundly I was not at all sure of just how it had happened. While I should have been thinking about how I was going to handle my noon visitor, my mind was playing erotic reruns of warm kisses, gentle caresses, expectant sighs, moans of pleasure, and after-the-act endearments. It was all I could do to refrain from awakening her with furtive movements. She was sleeping so peacefully that no matter how much I wanted her, I refrained.

I found myself wide awake, and resting so closely to her, and so much aware of the totality of our union, I could not slip back into sleep. So I slowly and quietly move away from her, got up from the bed, and went into the bat I ran hot water into the tub, and slipped in.

For a while, I reclined in the steaming water, letting m mind free to wander. But my mind wasn't cooperating. kept going back to the lady in the bed in the next roon After a while I gave up and pulled myself from the tu dried off quickly, and returned to her.

This time I did touch her. Brenda came awak immediately, stretching her arms out, murmurin something unintelligible. When I touched her at the preci place that always made her tremble with expectancy, h arms reached out for me. Sleepily, she uttered h acquiescence, repositioned herself, and pulled me atop he It was a wonderful way to begin the day.

I dragged Brenda from the motel room at eight, and w had breakfast in the motel dining room. When we ha finished our meal, I led her back to the room, gave her long kiss, and collected her things. When I handed them her, I didn't give her the opportunity to ask me somethir for which I had no answer. "You are going to go out, get your car, and go away until noon. Gloria doesn't kno you, so if she sees you as you are pulling back into th parking lot at exactly ten minutes of twelve, it won't spc our visit." Her eyes went wide, so I said, "I don't want ar arguments on this, Brenda. We have to do it my way. Ju park your car close enough so you can watch this room, ar sit tight. If you see anything that looks suspicious, get c the phone and call for some backup, and I don't care whe it comes from, just as long as they get here quickly."

She looked as though she was going to protest, bu instead, after a long pause and a loud, exasperated sigh, sh said, "I don't like this one bit, David. You know how I fe about you going into this alone."

"It has to be this way, Brenda," I responded.

She looked at me, then after a long moment, nodded. "Okay, we'll do it your way."

I opened the door and pushed her out and toward her car, suddenly feeling less than optimistic about how the day would turn out.

I was seated in one of the recliners when there was a knock on the door of the motel room. My heart gave a start, but I recovered quickly enough. As I got up from the chair, I glanced at my watch. It was ten minutes of noon.

I opened the door about six inches and saw Gloria standing there. She was smiling up at me. As I pushed the door wider, Dubois stepped into view, a nasty looking automatic in his hand. "Just step on back and we'll come in nice and friendly like." He brought the muzzle of the auto up to point at a spot somewhere between my chest and my forehead. I smiled and stepped back a half-step.

As I looked from the gun to Dubois' face, I noticed Brenda sitting behind the wheel of her car in a spot two paces down from the room. She nodded as I shook my head slowly, hoping that neither Gloria nor Dubois saw me.

They obviously hadn't seen me because as they entered the room, Dubois said, "You just back on up and take a seat on the bed, MacGruder." Then, his eyes sparkling, "But if you think you can move fast enough, you just go right on and try it. I'd like nothing better than to whack you across the side of the head with the barrel of this gun."

I didn't relish a lump on my head, so I did as I was told. When I was seated on the bed, I looked at Gloria plaintively. "I thought we were going to have some fun."

She smiled at me. "I think I'm going to have some fun, cop, but I doubt if you will."

Dubois spent a few seconds wrapping my wrists with duct tape. I sat there patiently and quietly like an obedient child as I sure didn't want to give him an opportunity to use that gun on me. When my hands were securely bound, he roughly searched me, but like the movie detectives so apt[ly] put it, I wasn't carrying.

When Dubois finished his task, Gloria sat beside me o[n] the bed. She reached over and stroked my face with he[r] hand. "MacGruder, tell me something."

I looked at her, trying to keep my voice even. "What?" I asked.

She let her hand drop to my lap. "Did you really think [I] was stupid enough to come here alone?" She squeezed m[e] painfully. "And for this?" Then she laughed, letting he[r] hand relax. "Men! You think that all you have to do [is] handle a girl a little and she'll fall right over on her bac[k] and beg for it. Cleet here is the only man who can mak[e] me scream, and he can only do it when he's been at me fo[r] two or three hours." She leaned close to me and spoke, he[r] mouth only an inch from my ear. "But I did think about [it] with you, MacGruder. Something about you makes m[e] think that we would have been really good together." Sh[e] moved back. "Then I thought about you being a cop, and [I] got more excited thinking about watching Cleet kill you." Then she moved away from me and stood up.

I shrugged, thinking just how unheroic I was feeling "You can't do it here. You'll have every cop within te[n] miles down on your back before the sounds of the shots di[e] away."

Gloria reached out and placed her hand against my face "Oh, MacGruder, we have no intention of killing you her[e]. And maybe if you are really good, I won't let Cleet hurt yo[u] at all." She knelt in front of me, her eyes mocking min[e]. "Think maybe you can convince me that I shouldn't l[et] Cleet beat on you?"

Dubois cut in. "Glory-Oh, we better get him on out o[f] here before someone comes knocking at the door."

Gloria's eyes went dull and she stood. "I guess you'[re] right."

Dubois lifted me roughly from the bed and I asked, What are you going to do?" I watched the two of them, aiting for an answer to my question. I knew that I was ving in to an uncontrollable urge to stall for time. All the hile a voice in my brain was telling me that Brenda was n her car phone, calling for some backup. Another voice as screaming that I should have asked Wiley to come over nd sit with Brenda.

After what seemed an eternity, but was only a few :conds, Dubois answered my question. "You and us are oing to take a ride, MacGruder. We're going to take you ack out to my place where we can have a nice long talk, nd where there ain't nobody who can disturb us."

I felt a slow numbing as his words sank in. I had no oubt that he would be remembering the way I had beaten im the afternoon before. I felt myself shiver as thoughts f what he might do ran through my brain.

I looked from Gloria to Dubois. "I have one question to sk," I said. "You owe me that."

Dubois started to speak, but Gloria cut him off. "Go head and ask it."

"Which of you is going to take the rap for Ben's aurder?"

Gloria laughed. "I don't think either Cleet or I will ever e convicted of that murder."

"Then it was Marvin?"

Gloria looked at me steadily. "You can forget about Iarvin." I think she knew that I had already forgotten bout him, because she said, "But you already know he's ead, don't you?" After a moment during which I tried to ɔok surprised, Gloria said, "He met with a tragic accident .." She paused and turned her head toward Dubois. "Or vas it suicide?"

He gave her a toothy grin and she turned back to me. Whichever it was, it happened a week before Ben ... fell from that cliff." This time, the surprised look I gave her wasn't put on. "Oh, yes, of course, how could you know. You see, MacGruder, Ben found out that I ... persuaded Marvin to withdraw all the money. It wasn't hard. All I had to do was do what I'm really good at, and Marvin agreed so quickly even I was surprised. Trouble is, I thought that I could do it without Ben knowing it, but I was wrong."

"And so you had this big ape kill him," I said.

She shook her head. "Don't rush me, or you won't hear the whole story." I shut my mouth, and listened. "See, MacGruder, I had to make Marvin believe that he and I were going to run away together. That way, he would do whatever I asked him to do. So I made him believe it, and he withdrew the money from the account."

I remembered that Ben's signature had to be on the withdrawal slip, and I shook my head. "You'll never make me believe Ben Guron had anything to do with any of that."

Gloria gave me a puzzled look. "I didn't say Ben had anything to do with it." A second later her face cleared and she laughed. "Oh, I see what you're getting at. The signature. You're thinking that Ben had to sign the slip." She gave me a condescending look. "MacGruder, I was a hooker for a long time. I learned the ropes, and one of the easiest things to learn was how to forge someone's signature. It took me fifteen minutes to master Ben's signature. When he found out, he thought it was funny. He used to sit and watch me sign his name to checks, and he didn't care. He even let me sign his name to his pension checks. It got so he never even bothered to sign anything. He would just drop whatever it was in front of me and go away knowing no one would ever question his signature. So you can see it was an easy matter to sign his name to that account release."

I had it all figured out. "So he found out about what ou and Marvin did, and how Cleet killed his brother, and nat's why Cleet killed him."

Gloria Dubois threw her head back and laughed. It)ok her a full minute to regain her composure. MacGruder," she said. "You really aren't very smart, are ou?" When I stared up at her defiantly, she said, "Lover, en never knew about the money. Marvin and I were very areful not to let anyone know. I didn't even tell Cleet bout it, even though he and I were making love every hance we could get." She looked sad, but only briefly. Poor Ben did find out about Marvin's death, though. The illy thing told me he was going to the police. I couldn't let nat happen, could I, especially as it was me who killed Marvin."

"You?" I asked incredulously.

Her eyes went hard. "You bet it was me. Marvin was ick, and there was no way I was ever going to run away vith him. But he had all the money, and I had to get it way from him. But even that was easy. I mean, it isn't ike I haven't done it before. I just offered myself to him, old him to bring the money and we would go away ogether, and he came running."

Again she sat beside me, soothingly stroking the umbing flesh of my wrists. "See, MacGruder, Cleet and I lanned the whole thing. I made him sit and listen to my lan until I had everything worked out perfectly. When I vas certain that nothing could go wrong, I told Marvin to neet me out on an old deserted logging road south of Boydville. When he got there, I got into his car, took off ny clothes and got him all hot. I kept at him, getting him lmost there until he was all goggle-eyed and sweating. I ever let him get too far along." Her eyes went dreamy. "I ad a friend once — she helped me get into the big money. he told me if I ever wanted to get the ones who paid two hundred a night and never asked questions to come back, had to learn to make it last for them. We doubled a coupl of times, and she showed me how to make them get almo there, then let them down real easy, bring them back u then down again, and keep doing it until they were goin crazy. When she had them begging, she would let them ge and when it was over, they would hand her twice th amount they had agreed upon, and they would always com back to her. So I copied her, and I learned real well. Aft a while, I was better than she ever was, and my johns pai more and came back. With Marvin, him being sick and al it was easier than it had been with my ... clients — easi even than it ever was with Ben." Her eyes came back int focus. "So I did what I do best to him, and when he was s ready he could scream, I told him that it would be a l better for him if we stopped for a while. He let me bac away, and so naturally I offered him a drink. I poured tw — yes, I had one, only mine didn't have any valium in i His did, though, and it was his wife's prescription in cas they found him. That's where Cleet helped — getting th prescription, I mean. I crushed two or three up and while was mixing his drink, I poured all that powder into the cu Just to make sure he drank it all, I kept telling him what was going to do just as soon as he finished his drink. And did some of it, too, only he passed out before I could finis After that, I started the engine and put that hose from th tailpipe into the car. Then I just walked away. If the found him, it would look like suicide. But they haven found him yet. Just as well, though."

I looked over at Dubois. "What the hell is wrong wit you? She killed your brother."

He grinned boyishly. "Don't matter none to me, boy The way I see it, Marvin was wrong, and he got what h deserved."

"All right, you've convinced me that I never should ave trusted you. So what are you going to do with me ow?"

It was Gloria who spoke. "Like Cleet told you, the first ing we are going to do is get you back over to Cleet's ouse. After that, we'll talk about what you know, and how uch evidence you've got."

I made my voice soft. "You know that we could have ad a good time together. We still can if you'll cut this tape nd get rid of the ape."

Gloria moved close to me, reached down and pulled her kirt up, exposing herself to me. "MacGruder, you take a eal good look at this." She fondled herself crudely. "You ant it so bad, maybe you can convince me that I should let ou have some of this before you die." Then she laughed nd let her skirt drop. "No, not you. I'll get more out of atching what Cleet does to you." She reached her hand ut and slapped me on the cheek. "You'll never get more nan just that one look."

Gloria stood and turned to Cleet. "You better put him ut so we can carry him out of this room like he's drunk."

Dubois came at me, his hands working fast, crashing nto my head so quickly I couldn't react. Most of the unches were aimed high so that I could turn my head a ttle and catch them on the hard bone above my ears. Then ame one that I didn't see, and he caught me in the left eye. Iy vision blurred, and I couldn't see to flinch at the next unches. At least one landed dead on my chin and my rain began the slow slip into darkness.

The last thing I remember was Cleet Dubois, standing ver me, the automatic in his hand, held butt outward. I aw the long, slow arc toward my head, tried to turn away, ut caught the butt against my temple, and completed the lip into the dark abyss of unconsciousness.

Chapter Nineteen

A searing pain brought me up flailing to the surface of consciousness as someone tugged at my hands. A voice in my aching head told me I knew who it was, but I couldn't put a face or name on the nightmarish thing that strained at what felt like wire wrapped tightly around my wrists. I tried to open my eyes and only the right one responded to the signal from my brain. Even with my one good eye open, there was darkness all around me. When I forced my eye to focus, it was like looking down a long tunnel where all you can see is darkness and a small circle of light way off in the distance. Try as you may, all you can see is the light. Through my eye, I saw the dark tunnel and I saw the circle of light a million miles off in the distance. In the light, I could see a shape. My brain told me I was wasting my time, but I tried to see who it was. I got the vague impression I should have known this person, but the impression faded as I felt the sting of something sharp and pointed bite into the flesh of my wrists.

Sometime later — maybe only a second — through the black clouds of mist that shrouded my brain, I heard a voice cry out, and then a scream. The voice seemed somehow familiar, but I could not place it. I knew that it was female, and I knew that I had heard that voice many times in the past, but I could not place the voice. Then I slipped back into the warm blackness.

When I came to the second time, I didn't know where I was or what had happened to me. I shook my head to clear some of the cobwebs. A pain shot through my head,

crashing into the bone just behind my eyes. My left eye
was swollen shut, so I closed my good eye until the pain
passed. It took what seemed to be a few years. I used the
time to recall what had happened. First it was Gloria
smiling up at me from the doorway. Then it was Dubois
standing behind her in the open doorway. I could vaguely
remember the conversation. After that, the cobwebs started
cluttering my brain and the rest was all a blur. I closed my
eye and drifted back off, a vision of Brenda filling the
screen in my head.

I didn't have any idea how long I was out, but when I
could open my eye, I found myself sitting on the ground
behind the Mercedes I had seen parked at the rear of the
house. The first thing I did was look down at my hands.
At first I was delighted to see that the tape had been
removed, but my elation vanished when I realized that I
still could not move my hands. It took me a moment to
realize that someone — probably Dubois — had wired my
hands together. I focused my one good eye on my wrists
until my vision cleared. And then I saw the rest of my
dilemma. Another wire was looped over the middle
between my hand and led up to my neck. I could see a
small closure in the wire about halfway between my hand
and my neck, and when I moved my arms out to increase
circulation, the closure moved upward. A small but stout
chain was tied around my forearms and led to the
undercarriage of the car.

Cleet Dubois gave me a knowing smile. "See, boy,
what we going to do is drag you around through them
briars out in the woods. I left your feet untied so maybe
you can run for a while. Matter of fact, I hope you can.
That way when you go down, your neck will get cut clean
through, and I can just leave you out there to rot. But
maybe you don't feel like running so you just lay down and
I drag you for a ways. If you're lucky, that wire I got

242

ound your neck will tighten up and you'll be dead before
ou get all cut up. Or maybe that wire around your hands
ill cut deep enough so's one of your hand will get cut
ean off. If that happens, you'll be able to get right up and
un away. If none of them things happen, a few hundred
ards through them briars and you'll be talking like there
in't no tomorrow." Then he laughed as though he had told
 joke. "Now that I think about it, there ain't going to be no
omorrow for you, boy."

He came over to me and squatted beside me. "You see
hat license plate she got on that car of hers?" When I
idn't respond he laughed. "*Glory-O*, that's what it says.
 now how she got that name?" Again I didn't respond.
t's cause of what she can do with that little mouth of hers,
oy. She can make a man lose all control before he knows
hat's happening to him. That's what she can do,
lacGruder. That's how she got that Guron fellow. She
ist kinda snaked herself against him and unzipped his
ants and put her little hand inside and before he knew
hat was happening, she was *Glory-O*'ing him." He
ughed nastily. "She sure do know how to do that right,
oy. I mean she does. There ain't no man from here down
 Jacksonville that can do nothing to stop it when she does
at. Know what I mean?" He let his eyes grow sad. "No,
 don't reckon you do at that. But maybe if you do your
lking right now before I have to waste any gas, maybe I'll
et Gloria to show you just how good she can be."

He laughed. "She was doing that to your friend that
orning she pushed him over the edge. She told me all
bout it that night while she and me were bouncing all over
er bed. She told me one minute he was telling her how
uch he loved her and promising that he would stand
eside her even though he had to tell the cops about what
he did to Marvin. Then she's down on her knees in front
f him and he's just standing there, doing nothing but

243

loving what she's doing to him. When it was all ove
Gloria slipped behind him, rubbing herself up against hir
and then gave him a little shove. She was going to g
down and make sure he was dead, but she heard someor
coming — that was you, I reckon. Anyway, she crawle
back up and left."

He moved his mouth close to my ear and said, "No
don't that make you want her? Every time I think abo
what she did to Marvin and Ben, I get to wanting he
Right now, she's in that house waiting for me to come bac
so why don't you and me get this over with?"

He put his big paw on my throat and squeezed, h
voice soft and soothing in my ear. "Know what we four
us, boy? While I was wrapping you all nice and snug to th
frame of this car, I heard a bush rattling over yonder. I ju
kept right on doing what I was doing, kind of hummir
softly to myself. Then I got myself up and went back on
the house and right out the back door. I circled around ar
came in from the back. And there she was, trying to co
through all that wire with a little pocket knife. She was s
worked up at seeing you bound up this way, she neve
heard me coming up behind her. Easy enough to reach ov
and grab her."

I tensed, tightening the noose around my neck. When
spoke, my voice croaked, "You hurt Brenda and I'll ki
you."

"Is that her name?" He ignored my threat. "I'll b
going on in the house to have some fun with her soon a
I'm finished here with you."

"She better be all right, Dubois."

He laughed, only there was no mirth in it. "She's fine
boy. Her and Gloria are in there. Gloria is teaching he
some of the things she learned while she was up there i
Washington, when she was doing all them big, importar
politicians. You just keep that in mind and you don't worr

bout that little lady. Me and Gloria will make her forget
ou real quick."

I felt anger welling up inside me, flooding me, taking
ver my mind and my body. Things raced through my
ind so quickly that I could not grasp them. Then an idea
rifted through a little slower than the rest. My brain
ached out, grabbed it and slowly flashed it over the
creen behind my eyes.

Awareness comes slow when you have been beaten,
specially when a wire noose cuts into your air supply. But
e anger I was feeling cleared my mind and I saw the idea,
orted it, graded it, removed the parts that would not work,
nd replaced them with things that would. When I was
eady to put the plan into action, I forced myself to relax,
etting my shoulders slump.

Dubois' face was still close to my ear when he said,
You don't like it when I talk about how I'm going to make
hat little piece scream for mercy? If it makes you feel any
etter, boy, you won't have to worry about it none at all. I
igure you'll be dead long before I ever get into that one."
le moved away and stood, sneering down at me. "I was
oing to kill you right off, but I want to enjoy seeing you
ie. Dying too quick ain't good enough, so you and me,
e're going to have a time of it. Now you just sit there and
tay alive if you can. I'm just going to leave you out here
hile I go in there and see if I can make your girl-friend
appy. You listen real good, boy, and you might be able to
ear her." He laughed and turned, walking toward the
ouse.

My head was spinning. I had to do something, but all
ny mind would concentrate on was what Dubois was going
o do to Brenda. I tried to clear it, but it was not working.

Then it was too late. Gloria came grinning from the
ouse, her eyes staring directly at me. "MacGruder, that
voman is something else. Give me a few days with her

245

and she'll be a new toy for me to play with." When she g
close enough, I saw the butt of an automatic in h
waistband.

"You hurt her ... " Gloria's foot kicked out and struc
me on the side of the head, cutting my words off. It d
something else, too. It cleared my head so that I knew wh
I would do.

Gloria knelt beside me, her hand rubbing the bruise c
my temple. "You just as well be nice to me, MacGruder.
told Cleet not to mess with her too much, but if you dor
watch yourself, I'll turn him loose on her, and she'll nev
be any good to another man." She moved so that she coul
look into my eyes. "Oh, I see it all now. She's your gir
isn't she? And you are all tied up and you can't do nothin
to stop what Cleet's doing to her." She tilted her head bac
and laughed cruelly. "You just stop worrying about tha
woman. You got enough to worry about yourself. I g
back in there, Cleet's going to come out here and drag yo
halfway across this state, and you ain't going to be able t
do nothing about it."

I made my voice plaintive. "Gloria, don't hurt her. Yo
can do whatever you want to me, but please don't hurt he
Please don't let him ... " I didn't finish the statement.

She smiled. "Cleet ain't going to do nothing that wi
leave no scars, MacGruder. He knows how to cause pai
without hardly even touching someone."

At that precise moment, a scream came from the house
It went on for a long time, fading into a loud moan, the
expanding into a scream again. Tears burned in the back c
my eyes and I felt my heart throbbing against my chest.
knew that I would have to act soon.

Gloria was watching me, her eyes narrowed. "Tha
making you want to kill him, lover?" She leaned her fac
close and breathed heavily. "I give him long enough, he
scream will turn into a sigh. She'll get to liking what he'

246

ing to her." There was another loud scream, and Gloria's
es narrowed even more. "But I seen him go too far a
uple of times. He gets carried away and she might crack.
he does and she won't be any good to me or anyone else."
Gloria smiled and leaned her face close to mine. I think
he was going to kiss me, but she never got the chance. I
ocked my head away from her and to the side, then
ought it back against hers. There was a loud, crunching
ound and I felt cartilage give. Then I heard a crack and
Gloria screamed. I jacked my head over again and
ounded it into her face. She went backward, blood
reaming from her nose. I rolled to the side until my feet
ere close enough to her head. Even though I was careful
ot to pull my arms downward, I felt the wire noose
ipping up against my neck. *Oh well*, I thought. *If I had to
o, I would take Gloria Guron with me.*

I brought my legs up and kicked out against her head.
he first kick put her out.

I lay still long enough to catch my breath. When I was
reathing more or less normally, I shook my hands as hard
s I could until I felt the knot in the chain come free. Then
was up and running, loosening the noose around my neck
s I ran. I had to put some distance between the house and
e, at least until I freed myself. Gloria was still very much
live, even though she was out cold. Somehow I knew she
as even more dangerous than Cleet would be.

I ran about two hundred yards into the woods and found
pine sapling that had been broken off about four feet from
e ground. I stretched my arms out and hooked one of the
ire strands over the broken tip of the tree. I began pulling
t the wire, feeling the strands closer to my hands begin to
ite in. I forced the pain from my mind, concentrating on
e agonies Brenda must be going through.

It was a long, tedious and painful process, but I finally
anaged to worked the twisted end of the wire free, and

247

using my legs as a snag, I unwrapped the wire until n
hands were free. It was at that moment I remembered t
automatic, and mentally kicked myself for not removing i

I looked around at the dense forest, suddenly aware th
I had not taken note of any landmarks as I ran into t
woods. I could feel my heart pounding as I stared intent
into the thick growth, trying to see something that wou
point out the path back to the house.

I felt my spirits sag as I sensed that it was no use. I w
lost, and there was no way I could find my way out of th
before the inevitable happened. I knew that Dubois wou
go out to the car sooner or later. When he went out,
would find Gloria. And if I knew him, he would take o
his anger on Brenda. It would be a quick death, and th
might be more merciful than what he was doing to her rig
then.

Then I heard Brenda scream again. As before, t
scream began loudly, then got lower until it was mere
uncontrollable gasps of pain. My ears caught the directic
from which they came, and my legs started propelling n
toward them almost before I knew what they were doing.
crashed through underbrush and briars, their thorns tearir
into my flesh, but I never felt the pain. I just kept runnir
toward the gut-wrenching sounds.

When I came out of the forest, I was fifty feet from t
rear of the car. Gloria was still where I had left he
vacantly unconscious eyes staring up at the sky. I had
get the gun, but when I started toward her, she sighe
loudly and moved her head. I thought about placing a we
aimed punch into the side of her head, but another screa
from the house cut that thought short. All thoughts of t
weapon disappeared and I made my way around the hou
until I stood beneath an open window. From inside, I cou
hear Brenda crying softly, muttering "No, please no. I ca
... " Then, another voice said, "Yes, you can, and you wi

248

Maybe if I do this ... " Then a scream of pain came from the first voice, and my heart sank.

I fought back tears and made my way to the rear of the house. I tried the door handle, and I felt it turn in my hand. I pushed the door open, and crept inside. I was in the kitchen. I moved to my right and through a door that led into the dining room. There was an open door off to my left. I could hear whimpering from somewhere in the house. The doorway led into a hall. I moved slowly until I was standing outside a door, behind which were the sounds of painful sobbing.

I tried the doorknob. It was locked. I remember thinking Dubois had not meant for Gloria to share the pleasure until he was through with it. From somewhere in my mind, I heard myself say that he did not have to worry about Gloria. I tensed myself, backed off a step, and then went crashing through the doorway and into the room.

Dubois turned sharply. "You bastard!" he shouted, and jumped from the bed.

I had just enough time to catch a quick glimpse of Brenda. She was in an old bed. It was one of those that had the tall posts at the corners of the headboard; shorter ones at the corners of the footboard. The posts came to blunt points at their tips. I forced my eyes down on Brenda. Her hands were taped to the headboard; her feet tied to the footboard. The white jumpsuit she was wearing was torn from the neckline down to her waist. Her hair was disheveled. Her face was contorted into an ugly mask of pain. There were angry red welts on the soft skin of her breast.

When I turned my eyes toward Dubois, he was grinning widely at me. "So you want to play with old Cleet?" He took a step toward me, stooped low, his arms outspread like a wrestler's.

The room was too small for me to go at Dubois. hurriedly looked around for something to use as a weapo There was nothing. I looked down at the floor in case I had dropped something there. There was only an old ar worn rug. Dubois was standing on the end closer to th bed.

He was bouncing up and down, flexing his leg "Come on, boy. I don't know how you got out of all thos wires and that chain, but this is better. I'm going to brea your neck nice and slow so you can die real slow an painful like."

When he leaned forward to take a step, I dropped to th floor and grabbed at the rug, hoping to pull him o balance. It was the only thing I could think of to do. jerked at the material, and felt it slip toward me. I looke up at Dubois, thinking that he might come tumbling dow on me. I didn't have to worry.

In his attempts to regain his footing, he steppe backward, his foot on the very edge of the rug. It slippe out from under him, and for a moment, he was balanced i midair, his arms flailing, his legs straight out in front o him. Then he came crashing down on the edge of the bed.

I scurried to my feet, expecting Dubois to be up and a me. But as I braced myself for his onslaught, I saw hir give a huge push to raise himself from the bed. Then h cried out a soft moan, tried to raise his head, then fell bac and relaxed. His chest heaved once, then rose slightly, the caved in on itself.

I took the three steps to the bed in one bound, ready t bash my fist into his face if he moved. He didn't. I presse my fingers to his neck and felt nothing. I looked down a him and saw the red stain beginning to creep its wa outward on the front of his shirt. In the center of the stain, could see the blunt end of the footboard post. In hi contortions while falling, Dubois had impaled himself.

I was about to go to Brenda when I heard an angry
out from behind me. When I turned, Gloria was grabbing
the automatic in her belt. I remember thinking it was the
me one Dubois had been holding back in my motel room.
eapt at her, catching her wrist as she turned to aim the
n at me. She was stronger than I thought she could be,
cking out at me, her arm almost too much for me to
ntrol as she forced the barrel around to point at me. I
is intent on folding over so that her kicks could not land
nen I caught sight of her left hand coming around at my
ad. I had just enough time to draw my head down
tween my shoulders when her fist careened off the top of
y skull. I fell backward, pushing at the gun in her hand at
e same time.

Then I heard the boom as the gun fired, and I braced
yself for the impact of the bullet, my brain was screaming
Brenda that I was sorry I was leaving her to the horrible
te that was awaiting her at the hands of Gloria Guron.
nen the hand I was holding went limp, and as I crashed to
e floor, I looked up at Gloria.

Her face was a crimson gash. The bullet had caught her
st below the chin, and had torn through her lower jaw,
pping its way upward, carving a deep crevice into what
d once been a beautiful face. I lay on my back, watching
she crumpled to the floor, the quick and acrid smell of
r death already filling the room.

For a moment, I lay there looking at what had once
en the wife of my friend Ben. She had come to rest on
e floor, no longer a creature of wanton pleasure. Now
e was but a slab of human meat, decay already setting in.
ne eye rested precariously on what had been her cheek,
aring out at me without life; the other looked at me over
eless lashes, still the dark shade of blue, but now without
e auburn glints. The bullet had finally torn through the
p of her head, taking a three-inch shard of her skull with

it. There was a red-gray sticky mass of tissue plastered the wall above where she was lying.

Then I heard Brenda sob, and came to my feet. I w to her, removed the tape from her wrists and untied binds that held her feet to the post. When she was free, s curled herself into the fetal position on the edge of the b at the far side away from where Dubois was impaled on post, and from where Gloria now lay. When I sat on bed next to her, she cast fright-filled eyes at me, and cri "No, please no more. I can't ... "

I leaned close, careful not to touch her, and whisper "It's over now, Brenda. He can't hurt you any more."

After a few seconds, I put my hand out. When touched her shoulder, she flinched, bared her teeth in a c like snarl, and opened her eyes widely. At first, they star out, seeing nothing but the horror she had been forced endure. Then they seemed to focus on me, and s murmured, "David?"

"Yes, love, it's me. It's over."

The fright gave way to despair and she said, "David, ... he ... I didn't want him to ... to do it, but when I foug him, he ... he ... "

Then she started to cry and I held her, gently at fir When the sobs began and she shook uncontrollably, I he her more tightly. I whispering soothingly, "It's ok; Brenda. Let it out. Let it go."

Chapter Twenty

There were a few visible scars, but none was very deep, d all would fade eventually. That's my translation of hat the doctors told me when I wheeled Brenda from the spital in Atlanta. Virginia said it better. "David, you ke that lady off somewhere, and you be good to her. Let r be the one to make the first move. Maybe she'll make Maybe she won't, but if she does, and if she decides terward it isn't what she wants, you hold her and tell her s okay." So that's exactly what I did.

There were a few days of silence, bundled up in the bed the forward stateroom. And then there were a few ntative touches, some mere accidental caresses followed quick tears and quicker feet, carrying Brenda back into e stateroom and away from me.

Then one evening, as I rolled and tumbled alone in my vn bed, Brenda came to me. When she slipped into bed side me and molded herself to me, I knew that she would okay. A few days of closeness, and then one glorious ght she came alive again.

Brenda and I had not discussed that afternoon up in the oods. I figured she had either erased the scene from her ind, or simply chose not to discuss it. And that was just ne by me. Out of sight, out of mind, or something like at.

It was a warm September morning. Brenda came from e shower, hair wet, face washed clean. She smiled at me I handed her a steaming cup of coffee. "You know, avid, what happened was ugly. It was a nightmare, and I

253

wish I could erase it from my memory, but I can't.
happened, and whether I like it or not, I have to live w
that fact." She sipped at the dark brew, her eyes strange
distant. Then they cleared and she stared at me. "You'
been very supportive, and I love you for it." She put t
cup on the counter, came around to where I was standir
and put her arms around my neck, straining upward for t
kiss.

In the process, the bathrobe she was wearing fell op
I pushed her back half a step and eyed her. "Think may
you've got a problem, lady," I said.

She giggled, dropped her arms and shook the robe fro
her shoulders. "Maybe I do at that." Then she moved clo
again and pressed her hips against mine. "Oh, it isn't r
who has the problem, David."

"Care to ... " I began, but her lips against mine told r
she felt the same urgency as I did.

Brenda slipped into the new black bikini, and informed r
that she was going over to the beach to take advantage
the early morning sun. She gave me a promisingly war
kiss when she passed me, and I patted her butt as she we
out the door. I poured another cup of coffee and placed
call to Wiley's private line. "Frazier," he answered.

"It's Dave. How're things going?"

"You caught me on my way out the door. If you h
called a few minutes later, you wouldn't have caught me."

"Busy?" I asked.

I heard a rough snort. "We've either got to hire mo
people, or else I have to learn how to work twenty-fo
hours a day!"

"So hire more people. We can afford it."

After a moment, Wiley said, "It's probably just a fluk
I can hack it."

"Yeah, I guess it might be nice getting out into the field ce in a while. Hell, I don't know how you stood it as g as you did."

"How's Brenda?" he asked, quickly changing the ject.

"Mending nicely. I took her over into the 'Glades terday, and Billy Eagle had her handling his swamp ggy like a pro. His wife, Flo, wouldn't let us leave until had a try at the fishing. Brenda caught one of the gest largemouth bass of the season."

He laughed, and then said, "She planning to stay down re for a while?"

"The doctors tell her that she needs to rest for a while. at scene with Gloria Guron and Dubois left a deep otional scar. She's sleeping better now; only an casional nightmare. I figure she needs another two or ee months to heal." I paused, then I said, "So, I guess answer is yes. Well, maybe I should say I hope Brenda planning to stay for a while, at least she is if I have ything to say about it.

"That isn't what I meant," he said. Then after a ment, he went on. "Maybe I should have asked if you going to keep her there."

"Wiley, that's completely up to Brenda. I've let her ow she can stay for as long as she wants, and under atever conditions she sets."

Wiley was quiet for a while. Then, "Okay partner. hen she comes back to Atlanta, why don't you come with ?" He was a very intuitive person.

"I might do that."

I heard him laugh. "Sure, and the polar ice cap will be mpletely melted by tomorrow afternoon. Oh, well, in the antime and as long as you have her, Dave, take vantage of what you have."

"I will," I said, and then added, "And that's a promise."

I heard him chuckle into the phone. "You take c[a]
partner."

"I will. You do the same," I responded.

"Davie, I gotta run." Then, "Oh, yeah, why did [you]
call?"

I smiled. "Just to talk, Wiley."

After a few seconds, he said, "Thanks," and then h[ung]
up.

I was reclining on the couch when Brenda came in. [She]
came over and nestled down beside me. She smelled of [sea]
breezes and suntan oil. "Miss me?" she asked.

I reached up and pulled her down so that I could k[iss]
her on the mouth and said, "More than you'll ever know."

Her hand touched the faded bruise around my left e[ye.]
"Didn't anyone ever tell you to duck?"

I turned my head and kissed the palm of her ha[nd.]
"Yes, maybe they did, but you know me. I never t[ake]
advice." Then, remembering something Wiley had said [on]
the telephone, I straightened up, stood and bent over h[er,]
kissing her lightly on the lips. Then I lifted her into [my]
arms and started off toward the king-sized bed in the mas[ter]
stateroom.

"What's this?" she cooed, nestling her face against [my]
neck.

"A friend told me to take advantage of what I have."

When I placed her in the middle of the bed, she smi[led]
up at me, and there was a mischievous sparkle in her e[yes]
as she asked, "And do you have me?" When I nodded [my]
answer, she commanded, "So take advantage, Da[vid]
MacGruder."

That is exactly what I did.

The End

About the Book

Dewitt L. Edenfield, Jr. is a retired naval officer, ex-cop and deputy sheriff. This is his second book in the David MacGruder series.